D0098555

ALSO BY KAREN RUSSELL

Sleep Donation

Vampires in the Lemon Grove: Stories

Swamplandia!

St. Lucy's Home for Girls Raised by Wolves

Orange World

and Other Stories

Orange World

and Other Stories

KAREN RUSSELL

ALFRED A. KNOPF
New York
2019

THIS IS A BORZOI BOOK
PUBLISHED BY ALFRED A. KNOPF

All rights reserved. Published in the United States by
Alfred A. Knopf, a division of Penguin Random House LLC,
New York, and distributed in Canada by Penguin Random House
Canada Limited, Toronto.

www.aaknopf.com

Knopf, Borzoi Books, and the colophon are registered
trademarks of Penguin Random House LLC.

Several pieces originally appeared in the following publications:
The New Yorker: "The Bad Graft" (2014), "The Prospectors" (2015),
"Bog Girl" (2016), and "Orange World" (2018)
Tin House: "The Gondoliers" (summer 2019)
Zoetrope: "Madame Bovary's Greyhound" (Vol. 17, No. 2, 2013),
"The Tornado Auction" (Vol. 21, No. 2, 2017), and
"Black Corfu" (Vol. 22, No. 2, 2018)

Library of Congress Cataloging-in-Publication Data
Names: Russell, Karen, [date] author.
Title: Orange world and other stories / Karen Russell.
Description: First edition. | New York : Alfred A. Knopf, 2019. |
"This is a Borzoi book published by Alfred A. Knopf."
Identifiers: LCCN 2018054561 (print) | LCCN 2018059348 (ebook) |
ISBN 9780525656142 (ebook) | ISBN 9780525656135 (hardcover)
Subjects: LCSH: Short stories, American—21st century.
Classification: LCC PS3618.U755 (ebook) |
LCC PS3618.U755 A6 2019 (print) | DDC 813/.6—dc23
LC record available at https://lccn.loc.gov/2018054561

Jacket illustration and design by John Gall

Manufactured in the United States of America
First Edition

For Tony & Oscar

Will it always be this way? The warm sky
orangelit, another swarm mounting within the swarm.

—"Yellow Jackets and the Sting Repeats,"
Carey McHugh

We need to know where we live in order to imagine
living elsewhere. We need to imagine living elsewhere
before we can live there.

—*Ghostly Matters,* Avery Gordon

Contents

The Prospectors   3

The Bad Graft   37

Bog Girl: A Romance   67

Madame Bovary's Greyhound   95

The Tornado Auction   113

Black Corfu   147

The Gondoliers   193

Orange World   235

Acknowledgments   269

Orange World

and Other Stories

The Prospectors

The entire ride would take eleven minutes. That was what the boy had promised us, the boy who never showed.

To be honest, I hadn't expected to find the chairlift. Not through the maze of old-growth firs and not in the dwindling light. Not without our escort. A minute earlier, I'd been on the brink of suggesting that we give up and hike back to the logging road. But at the peak of our despondency we saw it: the lift, rising like a mirage out of the timber woods, its four dark cables striping the red sunset. Chairs were floating up the mountainside, forty feet above our heads. Empty chairs, upholstered in ice, swaying lightly in the wind. Sailing beside them, just as swiftly and serenely, a hundred chairs came down the mountain. As if a mirror were malfunctioning, each chair separating from a buckle-bright double. Nobody was manning the loading station; if we wanted to take the lift we'd have to do it alone. I squeezed Clara's hand.

A party awaited us at the peak. Or so we'd been told by

Mr. No-Show, Mr. Nowhere, a French boy named Eugene de La Rochefoucauld.

"I bet his real name is Burt," Clara said angrily. We had never been stood up before. "I bet he's actually from Tennessee."

Well, he had certainly seemed European, when we met him coming down the mountain road on horseback, one week ago this night. He'd had that hat! Such a convincingly stupid goatee! He'd pronounced his name as if he were coughing up a jewel. Eugene de La Rochefoucauld had proffered a nasally invitation: Would we be his guests next Saturday night, at the gala opening of the Evergreen Lodge? We'd ride the new chairlift with him to the top of the mountain and be among the first visitors to the marvelous new ski resort. The president himself might be in attendance.

Clara, unintimidated, had flirted back. "Two dates—is that not being a little greedy, Eugene?"

"No less would be acceptable," he'd said, smiling, "for a man of my stature." (Eugene was five foot four; we'd assumed he meant education, wealth.) The party was to be held seven thousand feet above Lucerne, Oregon, the mountain town where we had marooned ourselves, at nineteen and twenty-two; still pretty (Clara was beautiful), still young enough to attract notice, but penniless, living week to week in a "historic" boardinghouse. "Historic" had turned out to be the landlady's synonym for "haunted." "Turn-of-the-century sash windows," we'd discovered, meant "pneumonia holes."

We'd waited for Eugene for close to an hour, while Time went slinking around the forest, slyly rearranging its shadows; now a red glow clung to the huge branches of the Douglas firs. When I finally spoke, the bony snap in my voice startled us both.

"We don't need him, Clara."

"We don't?"

"No. We can get there on our own."

Clara turned to me with blue lips and flakes daggering her lashes. I felt a pang: I could see both that she was afraid of my proposal and that she could be persuaded. This is a terrible knowledge to possess about a friend. Nervously, I counted my silver and gold bracelets, meting out reasons for making the journey. If we did not make the trip, I would have to pawn them. I argued that it was riskier *not* to take this risk. (For me, at least; Clara had her wealthy parents waiting back in Florida. As much as we dared together, we never risked our friendship by bringing up that gulf.) I touched the fake red flower pinned to my black bun. What had we gone to all this effort for? We owed our landlady twelve dollars for January's rent. Did Clara prefer to wait in the drifts for our prince, that fake frog, Eugene, to arrive?

For months, all anybody in Lucerne had been able to talk about was this lodge, the centerpiece of a new ski resort on Mount Joy. Another New Deal miracle. In his Fireside Chats, Roosevelt had promised us that these construction projects would lift us out of the Depression. Sometimes I caught myself squinting hungrily at the peak, as if the government money might be visible, falling from the actual clouds. Out-of-work artisans had flocked to northern Oregon: carpenters, masons, weavers, engineers. The Evergreen Lodge, we'd heard, had original stonework, carved from five thousand pounds of native granite. Its doors were cathedral huge, made of hand-cut ponderosa pine. Murals had been commissioned from local artists: scenes of mountain wildflowers, rearing bears. Quilts covered the beds, hand crocheted by the New Deal men. I loved to picture their calloused black thumbs on the bridally white muslin. Architecturally, what was said to stun every visitor was the main hall: a huge hexagonal chamber, with a band platform and "acres for dancing, at the top of the world!"

WPA workers cut trails into the side of Mount Joy, assisted by the Civilian Conservation Corps boys from Camp Thistle and Camp Bountiful. I'd seen these young men around town, on leave from the woods, in their mud-caked boots and khaki shirts with the government logo. Their greasy faces clumped together like olives in a jar. They were the young mechanics who had wrenched the lift out of a snowy void and into skeletal, functioning existence. To raise bodies from the base of the mountain to the summit in eleven minutes! It sounded like one of Jules Verne's visions.

"See that platform?" I said to Clara. "Stand there, and fall back into the next chair. I'll be right behind you."

At first, the climb was beautiful. An evergreen army held its position in the whipping winds. Soon, the woods were replaced by fields of white. Icy outcroppings rose like fangs out of a pink-rimmed sky. We rose, too, our voices swallowed by the cables' groaning. Clara was singing something that I strained to hear, and failed to comprehend.

Clara and I called ourselves the Prospectors. Our fathers, two very different kinds of gambler, had been obsessed with the gold rush, and we grew up hearing stories about Yukon fever and the Klondike stampeders. We knew the legend of the farmer who had panned out a hundred and thirty thousand dollars, the clerk who dug up eighty-five thousand, the black-smith who discovered a haul of the magic metal on Rabbit Creek and made himself a hundred grand richer in a single hour. This period of American history held a special appeal for Clara's father, Mr. Finisterre, a bony-faced Portuguese immigrant to southwestern Florida who had wrung his modest fortune out of the sea-damp wallets of tourists. My own father had killed himself outside the dog track in the spring of 1931, and I'd been fortunate to find a job as a maid at the Hotel Finisterre.

Clara Finisterre was the only other maid on staff—a summer job. Her parents were strict and oblivious people. Their thousand rules went unenforced. They were very busy with their guests. A sea serpent, it was rumored, haunted the coastline beside the hotel, and ninety percent of our tourism was serpent driven. Amateur teratologists in panama hats read the newspaper on the veranda, drinking orange juice and idly scanning the horizon for fins.

"Thank you," Mr. Finisterre whispered to me once, too sozzled to remember my name, "for keeping the secret that there is no secret." The black Atlantic rippled emptily in his eyeglasses.

Every night, Mrs. Finisterre hosted a cocktail hour: cubing green and orange melon, cranking songs out of the ivory

gramophone, pouring bright malice into the fruit punch in
the form of a mentally deranging Portuguese rum. She'd
apprenticed her three beautiful daughters in the Light Arts,
the Party Arts. Clara was her eldest. Together, the Finisterre
women smoothed arguments and linens. They concocted
banter, gab, palaver, patter—every sugary variety of small talk
that dissolves into the night. I hated the cocktail hour, and,
whenever I could, I escaped to beat rugs and sweep leaves on
the hotel roof. One Monday, however, I heard footsteps ringing on the ladder. It was Clara. She saw me and froze.

Bruises were thickening all over her arms. They were
that brilliant pansy blue, the beautiful color that belies its
origins. Automatically, I crossed the roof to her. We clacked
skeletons—to call it an embrace would misrepresent the
violence of our first collision. To soothe her, I heard myself
making stupid jokes, babbling inanities about the weather,
asking in my vague and meandering way what could be done
to help her; I could not bring myself to say, plainly, *Who did
this to you?* Choking on my only real question, I offered her
my cardigan—the way you'd hand a sick person a tissue. She
put it on. She buttoned all the buttons. You couldn't tell that
anything was wrong now. This amazed me, that a covering
so thin could erase her bruises. I'd half expected them to bore
holes through the wool.

"Don't worry, okay?" she said. "I promise, it's nothing."

"I won't tell," I blurted out—although of course I had
nothing to tell beyond what I'd glimpsed. Night fell, and I
was shivering now, so Clara held me. Something subtle and
real shifted inside our embrace—nothing detectable to an
observer, but a change I registered in my bones. For the dura-

tion of our friendship, we'd trade off roles like this: anchor and boat, beholder and beheld. We must have looked like some Janus-faced statue, our chins pointing east and west. An unembarrassed silence seemed to be on loan to us from the distant future, where we were already friends. Then I heard her say, staring over my shoulder at the darkening sea: "What would you be, Aubby, if you lived somewhere else?"

"I'd be a prospector," I told her, without batting an eye. "I'd be a prospector of the prospectors. I'd wait for luck to strike them, and then I'd take their gold."

Clara laughed and I joined in, amazed—until this moment, I hadn't considered that my days at the hotel might be eclipsing other sorts of lives. Clara Finisterre was someone whom I thought of as having a fate to escape, but I would never have dignified my own prospects that way, by calling them "a fate." Things simply happened to me, and I didn't matter enough to anyone or any scheme for them to build into a destiny. When I thought about the future, it felt almost claustrophobically near at hand, as if my nose were bumping up against a dirty window. Next Monday. Next Wednesday. But that night I saw Clara's laughing face, and I realized with a shock that together we could lift the glass, and fly off.

Clara took me to a debutante ball at a tacky mansion that looked rabid to me, frothy with white marble balconies. She introduced me as "my best friend, Aubergine." Thus began our secret life. We sifted through the closets and the jewelry boxes of our hosts. Clara tutored me in the social graces, and I taught Clara what to take, and how to get away with it.

One night, Clara came to find me on the roof. She was blinking muddily out of two black eyes. Who was doing this—Mr. Finisterre? Someone from the hotel? She refused to say. I made a deal with Clara: she never had to tell me who, but we had to leave Florida.

The next day, we found ourselves at the train station, with all our clothes and savings.

Those first weeks alone were an education. The West was very poor at that moment, owing to the Depression. But it was still home to many aspiring and expiring millionaires, and we made it our job to make their acquaintance. One aging oil speculator paid for our meals and our transit and required only that we absorb his memories; Clara nicknamed him the "allegedly legendary wit." He had three genres of tale: business victories; sporting adventures that ended in the death of mammals; and eulogies for his former virility.

We met mining captains and fishing captains, whose whiskers quivered like those of orphaned seals. The freckled heirs to timber fortunes. Glazy baronial types, with portentous and misguided names—Romulus and Creon—who were pleased to invite us to gala dinners, and to use us as their gloating mirrors. In exchange for this service, Clara and I helped ourselves to many fine items from their houses. Clara had a magic satchel that seemed to expand with our greed, and we stole everything it could swallow: dessert spoons, candlesticks, a poodle's jeweled collar. We strode out of parties wearing our hostess's two-toned heels, woozy with adrenaline. Crutched along by Clara's sturdy charm, I was swung through doors that led to marmoreal courtyards and curtained salons and, in many cases, master bedrooms, where my skin glowed under the warm reefs of artificial lighting.

But winter hit, and our mining prospects dimmed considerably. The Oregon coastline was laced with ghost towns; two paper mills had closed, and whole counties had gone bankrupt. Men were flocking inland to the mountains, where the rumor was that the WPA had work for construction teams. I told Clara that we needed to follow them. So we thumbed a ride with a group of work-starved Astoria teenagers who had heard about the Evergreen Lodge. Gold dust had drawn the first prospectors to these mountains; those boys were after the weekly three-dollar salary. But if government money was snowing onto Mount Joy, it had yet to reach the town below. I'd made a bad miscalculation, suggesting Lucerne. Our first night in town, Clara and I stared at our faces superimposed over the dark storefront windows. In the boardinghouse, we lay awake in the dark, pretending to believe in each other's theatrical sleep; only our bellies were honest, growling at each other. *Why did you bring us here?* Clara never dreamed of asking me. With her generous amnesia, she seemed already to have forgotten that leaving home had been my idea.

Day after day, I told Clara not to worry: "We just need one good night." We kept lying to each other, pretending that our hunger was part of the game. Social graces get you meager results in a shuttered town. We started haunting the bars around the CCC camps. The gaunt men there had next to nothing, and I felt a pang lifting anything from them. Back in the boardinghouse, our fingers spidering through wallets, we barely spoke to each other. Clara and I began to disappear into adjacent rooms with strangers. *She was better off before,* my mind whispered. For the first time since we'd left Florida, it occurred to me that our expedition might fail.

The chairlift ascended seven thousand two hundred and fifty feet—I remembered this figure from the newspapers. It had meant very little to me in the abstract. But now I felt our height in the soles of my feet. For whole minutes, we lost sight of the mountain in an onrush of mist. Finally, hands were waiting to catch us. They shot out of the darkness, gripping me under the arms, swinging me free of the lift. Our empty chairs were whipped around by the huge bull wheel before starting the long flight downhill. Hands, wonderfully warm hands, were supporting my back.

"Eugene?" I called, my lips numb.

"Who's *You-Jean?*" a strange voice chuckled.

The man who was not Eugene turned out to be an ursine mountaineer. With his lantern held high, he peered into our faces. I recognized the drab green CCC uniform. He looked about our age to me, although his face kept blurring in the snow. The lantern, battery powered, turned us all jaundiced shades of gold. He had no clue, he said, about any *Eugene.* But he'd been stationed here to escort guests to the lodge.

Out of the corner of my eye, I saw tears freezing onto Clara's cheeks. Already she was fluffing her hair, asking this government employee how he'd gotten the enviable job of escorting beautiful women across the snows. How quickly she was able to snap back into character! I could barely move my frozen tongue, and I trudged along behind them.

"How old are you girls?" the CCC man asked, and "Where

are you from?" and every lie that we told him made me feel safer in his company.

The lodge was a true palace. Its shadow alone seemed to cover fifty acres of snow. Electricity raised a yellowish aura around it, so that the resort loomed like a bubble pitched against the mountain sky. Its A-frame reared out of the woods with the insensate authority of any redwood tree. Lights blazed in every window. As we drew closer, we saw faces peering down at us from several of these.

The terror was still with us. The speed of the ascent. My blood felt carbonated. Six feet ahead of us, Not-Eugene, whose name we'd failed to catch, swung the battery-powered lamp above his head and guided us through a whale-gray tunnel made of ice. "Quite the runway to a party, eh?"

Two enormous polished doors blew inward, and we found ourselves in a rustic ballroom, with fireplaces in each corner shooting heat at us. Amethyst chandeliers sent lakes of light rippling across the dance floor; the stone chimneys looked like indoor caves. Over the bar, a mounted boar grinned tuskily down at us. Men mobbed us, handing us fizzing drinks, taking our coats. Deluged by introductions, we started giggling, handing our hands around: "Nilson," "Pauley," "Villanueva," "Obadiah," "Acker . . ." Proudly, each identified himself to us as one of the CCC "tree soldiers" who had built this fantasy resort: masons and blacksmiths and painters and foresters. They were boys, I couldn't help but think, boys our age. More faces rose out of the shadows, beaming hard. I guessed that, like us, they'd been waiting for this night to come for some time. Someone lit two cigarettes, passed them our way.

I shivered now with expectation. Clara threaded her hand through mine and squeezed down hard—time to dive into the sea. We'd plunged into stranger waters, socially. How many nights had we spent together, listening to tourists speak in tongues, relieved of their senses by Mrs. Finisterre's rum punch? Most of the boys were already drunk—I could smell that. Some rocked on their heels, desperate to start dancing.

They led us toward the bar. Feeling came flooding back into my skin, and I kept laughing at everything these young men were saying, elated to be indoors with them. Clara had to pinch me through the puffed sleeve of my dress:

"Aubby? Are we the only girls here?"

Clara was right: Where were the socialites we'd expected to see? The Oregon state forester, with his sullen red-lipped wife? The governor, the bank presidents? The ski experts from the Swiss Alps? Fifty-two paying guests, selected by lottery, had rooms waiting for them—we'd seen the list of names in Sunday's Oregon *Gazette*.

I turned to a man with wise amber eyes. He had unlined skin and a wispy blond mustache, but he smiled at us with the mellow despair of an old goat.

"Excuse me, sir. When does the celebration start?"

Clara flanked him on the left, smiling just as politely.

"Are we the first guests to arrive?"

But now the goat's eyes flamed: "Whadda you talkin' about? This party is *under way,* lady. You got twenty-six dancing partners to choose from in here—that ain't enough?"

The strength of his fury surprised us; backing up, I bumped my hip against a banister. My hand closed on what turned out to be a tiny beaver, a carved ornament. Each cedar newel post had one.

"The woodwork is beautiful."

He grinned and relaxed, soothed by the compliment.

"My supervisor is none other than O. B. Dawson."

"And your name?"

The thought appeared unbidden: *Later, you'll want to know what to scream.*

"Mickey Loatch. Got a wife, girls, I'm chagrined to say. Got three kids already, back in Osprey. I'm here so they can eat." Casually, he explained to us the intensity of his loneliness, the loneliness of the entire corps. They'd been driven by truck, eight miles each day, from Camp Thistle to the deep woods. For months at a time, they lived away from their families. Drinking water came from Lister bags; the latrines were saddle trenches. Everyone was glad, glad, glad, he said, to have the work. "There wasn't anything for us, until the Emerald Lodge project came along."

Mr. Loatch, I'd been noticing, had the strangest eyes I'd ever seen. They were a brilliant dark yellow, the color of that magic metal, gold.

Swallowing, I asked the man, "Excuse me, but I'm a bit confused. Isn't this the *Evergreen* Lodge?"

"The Evergreen Lodge?" the man said, exposing a mouthful of chewed pink sausage. "Where's dat, gurrls?" He laughed at his own cartoony voice.

A suspicion was coming into focus, a dreadful theory; I tried to talk it away, but the harder I looked, the keener it became. A quick scan of the room confirmed what I must have registered and ignored when I first walked through

those doors. Were all of the boys' eyes this same hue? Trying
to stay calm, I gripped Clara's hand and spun her around like
a weather vane: gold, gold, gold, gold.

"Oh my God, Clara."

"Aubby? What's wrong with you?"

"Clara," I murmured, "I think we may have taken the
wrong lift."

<hr />

Two lodges existed on Mount Joy. There was the Evergreen
Lodge, which would be unveiled tonight, in a ceremony of
extraordinary opulence, attended by the state forester and the
president. Where Eugene was likely standing, on the balcony
level, raising a flute for the champagne toast. There had once
been, however, on the southeastern side of this same mountain, a second structure. This place lived on in local memory
as a demolished hope, an unconsummated blueprint. It was
the failed original, crushed by an avalanche two years earlier, the graveyard of twenty-six workers from Company 609
of the Oregon Civilian Conservation Corps.

"Unwittingly," our landlady, who loved a bloody and
unjust story, had told us over a pancake breakfast, "those
workers were building their own casket." With tobogganing
runs and a movie theater, and more windows than Versailles,
it was to have been even more impressive than the Evergreen
Lodge. But the unfinished lodge had been completely covered
in the collapse.

Mickey Loatch was still steering us around, showing off
the stonework.

"Have you gals been to the Cloud Cap Inn? That's hitched to the mountain with wire cables. See, what we done is—"

"Mr. Loatch?" Swilling a drink, I steadied my voice. "How late does the chairlift run?"

"Oh dear." He pursed his lips. "You girls gotta be somewhere? I'm afraid you're stuck with us, at least until morning. You're the last we let up. They shut that lift down until dawn."

Next to me, I heard Clara in my ear: "Are you crazy? We just got here, and you're talking about leaving? Do you know how rude you sound?"

"They're dead."

"What are you talking about? Who's dead?"

"Everyone. Everyone but us."

Clara turned from me, her jaw tensing. At a nearby table, five green-clad boys were watching our conversation play out with detached interest, as if it were a sport they rarely followed. Clara wet her lips and smiled down at them, drumming her red nails on their table's glossy surface.

"This is so beautiful!" she cooed.

All five of the dead boys blushed.

"Excuse us," she fluttered. "Is there a powder room? My friend here is just a mess!"

———————

THE LADIES ROOM read a bronzed sign posted on an otherwise undistinguished door. At other parties, this room had always been our sanctuary. Once the door was shut, we stared at each other in the mirror, transferring knowledge across the glass.

Her eyes were still brown, I noted with relief, and mine were blue. I worried that I might start screaming, but I bit back my panic, and I watched Clara do the same for me. "Your nose," I finally murmured. Blood poured in two bright bars down her upper lip.

"I guess we must be really high up," she said, and started to cry.

"Shh, shh, shh . . ."

I wiped at the blood with a tissue.

"See?" I showed it to her. "At least we *are,* ah, at least we can still . . ."

Clara sneezed violently, and we stared at the reddish globules on the glass, which stood out with terrifying lucidity against the flat, unreal world of the mirror.

"What are we going to do, Aubby?"

I shook my head; a horror flooded through me until I could barely breathe.

Ordinarily, I would have handled the logistics of our escape—picked locks, counterfeited tickets. Clara would have corrected my lipstick and my posture, encouraging me to look more like a willowy seductress and less like a baseball umpire. But tonight it was Clara who formulated the plan. We had to tiptoe around the Emerald Lodge. We had to dim our own lights. And, most critical to our survival here, according to Clara: we had to persuade our dead hosts that we believed they were alive.

At first, I objected; I thought these workers deserved to know the truth about themselves.

"Oh?" Clara said. "How principled of you."

And what did I think was going to happen, she asked, if we told the men what we knew?

"I don't know. They'll let us go?"

Clara shook her head.

"Think about it, Aubby—what's keeping this place together?"

We had to be very cautious, very *amenable,* she argued. We couldn't challenge our hosts on any of their convictions. The Emerald Lodge was a real place, and they were breathing safely inside it. We had to admire their handiwork, she said. Continue to exclaim over the lintel arches and the wrought-iron grates, the beams and posts. As if they were real, as if they were solid. Clara begged me to do this. Who knew what might happen if we roused them from their dreaming? The CCC workers' ghosts had built this place, Clara said; we were at their mercy. If the men discovered they were dead, we'd die with them. We needed to believe in their rooms until dawn—just long enough to escape them.

"Same plan as ever," Clara said. "How many hundreds of nights have we staked a claim at a party like this?"

Zero, I told her. On no occasion had we been the only living people.

"We'll charm them. We'll drink a little, dance a little. And then, come dawn, we'll escape down the mountain."

Somebody started pounding on the door: "Hey! What's the holdup, huh? Somebody fall in? You girls wanna dance or what?"

"Almost ready!" Clara shouted brightly.

On the dance floor, the amber-eyed ghosts were as awkward and as touching, as unconvincingly brash, as any boys in history on the threshold of a party. Innocent hopefuls with their hats pressed to their chests.

"I feel sorry for them, Clara! They have no idea."

"Yes. It's terribly sad."

Her face hardened into a stony expression I'd seen on her only a handful of times in our career as prospectors.

"When we get back down the mountain, we can feel sad," she said. "Right now, we are going to laugh at all their jokes. We are going to celebrate this stupendous American land-mark, the Emerald Lodge."

Clara's mother owned an etiquette book for women, the first chapter of which advises, *Make Your Date Feel Like He Is the Life of the Party!* People often mistake laughing girls for foolish creatures. They mistake our merriment for nerves or weakness, or the hysterical looning of desire. Sometimes, it is that. But not tonight. We could hold our wardens hostage, too, in this careful way. Everybody needs an audience.

At other parties, our hosts had always been very willing to believe us when we feigned interest in their endless rehears-als of the past. They used our black pupils to polish up their antique triumphs. Even an ogreish salmon-boat captain, a bachelor again at eighty-seven, was convinced that we were both in love with him. Nobody ever invited Clara and me to a gala to hear our honest opinions.

At the bar, a calliope of tiny glasses was waiting for me: honey and cherry and lemon. Flavored liquors, imported from

Italy, the bartender smiled shyly. "Delicious!" I exclaimed, touching each to my lips. Clara, meanwhile, had been swept onto the dance floor. With her mauve lipstick in place and her glossy hair smoothed, she was shooting colors all around the room. Could you scare a dead boy with the vibrancy of your life? *Be careful,* I mouthed, motioning her into the shadows. Boys in green beanies kept sidling up to her, vying for her attention. It hurt my heart to see them trying. Of course, news of their own death had not reached them— how could that news get up the mountain, to where the workers were buried under snow?

Perched on the barstool, I plaited my hair. I tried to think up some good jokes.

"Hullo. Care if I join you?"

This dead boy introduced himself as Lee Covey. Black bangs flopped onto his brow. He had the small, recessed, comically despondent face of a pug dog. I liked him immediately. And he was so funny that I did not have to theatricalize my laughter. Lee's voluble eyes made conversation feel almost unnecessary; his conviction that he was alive was contagious.

"I'm not much of a dancer," Lee apologized abruptly. As if to prove his point, he sent a glass crashing off the bar.

"Oh, that's okay. I'm not, either. See my friend out there?" I asked. "In the green dress? She's the graceful one."

But Lee kept his golden eyes fixed on me, and soon it became difficult to say who was the mesmerist and who was succumbing to hypnosis. His Camp Thistle stories made me laugh so hard that I worried about falling off the barstool. Lee had a rippling laugh, like summer thunder; by this point I was very drunk. Lee started in on his family's sorry history:

"Daddy the Dwindler, he spent it all, he lost everything we had, he turned me out of the house. It fell to me to support the family . . ."

I nodded, recognizing his story's contours. How had the other workers washed up here? I wondered. Did they remember their childhoods, their lives before the avalanche? Or had those memories been buried inside them?

It was the loneliest feeling, to watch the group of dead boys dancing. Coupled off, they held on to each other's shoulders. "For practice," Lee explained. They steered each other uncertainly around the hexagonal floor, swaying on currents of song.

"Say, how about it?" Lee said suddenly. "Let's give it a whirl—you only live once."

Seconds later, we were on the floor, foxtrotting in the center of the hall.

"Oh, oh, oh," he crooned.

When Lee and I kissed, it felt no different from kissing a living mouth. We sank into the rhythms of horns and strings and harmonicas, performed by a live band of five dead mountain brothers. With the naïve joy of all these ghosts, they tootled their glittery instruments at us.

A hand grabbed my shoulder.

"May I cut in?"

Clara dragged me off the floor.

———

Back in the powder room, Clara's eyes looked shiny, raccoon-beady. She was exhausted, I realized. Some grins are only reflexes, but others are courageous acts—Clara's was the latter. The clock had just chimed ten-thirty. The party showed no signs of slowing. At least the clock is moving, I pointed out. We tried to conjure a picture of the risen sun, piercing the thousand windows of the Emerald Lodge.

"You doing okay?"

"I have certainly been better."

"We're going to make it down the mountain."

"Of course we are."

———

Near the western staircase, Lee waited with a drink in hand. Shadows pooled unnaturally around his feet; they reminded me of peeling paint. If you stared too long, they seemed to curl slightly up from the floorboards.

"Jean! There you are!"

At the sound of my real name, I felt electrified—hadn't I introduced myself by a pseudonym? Clara and I had a telephone book of false names. It was how we dressed for parties. We chose alter egos for each other, like jewelry.

"It's Candy, actually." I smiled politely. "Short for Candace."

"Whatever you say, *Jean,*" Lee said, playing lightly with my bracelet.

"Who told you that? Did my friend tell you that?"

"You did."

I blinked slowly at Lee, watching his grinning face come in and out of focus.

I'd had plenty more to drink, and I realized that I didn't

remember half the things we'd talked about. What else, I wondered, had I let slip?

"How did you get that name, huh? It's a really pretty name, Jeannie."

I was unused to being asked personal questions. Lee put his arms around me, and then, unbelievably, I heard my voice in the darkness, telling the ghost a true story.

Jean, I told him, is what I prefer to go by. In Florida, most everybody called me Aubby.

My parents named me Aubergine. They wanted me to have a glamorous name. It was a luxury they could afford to give me, a spell of protection. "Aubergine" was a word that my father had learned during his wartime service, the French word for "dawn," he said. A name like that, they felt, would envelop me in an aura of mystery, from swaddling to shroud. One night, on a rare trip to a restaurant, we learned the truth from a fellow diner, a bald, genteel eavesdropper.

"Aubergine," he said thoughtfully. "What an *interesting* name."

We beamed at him eagerly, my whole family.

"It is, of course, the French word for 'eggplant.'"

"Oh, darn!" my mother said, unable to contain her sorrow.

"Of course!" roared old dad.

But we were a family long accustomed to reversals of fortune; in fact, my father had gone bankrupt misapprehending various facts about the dog track and his own competencies.

"It suits you," the bald diner said, smiling and turning the pages of his newspaper. "You are a little fat, yes? Like an eggplant!"

"We call her Jean for short," my mother had smoothly replied.

———

Clara was always teasing me. "Don't fall in love with anybody," she'd say, and then we'd laugh for longer than the joke really warranted, because this scenario struck us both as so unlikely. But as I leaned against this ghost, I felt my life falling into place. It was the spotlight of his eyes, those radiant beams, that gently drew motes from the past out of me—and I loved this. He had gotten me talking, and now I didn't want to shut up. His eyes grew wider and wider, golden nets woven with golden fibers. I told him about my father's suicide, my mother's death. At the last second, I bit my tongue, but I'd been on the verge of telling him about Clara's bruises, those mute blue coordinates. Not to solicit Lee's help—what could this phantom do? No, merely to keep him looking at me.

Hush, Aubby, I heard in Clara's tiny, moth-fluttery voice, which was immediately incinerated by the hot pleasure of Lee's gaze.

We kissed a second time. I felt our teeth click together; two warm hands cupped my cheeks. But when he lifted his face, his anguish leapt out at me. His wild eyes were like bees trapped on the wrong side of a window, bouncing along the glass. "You . . . ," he began. He stroked at my cheek. "You feel . . ." Very delicately, he tried kissing me again. "You taste . . ." Some bewildered comment trailed off into silence.

One hand smoothed over my dress, while the other rose to claw at his pale throat.

"How's that?" he whispered hoarsely in my ear. "Does that feel all right?"

Lee was so much in the dark. I had no idea how to help him. I wondered how honest I would have wanted Lee to be with me, if he were in my shoes. *Put him out of his misery,* country people say of sick dogs. But Lee looked very happy. Excited, even, about the future.

"Should we go upstairs, Jean?"

"But where did Clara go?" I kept murmuring.

It took great effort to remember her name.

"Did she disappear on you?" Lee said, and winked. "Do you think she's found her way upstairs, too?"

Crossing the room, we spotted her. Her hands were clasped around the hog stubble of a large boy's neck, and they were swaying in the center of the hexagon. I waved at her, trying to get her attention, and she stared right through me. A smile played on her face, while the chandeliers plucked up the red in her hair, strumming even the subtlest colors out of her.

Grinning, Lee lifted a hand to his black eyebrow in a mock salute. His bloodless hand looked thin as paper. I had a sharp memory of standing at a bay window, in Florida, and feeling the night sky change direction on me—no longer lapping at the horizon but rolling inland. Something was pouring toward me now, a nothingness exhaled through the floury membrane of the boy. If Lee could see the difference in the transparency of our splayed hands, he wasn't letting on.

Now Clara was kissing her boy's plush lips. Her fingers were still knitted around his tawny neck. *Clara, Clara, we have abandoned our posts.* We shouldn't have kissed them; we shouldn't have taken that black water onboard. Lee may not have known that he was dead, but my body did; it seemed to be having some kind of stupefied reaction to the kiss. I felt myself sinking fast, sinking far below thought. The two boys swept us toward the stairs with a courtly synchronicity, their uniformed bodies tugging us into the shadows, where our hair and our skin and our purple and emerald party dresses turned suddenly blue, like two candles blown out.

And now I watched as Clara flowed up the stairs after her stocky dancing partner, laughing with genuine abandon, her head flung back and her throat exposed. I followed right behind her, but I could not close the gap. I watched her ascent, just as I had on the lift. Groggily, I saw them moving down a posy-wallpapered corridor. Even squinting, I could not make out the watery digits on the doors. All these doors were, of course, identical. One swung open, then shut, swallowing Clara. I doubted we would find each other again. By now, however, I felt very calm. I let Lee lead me by the wrist, like a child, only my bracelets shaking.

Room 409 had natural wood walls, glowing with a piney shine in the low light. Lee sat down on a chair and tugged off his work boots, flushed with the yellow avarice of 4 a.m. Darkness flooded steadily out of him, and I absorbed it. "Jean," he kept saying, a word that sounded so familiar, although its meaning now escaped me. I covered his mouth with my mouth. I sat on the ghost boy's lap, kissing his neck, pretending to feel a pulse. Eventually, grumbling an apology, Lee stood and disappeared into the bathroom. I heard a faucet turn on; Lord knows what came pouring out of it. The room had a queen bed, and I pulled back a corner of the soft cotton quilt. It was so beautiful, edelweiss white. I slid in with my dress still pinned to me. I could not stop yawning; seconds from now, I'd drop off. I never wanted to go back out there, I decided. Why lie about this? There was no longer any chair-lift waiting to carry us home, was there? No mountain, no fool's-gold moon. The Earth we'd left felt like a photograph. And was it such a terrible thing, to live at the lodge?

Something was descending slowly, like a heavy theater curtain, inside my body; I felt my will to know the truth ebbing into a happy, warm insanity. We could all be dead—why not? We could be in love, me and a dead boy. We could be sisters here, Clara and me, equally poor and equally beautiful.

Lee had come back and was stroking my hair onto the pillow. "Want to take a little nap?" he asked.

I had never wanted anything more. But then I looked down at my red fingernails and noticed a tiny chip in the polish, exposing the translucent surface below. Clara had painted them for me yesterday morning, before the party—eons ago. *Clara,* I remembered. *What is happening to Clara?* I dug out of the heavy coverlet, struggling up. At precisely that moment, the door began to rattle in its frame; outside, a man was calling for Lee.

"He's here! He's here! He's here!" a baritone voice growled happily. "Goddammit, Lee, button up and get downstairs!"

Lee rubbed his golden eyes and palmed his curls. I stared at him uncomprehendingly.

"I regret the interruption, my dear. But this we cannot miss." He grinned at me, exposing a mouthful of holes. "You wanna have your picture taken, doncha?"

———

Clara and I found each other on the staircase. What had happened to her, in her room? That's a lock I can't pick. Even on ordinary nights, we often split up, and afterward in the boardinghouse we never discussed those unreal intervals. On our prospecting expeditions, whatever doors we closed stayed shut. Clara had her arm around her date, who looked doughier than I recalled, his round face almost featureless, his eyebrows vanished; even the point of his green toothpick seemed blurred. Lee ran up to greet him, and we hung back while the two men continued downstairs, racing each other to reach the photographer. This time we did not try to disguise our relief.

"I was falling asleep!" Clara said. "And I wanted to sleep so badly, Aubby, but then I remembered you were here somewhere, too."

"I was falling asleep," I said, "but then I remembered your face."

Clara redid my bun, and I straightened her hem. We were fine, we promised each other.

"I didn't get anything," Clara said. "But I'm not leaving empty-handed."

I gaped at her. Was she still talking about prospecting?

"You can't steal from this place."

Clara had turned to inspect a sculpted flower blooming

from an iron railing; she tugged at it experimentally, as if she thought she might free it from the banister.

"Clara, wake up. That's not—"

"No? That's not why you brought me here?"

She flicked her eyes up at me, her gaze limpid and accusatory. And I felt I'd become fluent in the language of eyes; now I saw what she'd known all along. What she'd been swallowing back on our prospecting trips, what she'd never once screamed at me, in the freezing boardinghouse: *You use me. Every party, you bait the hook, and I dangle. I let them, I am eaten, and what do I get? Some scrap metal?*

"I'm sorry, Clara . . ."

My apology opened outward, a blossoming horror. I'd used her bruises to justify leaving Florida. I'd used her face to open doors. Greed had convinced me I could take care of her up here, and then I'd disappeared on her. How long had Clara known what I was doing? I'd barely known myself.

But Clara, still holding my hand, pointed at the clock. It was 5 a.m.

"Dawn is coming." She gave me a wide, genuine smile. "We are going to get home."

Downstairs, the CCC boys were shuffling around the dance floor, positioning themselves in a triangular arrangement. The tallest men knelt down, and the shorter men filed behind them. When they saw us watching from the staircase, they waved.

"Where you girls been? The photographer is *here*."

The fires were still burning, the huge logs unconsumed. Even the walls, it seemed, were trembling in anticipation. This place wanted to go on shining in our living eyes, was that it? The dead boys feasted on our attention, but so did the entire structure.

Several of the dead boys grabbed us and hustled us toward the posed and grinning rows of uniformed workers. We spotted a tripod in the corner of the lodge, a man doubled over, his head swallowed by the black cover. He was wearing a flamboyant costume: a ragged black cape, made from the same smocky material as the camera cover, and bright-red satin trousers.

"Picture time!" his voice boomed.

Now the true light of the Emerald Lodge began to erupt in rhythmic bursts. We winced at the metallic flash, the sun above his neck. The workers stiffened, their lean faces plumped by grins. It was an inversion of the standard firing squad: two dozen men hunched before the photographer and his mounted cannon. *"Cheese!"* the CCC boys cried.

We squinted against the radiant detonations. These blasts were much brighter and louder than any shutter click on the Earth.

With each flash, the men grew more definite: their chins sharpening, cheeks ripening around their smiles. Dim brows darkened to black arcs; the gold of their eyes deepened, as if each face were receiving a generous pour of whiskey. Was it life that these ghosts were drawing from the camera's light? No, these flashes—they imbued the ghosts with something else.

"Do not let him shoot you," I hissed, grabbing Clara by the elbow. We ran for cover. Every time the flashbulb illuminated the room, I flinched. "Did he get you? Did he get me?"

With an animal terror, we knew to avoid that light. We

could not let the photographer fix us in the frame, we could not let him capture us on whatever film still held them here, dancing jerkily on the hexagonal floor. *If that happens, we are done for,* I thought. *We are here forever.*

With his unlidded eye, the photographer spotted us where we had crouched behind the piano. Bent at the waist, his head cloaked by the wrinkling purple-black cover, he rotated the camera. Then he waggled his fingers at us, motioning us into the frame.

"Smile, ladies," Mickey Loatch ordered as we darted around the cedar tables.

We never saw his face, but he was hunting us. This devil— excuse me, let us continue to call him "the party photographer," as I do not want to frighten anyone unduly—spun the tripod on its rolling wheels, his hairy hands gripping its sides, the cover flapping onto his shoulders like a strange pleated wig. His single blue lens kept fixing on our bodies. Clara dove low behind the wicker chairs and pulled me after her.

The CCC boys who were assembled on the dance floor, meanwhile, stayed glacially frozen. Smiles floated muzzily around their faces. A droning rose from the room, a sound like dragonflies in summer, and I realized that we were hearing the men's groaning effort to stay in focus: to flood their faces with ersatz blood, to hold still, hold still, and smile.

Then the chair tipped; one of our pursuers had lifted Clara up, kicking and screaming, and began to carry her back to the dance floor, where men were shifting to make a place for her.

"Front and center, ladies," the company captain called urgently. "Fix your dress, dear. The straps have gotten all twisted."

I had a terrible vision of Clara caught inside the shot with them, her eyes turning from brown to umber to the deathlessly sparkling gold.

"Stop!" I yelled. "Let her go! She—"

She's alive, I did not risk telling them.

"She does not photograph well!"

With aqueous indifference, the camera lifted its eye.

"Listen, forgive us, but we cannot be in your photograph!"

"Let *go*!" Clara said, cinched inside an octopus of the men's restraining arms, every one of them pretending that this was still a game.

We used to pledge, with great passion, always to defend each other. We meant it, too. These were easy promises to make, when we were safely at the boardinghouse; but on this mountain even breathing felt dangerous.

But Clara pushed back. Clara saved us.

She directed her voice at every object in the lodge, screaming at the very rafters. Gloriously, her speech gurgling with saliva and blood and everything wet, everything living, she began to howl at them, the dead ones. She foamed red, my best friend, forming the words we had been stifling all night, the spell-bursting ones:

"It's done, gentlemen. It's over. Your song ended. You are news font; you are characters. I could read you each your own obituary. None of this—"

"Shut her up," a man growled.

"Shut up, shut up!" several others screamed.

She was chanting, one hand at her throbbing temple: "None of this, none of this, none of this *is*!"

Some men were thumbing their ears shut. Some had braced

themselves in the doorframes, as they teach the children of the West to do during earthquakes. I resisted the urge to cover my own ears as she bansheed back at the shocked ghosts:

"Two years ago, there was an avalanche at your construction site. It was terrible, a tragedy. We were all so sorry . . ."

She took a breath.

"You are dead."

Her voice grew gentle, almost maternal—it was like watching the wind drop out of the world, flattening a full sail. Her shoulders fell, her palms turned out.

"You were all buried with this lodge."

Their eyes turned to us, incredulous. Hard and yellow, dozens of spiny armadillos. After a second, the CCC company burst out laughing. Some men cried tears, they were howling so hard at Clara. Lee was among them, and he looked much changed, his face as smooth and flexibly white as an eel's belly.

These men—they didn't believe her!

And why should we ever have expected them to believe us, two female nobodies, two intruders? For these were the master carpenters, the master stonemasons and weavers, the master self-deceivers, the ghosts.

"Dead," one sad man said, as if testing the word out.

"Dead. Dead. Dead," his friends repeated, quizzically.

But the sound was a shallow production, as if each man were scratching at topsoil with the point of a shovel. Aware, perhaps, that if he dug with a little more dedication, he would find his body lying breathless under this world's surface.

"Dead."   "Dead."

"Dead."   "Dead."   *"Dead."*

"Dead."

They croaked like pond frogs, all across the ballroom. "Dead" was a foreign word, which the boys could pronounce perfectly, soberly, and matter-of-factly, without comprehending its meaning.

One or two of them, however, exchanged a glance; I saw a burly blacksmith cut eyes at the ruby-cheeked trumpet player. It was a guileful look, a what-can-be-done look.

So they knew; or they almost knew; or they'd buried the knowledge of their deaths, and we had exhumed it. Who can say what the dead do or do not know? Perhaps the knowledge of one's death, ceaselessly swallowed, is the very food you need to become a ghost. They burned that knowledge up like whale fat and continued to shine on.

But then a quaking began to ripple across the ballroom floor. A chandelier, in its handsome zigzag frame, burst into a spray of glass above us. One of the pillars, three feet wide, cracked in two. Outside, from all corners, we heard a rumbling, as if the world were gathering its breath.

"Oh, God," I heard one of them groan. "It's happening again."

My eyes met Clara's, as they always do at parties. She did not have to tell me: *Run.*

On our race through the lodge, in all that chaos and din, Clara somehow heard another sound. A bright chirping. A sound like gold coins being tossed up, caught, and fisted. It stopped her cold. The entire building was shaking on its foundations, but through the tremors she spotted a domed cage, hanging in the foyer. On a tiny stirrup, a yellow bird was swinging. The cage was a wrought-iron skeleton, the handiwork of phantoms, but the bird, we both knew instantly, was real. It was agitating its wings in the polar air, as alive as we were. Its shadow was denser than anything in that ice palace. Its song split our eardrums. Its feathers burned into our retinas, rich with solar color, and its small body was stuffed with life.

At the Evergreen Lodge, on the opposite side of the mountain, two twelve-foot doors, designed and built by the CCC, stand sentry against the outside air—seven hundred pounds of hand-cut ponderosa pine, from Oregon's primeval woods. Inside the Emerald Lodge, we found their phantom twins, the dream originals. Those doors still worked, thank God. We pushed them open. Bright light, real daylight, shot onto our faces.

The sun was rising. The chairlift, visible across a pillowcase of fresh snow, was running.

We sprinted for it. Golden sunlight painted the steel cables. We raced across the platform, jumping for the chairs, and I will never know how fast or how far we flew to get back to the Earth. In all our years of prospecting in the West, this was our greatest heist. Clara opened her satchel and lifted the yellow bird onto her lap, and I heard it shrieking the whole way down the mountain.

The Bad Graft

The land looked flattened, as if by a rolling pin. All aspects, all directions. On either side of Highway 62, the sand cast up visions of evaporated civilizations, dissolved castles that lay buried under the desert. Any human eye, goggled by a car's windshield, can graft such fantasies onto the great Mojave. And the girl and the boy in the Dodge Charger were exceptionally farsighted. Mirages rose from the boulders, a flume of dream attached to real rock.

And hadn't their trip unfolded like a fairy tale? the couple later quizzed each other, recalling that strange day, their first in California, hiking among the enormous apricot boulders of Joshua Tree National Park. The girl had gotten her period a week early and was feeling woozy; the boy kept bending over to remove a pebble from his shoe, a phantom that he repeatedly failed to find. Neither disclosed these private discomforts. Each wanted the other to have the illusion that they might pause, anywhere, at any moment, and make love.

And while both thought this was highly unlikely—not in this heat, not at this hour—the possibility kept bubbling up, everyplace they touched. This was the only true protection they'd brought with them as they walked deeper into the blue-gold Mojave.

On the day they arrived in Joshua Tree, it was a hundred and six degrees. They had never been to the desert. The boy could scarcely believe the size of the boulders, clustered under the enormous sun like dead red rockets awaiting repair, or the span of the sky, a cheerfully vacant blue dome, the desert's hallucinatory choreography achieved through stillness, brightness, darkness, distance—and all of this before noon. It was a big day, they agreed. It was a day so huge, in fact, that its real scale would always elude them. Neither understood that a single hour in the desert could mutate their entire future as a couple. In a sense, they will never escape this trail loop near Black Rock Canyon. They had prepared for the hike well, they thought, with granola bars, water, and an anti-UV sunscreen so powerful that its SPF seemed antagonistic. "Albino spring break," the boy said, rubbing the cream onto her nose. They'd heard about the couple who had died of dehydration six miles from where they were standing. They congratulated themselves on being unusually responsible and believed themselves to be at the start of a long journey, weightless spores blowing west.

The trip was a kind of honeymoon. The boy and girl were eloping. They weren't married, however, and had already agreed that they never would be—they weren't that kind of couple. The boy, Andy, was a reader; he said that they were seafarers, wanderers. EVER UNFIXED, a line from Melville, was scraped in red ink across the veins of his arm. The girl, Angie, was three years sober and still struggling to find her mooring on dry land. On their first date they had decided to run away together.

Andy bought a stupidly huge knife; Angie had a tiny magenta flashlight suspended on a gold chain, which she wore around her throat. He was twenty-two; she had just turned twenty-six. Kids were for later, maybe. They could still see the children they had been: their own Popsicle-red smiles haunting them. Still, they'd wanted to celebrate a beginning. And the Mojave was a good place to launch into exile together; already they felt their past lives in Pennsylvania dissolving into rumor, sucked up by the hot sun of California and the perfectly blue solvent of the sky.

They'd been driving for three days; almost nobody knew yet that they were gone. They'd cashed old checks. They'd quit their jobs. Nothing was planned. The rental Dodge Charger had been a real steal, because the boy's cousin Sewell was a manager at the Zero to Sixty franchise, and because it smelled like decades of cigarettes. Between them they had nine hundred and fifty dollars left now. Less, less, less. At each rest stop, Angie uncapped the ballpoint, did some nauseating accounting. Everything was going pretty fast. By the time they reached Nevada, they had spent more than eight hundred dollars on gasoline.

———

Near Palm Springs, they stop to eat at a no-name diner and nearly get sick from the shock of oxygen outside the stale sedan. The night before, just outside Albuquerque, they parked behind a barbecue restaurant and slept inside a cloud of meat smells. The experience still has the sizzle of a recent hell in Angie's memory. Will they do this every night? She wants to believe her boyfriend when he tells her they are gypsies, two moths drunk on light, darting from the flower of one red sunset to the next; but several times she's dozed off in the passenger seat and awakened from traitorous dreams of her old bedroom, soft pillows.

After dinner, Andy drives drowsily, weaving slightly. Sand, sand, sand—all that pulverized time. Eons ago, the world's burst hourglass spilled its contents here; now the years pile and spin, waiting with inhuman patience to be swept into some future ocean. Sand washes right up to the paved road, washes over to the other side in a solid orange current, illuminated by their headlights.

"Who lives way out like that?" Angie says, pointing through the window at a line of trailer homes. *Why* is the implied question. Thirteen-foot saguaro cacti look like enormous roadside hitchhikers, comical and menacing. Andy is drifting off, his hand on Angie's bare thigh, when a streak of color crosses the road.

"Jesus! What was that?"

A parade of horned beasts. Just sheep, Angie notes with relief.

Andy watches each animal go from sheep to cloud in the side mirror, reduced immediately into memory. The radio blares songs about other humans' doomed or lost loves, or their bombastic lusts in progress. Andy watches his girlfriend's red lips move, mouthing the lyrics to a song Andy

didn't realize he knew. *My wife's lips,* he thinks, and feels
frightened by the onslaught of an unexpected happiness.
Were they serious, coming out here? Were they kidding
around? Are they getting more serious? Less? Perhaps they'll
sort it all out at the next rest stop.

That night, they stay in a fifty-dollar motel. By dawn, they
are back on the highway. They don't try to account for their
urgency to be gone. Both feel it; neither can resist it.

At 10 a.m., Angie lifts her arm to point at the western sky.
There is a pale rainbow arcing over the desert. It looks as if
God had made a bad laundry error, mixed his colors with his
whites. *How could even the rainbow be faded?* she wonders.

"Look!" she blurts. "We're here."

The sign reads ENTERING JOSHUA TREE NATIONAL PARK.

Quietly, they roll under the insubstantial archway of the
rainbow. Andy slows the Charger. He wants to record this
transition, which feels important. Usually, you can only catch
the Sasquatch blur of your own legendary moments in the
side mirrors.

More and more slowly, they drive into the park. Sand
burns outside their windows in every direction. Compass
needles spin in their twinned minds: everywhere they look,
they are greeted by horizon, deep gulps of blue. People think
of the green pastoral when they think of lovers in nature.
Those English poets used the vales and streams to douse their
lusts into verse. But the desert offers something that no forest
brook or valley ever can: distance. A cloudless rooming house
for couples. Skies that will host any visitors' dreams with the
bald hospitality of pure space. In terms of an ecology that
can support two lovers in hot pursuit of each other, this is the

place; everywhere you look, you'll find monuments to fevered longing. Craters beg for rain all year long. Moths haunt the succulents, winging sticky pollen from flower to flower.

Near the campground entrance, they are met by a blue-eyed man of indeterminate age, a park employee, who comes lunging out of the infernal brightness with whiskery urgency. His feet are so huge that he looks like a jackrabbit, even in boots.

"Where did you folks wash up from?" he asks.

Their answer elicits a grunt.

"First timers to the park?"

The boy explains that they are on their honeymoon, watches the girl redden with pleasure.

Up close, the ranger has the unnervingly direct gaze and polished bristlecone skin of so many outdoorsmen. A large bee lifts off a cactus, walks the rim of his hat, and he doesn't flick it off, a show of tolerance that is surely for their benefit.

"Do Warren Peak. Go see the Joshua trees. Watch the yucca moths do their magic. You're in luck—you've come smack in the middle of a pulse event. As far as we can tell, the entire range of Joshuas is in bloom right now. You think *you're* in love? The moths are smitten. In all my years, I've seen nothing to rival it. It's a goddamn orgy in the canyon."

It turns out that their visit has coincided with a tremendous blossoming, one that is occurring all over the Southwest. Highly erotic, the ranger says, with his creepy bachelor smile. A record number of greenish-white flowers have erupted out of the Joshuas. Pineapple-huge, they crown every branch.

"Now, there's an education for a couple, huh? Charles Darwin agrees with me. Says it's the most remarkable pollination system in nature. 'There is no romance more dire and pure than that of the desert moth and the Joshua.'"

"Dire?" the girl asks. And learns from the ranger that the Joshua trees may be on the brink of extinction. Botanists believe they are witnessing a coordinated response to crisis. Perhaps a drought, legible in the plants' purplish leaves, has resulted in this push. Seeds in abundance. The ancient species' Hail Mary pass. Yucca moths, attracted by the flowers' penetrating odor, are their heroic spouses, equally dependent, equally endangered; their larval children feast on yucca seeds.

"It's an obligate relationship. Each species' future depends entirely on the other," the ranger says, and then grins hugely at them. The boy is thinking that the math sounds about right: two species, one fate. The girl wonders, of their own elopement: Who is more dependent on whom? What toast might Charles Darwin make were they to break their first vows and get married?

So they obey the ranger, drive the Charger another quarter mile, park at the deserted base of Warren Peak.

Angie says she has to pee, and Andy sits on the hood and watches her.

They set off along the trail, which begins to ascend the ridgeline east of Warren Peak. Now Joshua woodland sprawls around them.

This is where the bad graft occurs.

For the rest of her life, she will be driven to return to the park, searching for the origin of the feeling that chooses this day to invade her and make its home under her skin.

Before starting the ascent, each pauses to admire the plant that is the park's namesake. The Joshua trees look *hilariously* alien. Like Satan's telephone poles. They're primitive, irregularly limbed, their branches swooning up and down, sparsely covered with syringe-thin leaves—more like spines, Angie notes. Some mature trees have held their insane poses for a thousand years; they look as if they were on drugs and hallucinating themselves.

The ranger told them that the plant was named in the nineteenth century by a caravan of Mormons, passing through what they perceived to be a wasteland. They saw a forest of hands, which recalled to them the prayers of the prophet Joshua. But the girl can't see these plants as any kind of holy augury. She's thinking: *Dr. Seuss. Timothy Leary.*

"See the moths, Angie?"

No wonder they call it a pulse event—wings are beating everywhere.

Unfortunately for Angie, the ranger they encountered had zero information to share on the ghostly Leap. So he could not warn her about the real danger posed to humans by the pulsating Joshuas. Between February and April, the yucca moths arrive like living winds, swirling through Black Rock Canyon. Blossoms detonate. Pollen heaves up.

Then the Joshua tree sheds a fantastic sum of itself.

Angie feels dizzy. As she leans out to steady herself against a nearby Joshua tree, her finger is pricked by something sharp. One of the plant's daggerlike spines. Bewildered, she stares at the spot of red on her finger. Running blood looks exotic next to the etiolated grasses.

Angie Gonzalez, wild child from Nestor, Pennsylvania, pricks her finger on a desert dagger and becomes an entirely new creature.

When the Leap occurs, Angie does not register any change whatsoever. She has no idea what has just added its store of life to hers.

But other creatures of the desert *do* seem to apprehend what is happening. Through the crosshairs of its huge pupils, a tarantula watches Angie's skin drink in the danger: the pollen from the Joshua mixes with the red blood on her finger. On a fuchsia ledge of limestone, a dozen lizards witness the Leap. They shut their gluey eyes as one, sealing their lucent bodies from contagion, interkingdom corruption.

During a season of wild ferment, a kind of atmospheric accident can occur: the extraordinary moisture stored in the mind of a passing animal or hiker can compel the spirit of a Joshua to Leap through its own membranes. The change is metaphysical: the tree's spirit is absorbed into the migrating consciousness, where it lives on, intertwined with its host.

Instinct guides its passage now, through the engulfing darkness of Angie's mind. Programmed with the urgent need to plug itself into some earth, the plant's spirit goes searching for terra firma.

Andy unzips his backpack, produces Fiji water and a Snoopy Band-Aid.

"Your nose got burned," he says, and smiles at her.

And, at this juncture, she can smile back.

He kisses the nose.

"C'mon, let's get out of here."

Then something explodes behind her eyelids into a radial green fan, dazzling her with pain. Her neck aches, her abdomen. The pain moves lower. It feels as if an umbrella were opening below her navel. *Menstrual cramps,* she thinks. Seconds later, as with a soldering iron, an acute and narrowly focused heat climbs her spine.

At first, the Joshua tree is elated to discover that it's alive: *I survived my Leap. I was not annihilated. Whatever "I" was.*

Grafted to the girl's consciousness, the plant becomes aware of itself. It dreams its green way up into her eyestalks, peers out:

Standing there, in the mirror of the desert, are a hundred versions of itself. Here is its home: a six-armed hulk, fibrous and fruiting obscenely under a noon sun. Here is the locus that recently contained this tree spirit. For a tree, this is a dreadful experience. Its uprooted awareness floats throughout the alien form. It concentrates itself behind Angie's eyeballs, where there is moisture. This insoluble spirit, this refugee from the Joshua tree, understands itself to have leapt into hell. The wrong place, the wrong vessel. It pulses outward in a fuzzy frenzy of investigation, flares greener, sends out feelers. Compared with the warm and expansive desert soil, the human body is a cul-de-sac.

This newborn ghost has only just begun to apprehend itself when its fragile tenancy is threatened: Angie sneezes, rubs at her temple. Unaware that this is an immunologic reflex, she is convulsed by waves of nostalgia for earlier selves, remote homes. Here, for some reason, is her childhood backyard, filled with anarchic wildflowers and bordered by Pennsylvania hemlock.

Then the pain dismantles the memory; she holds her head in her hand, cries for Andy.

This is the plant, fighting back.

The girl moans.

"Andy, you don't have any medicine? Advil ... something?"

The vegetable invader feels the horror of its imprisonment. Its new host is walking away from the Joshua-tree forest, following Andy. What can this kind of survival mean?

Although they don't know it, escape is now impossible for our vagabonding couple. Andy opens the sedan door, Angie climbs in, and in the side mirrors the hundreds of Joshuas shrink away into hobgoblin shapes.

"Angie? You got so quiet."

"It's the sun. My head is killing me, honey."

Dispersed throughout her consciousness, the tree begins to grow.

Andy has no clue that he is now party to a love triangle. What he perceives is that his girlfriend is acting very strangely.

"Do you need some water? Want to sit and rest awhile?"

At the motel, the girl makes straight for the bathroom faucet. She washes down the water with more water, doesn't want to eat dinner. When Andy tries to undress her, she fights him off. Her movements seem to him balletic, unusually nimble; yet, walking across the room, she pauses at the oddest moments. That night, she basks in the glow of their TV as if it were the sun. Yellow is such a relief.

"I hate this show," the boy says, staring not at the motel TV but at her. "Let's turn it off?"

Who are you? he does not bother to ask.

Calmly, he becomes aware that the girl he loves has exited

the room. Usually, when this sensation comes over him, it means she's fallen asleep. Tonight she is sitting up in bed, eyes bright, very wide awake. Her eyes in most lighting are hazel; tonight they are the brightest green. As if great doors had been flung open onto an empty and electrically lit room.

The Joshua tree "thinks" in covert bursts of activity:

Oh, I have made a terrible mistake.

Oh, please get me out of it, get me out of it, send me home.

"The headache," she calls the odd pressure at first. "The green headache."

"Psychosis," at 4 a.m., when its power over her crests and she lies awake terrified. "Torpor" or "sluggishness" when it ebbs.

Had you told her, *The invader is sinking its roots throughout you, tethering itself to you with a thousand spectral feelers*—who knows what she would have done?

———

The next day, they wake at dawn, as per their original plan: to start every day at sunup and navigate by whim. They go north on 247, with vague plans to stop in Barstow for gas. The girl's eyes are aching. Partway across the Morongo Basin, she starts to cry so hard that the boy is forced to pull over.

"Forget it," she says.

"Forget what?"

"It. All of it. The seafaring stuff—I can't do it anymore."

The boy blinks at her. "It's been four days."

But her lips look blue, and she won't be reasonable.

"Leave me here."

"You don't have any money."

"I'll work. They're hiring everywhere in town, did you notice that?" A job sounds unaccountably blissful to the girl. Drinking water in the afternoon. Sitting at a desk.

"What? What the hell are you talking about?"

The boy scowls down at his arm, flipped outward against the steering wheel. She keeps talking to him in a new, low monotone, telling him that she loves the desert, she loves the Joshua trees, she wants to stay. Dumbly, he rereads his own tattoo: EVER UNFIXED. For some reason, he finds that he cannot quite blame the girl for ruining things. It's the plan he hates, their excellent plan, for capsizing on them.

The crumbly truth: the boy imagined that he'd be the one to betray the girl.

"Andy, I'm sorry. But I know that I belong here."

"Okay, just to be clear: When you say 'here,' you mean this parking lot?" The sedan is parked outside Cojo's Army Surplus and Fro-Yo; it's a place where you can purchase camo underwear and also a cup of unlicensed TCBY swirl. "Or do you mean this?" He waves his arms around to indicate the desert.

Had they continued, just a short distance northwest of Yucca Valley they would have reached the on-ramp to I-15 north and, beyond that, the pinball magic of the tollbooths, that multiverse of possible futures connected by America's interstate system.

For the next two hours, they fight inside the car.

Round clusters of leaves shake loose in front of her eyes,

greeny-white blossoms. If she could only show him the desert in her imagination, Angie thinks, the way she sees it.

When it becomes clear that she's not joking, the boy turns the car around. Calls Cousin Sewell in Pennsylvania, explains their situation. "We want to stay awhile," he says. "We like it here."

Sewell needs to know how long. They'll have to put the car on some conveyance, get it back to Pennsylvania.

"Indefinitely," the boy hears himself say. Her word, for what she claims to want.

They decide to pay the weekly rate at the motel. They go for walks. They go for drives. Her favorite thing seems to be sitting in a dry wreck of a turquoise Jacuzzi they discover on the edge of town, some luckless homesteader's abandoned pleasure tub. And he likes this, too, actually—sitting in the tub, he finds it easy to pretend that they aren't trapped in a tourist town, that they are sailing toward an elsewhere. And he loves what happens to her face right at sunset over the infinite desert. Moonlight, however, affects her in a way that he finds indescribably frightening. *The change is in the eyes,* he thinks.

II. EMERGENCE

Two weeks later, in late April, their money runs out. They've spent the days outside, Angie doing stretches in the motel courtyard, Andy reading his stolen library books from back east, waiting for the bad enchantment to break. Andy tells Angie he is leaving her. They have no vehicle, the rental

Dodge having been chauffeured east by a genial grifter pal of Sewell's. Angie nods, staring out the window of their room as the rain sweeps over the desert. All the muddy colors of the sky touch the earth.

"Did you hear me? I said I'm leaving, Angie."

That afternoon, Andy gets a job at the Joshua Tree Saloon.

Then there is a period of peace, coinciding with the Joshua tree's dormancy inside Angie, which lasts from April to mid-May. In the park, the Joshuas' blossoms have all dropped off, leaving dried stalks. Andy does not even suggest "moving on" anymore, so thrilled is he to laugh with Angie again. He comes home with green fistfuls of tourist cash, reeking of Fireball and Pine-Sol. *Okay,* he thinks. *Oh, thank God. We're getting back to normal.*

Then one day, after a spectacular freak thundershower, Angie tells him that he needs to go home. Or away. Elsewhere, a bedroom other than the motel.

She feels terrible, she doesn't know what she is saying.

Get me out of it, the plant keeps throbbing like a muscle in Angie's mind. A rustling sound in her inner ear, the plant's footsteps. A throaty appetite makes her imagine stuffing herself with hot mouthfuls of desert sand. Once Andy leaves her, she'll have a chance to inspect her interior, figure out what's gone haywire.

"Let's go to Reno," Andy says. He feels quite desperate now, spinning the radio dial through seas of static. His great success this week at work was formalizing, via generous pours of straight gin, a new friendship with Jerry the Mailman, who has given him access to his boxy truck.

"Go to Reno. Win big. I'll be right here. I don't want to leave the desert."

Why doesn't she? The girl grows hysterical whenever Andy drives toward the freeway that might carry them away from the Mojave. She feels best when they are close to Warren Peak and the Black Rock Canyon campground.

For the next two weeks, she keeps encouraging Andy to leave her. Sometimes she feels a lump in her throat that she can't swallow, and it's easy to pretend that this is a vestige of who she used to be, her Pennsylvania history, now compacted into a hard ball she cannot access or dissolve; for Andy's sake, she wishes she could be that girl again. Dimly she is aware that she used to crave travel, adventure. She can remember the pressure of Andy's legs tangled around her, but not what she held in her mind. The world has grown unwieldy, and there are days now when the only thing that appeals to her is pulling up her T-shirt and going belly flat on the burning pink sand beyond the motel walkway.

One night, Angie turns to face the wall. Golf-ball-sized orange-and-yellow flowers pattern their wallpaper. Plus water stains from ancient leaks. She has never noticed this before. Under the influence of the Joshua, she sees these water stains as beautiful. That Rorschach is more interesting than TV. "What do you see?" she asks the boy.

"I'm not in the mood," he says, having at last been granted the opportunity to have a mood, after days and hours spent trying to rekindle her appetite for pleasure, for danger. He realizes that he has cut all ties for her, that he has nothing he wants to return to in Pennsylvania. It's a liberating, terrifying feeling. If she leaves him—if he leaves her—what then?

Now the plant is catching on to something.

In its three months of incubation, it grows exponentially in its capacity for thought. Gradually, the plant learns to "think" blue, to "smell" rain through a nose.

Unfurling its languorous intelligence, it looks out through her eyes, hunting for meaning the way it used to seek out deep sun, jade dew, hunting now for the means of imagining its own life, comprehending what it has become inside the girl.

The Joshua tree discovers that it *loves* church! Plugging one's knees into the purple risers, lifting to enter a song. The apple-red agony painted onto the cheeks of the sallow man. All the light that fills the church drifts dreamily over the Joshua tree, which stretches to its fullest extension inside the girl during the slow-crawling time of the service. It approves of this place, which resembles a massive seed hull. Deeply, extrapolating from its forays into the earth, it understands the architecture and the impulse. Craving stillness, these humans have evolved this stronghold.

"How was it?" Andy asks, picking her up. He refused to go with her. Sundays are his day off. "Delicious God-bread? Lots of songs?"

"It was nice. What are you so jealous about?"

"Angie, you never said."

"Mmm?"

"I didn't know you were religious."

Her head bobs on the long stem of her neck, as if they were agreeing on a fascinating point.

"Yes. There's plenty we don't know about each other."

I can still get out of this, he thinks. Without understanding exactly how the trap got sprung, he can feel its teeth in him.

"You should come in next time," she offers. "You'd like the windows."

"I can see the windows right now."

"You'd like being on our side of them."

Seed hull, the girl thinks, for no reason.

———

Sometimes, to earn extra money, she watches kids who are staying at the motel. Six dollars an hour, four dollars for each additional kid. She is good at it, mostly.

Timmy Babson hates the babysitter. Sometimes her eyes are a dull, friendly brown and as kind as his sister's; sometimes they are twin vacuums. This is already pretty scary. But tonight, when he looks over, he sees the bad light flooding into them. Not yellow, not green. An older color, which Timmy recognizes on sight but cannot name. And this is much worse.

His own eyes prickle wetly. His blond hair darkens with sweat; pearls of water stand out on his smooth six-year-old forehead. The longer he stares back, the wider the gaze seems to get, like a grin. Her eyes radiate hard spines of heat, which drill into him. Timmy Babson feels punctured, "seen."

"Jane!" Timmy screams for his mother, calling for her by her first name for the first time. "Jane, Jane! It's looking at me again!"

On her good days, Angie tries to battle the invader. She thinks she's fighting against lethargy. She does jumping jacks in the motel courtyard, calls her best friend in Juneau from the motel pay phone, and anxiously tries to reminisce about their shitty high-school band. They sing an old song together, and she feels almost normal.

But, increasingly, she finds herself powerless to resist the warmth that spreads through her chest, the midday paralysis, the hunger for something slow and deep and unnameable. Some maid has drawn the blackout curtains. One lightbulb dangles. The dark reminds Angie of packed earth, moisture. What she interprets as sprawling emotion is the Joshua tree. Here was its birth, in the sands of Black Rock Canyon. Here was its death, and its rebirth as a ghostly presence in the human. Couldn't it perhaps Leap back into that older organism?

The lightbulb pulses in time with Angie's headache. It acquires a fetal glow, otherworldly.

Home, home, home.

Down, down, down.

Her heels grind uselessly into the carpet. Her toes curl at the fibers. She stands in the quiet womb of the room, waiting for a signal from the root brain, the ancient network from which the invader has been exiled. She lifts her arms until they are fully extended, her fingers turned outward. Her ears prick up like sharp leaves, alert for moisture.

She is still standing like that when Andy comes home with groceries at 10 p.m., her palms facing the droning lightbulb, so perfectly still that he yelps when he spots her.

How old such stories must be, legends of the bad romance between wandering humans and plants! How often these bad grafts must occur, and few people ever the wiser!

In 1852, the Mormon settlers who gave the Joshua tree its name reported every variety of disturbance among their party after hikes through the sparse and fragrant forests of Death Valley. One elder sat on a rock at the forest's edge and refused to move.

Eighteen seventy-three, in the lawless town of Panamint City. Darwin in 1874; Modoc in 1875. During the silver boom dozens of miners went missing. Many leapt to their deaths down the shafts. The silver rush coincided with a pulse event: the trees blossomed unstoppably, wept pollen, and Leapt, eclipsing the minds of these poor humans, who stood no chance against the vegetable's ancient spirit. Dying is one symptom of a bad graft. The invasive species coiled green around the silver miners' brains.

Eighteen seventy-nine: All towns abandoned. Sorted ore sat in wheelbarrows aboveground, winking emptily at the nearby Joshuas.

In 1922, in what is now the southern region of the park, near the abandoned iron mines of Eagle Mountain, a man was killed by the human host of a Joshua tree. It was not difficult to find the murderer, since a girl was huddled a few feet from the warm body, sobbing quietly.

"A crime of passion," the young officer, who tended to take a romantic view of motives, murmured. The grizzled elder on the call with him had less to say about what drove anyone to do anything.

All the girl could remember was the terrible, irremediable tension between wanting to be somewhere and wanting to be nowhere. And the plant, crazed by its proximity to rich familiar soil, tried repeatedly to Leap out of her. This caused her hand to lift, holding a long knife, and plummet earthward, rooting into the fleshy chest of her lover, feeling deeper and deeper for moisture.

———

The Joshua tree's greatest victory over the couple comes four months into their stay: they sign a lease. A bungalow on the outskirts of the national park, with an outdoor shower and a fence to keep out the coyotes.

When the shower water gets into their mouths, it tastes like poison. Strange reptiles hug the fence posts, like colorful olives on toothpicks. Andy squeezes Angie's hand and returns the gaze of these tiny monsters; he feels strangely bashful as they bugle their throats at him. Four months into his desert sojourn, and he still doesn't know the name of anything. Up close, the bungalow looks a lot like a shed. The bloated vowels of his signature on the landlord's papers make him think of a large hand blurring underwater.

Three Joshua trees grow right in their new backyard.

Rent, before utilities, is four hundred dollars.

"We can't afford this," he tells the girl, speaking less to her than to the quiet trees, wanting some court stenographer in the larger cosmos to record his protest.

The landlord, who is a native of Yucca Valley, is taking the young couple through the calendar. His name is Desert John, and he offers these eastern kids what he calls Desert John's Survival Tips. With laconic glee, he advises Andy to cut back the chaparral in their backyard to waist height in summer, to avoid the "minimal" danger of baby rattlesnakes. He tells Angie to hydrate "aggressively," especially if she's trying to get pregnant. (Angie starfishes a hand over her belly button and blanches; nobody has said anything to suggest this.) With polite horror, the couple nods along to stories of their predecessors, former tenants who collapsed from heat exhaustion, were bitten by every kind of snake and spider: "Fanged in the ankle and ass, I shit you not, kids. Beware the desert hammock."

Average annual rainfall: five inches. Eight-degree nights in December, one-hundred-and-twelve-degree July days. Andy is thinking of Angie's face on the motel pillow. He calculates they've slept together maybe fourteen times in four months. In terms of survival strategies, in a country hostile to growth? These desert plants, so ostentatiously alive in the Mojave, have got zero on Andy.

III. ESTABLISHMENT

Once, and only once, the three of them achieve a perfect union.

It takes some doing, but Andy finally succeeds in getting her out of the house.

"It's our anniversary," he lies, since they never really picked a day.

He's taking Angie to Pappy & Harriet's Pioneertown Palace, a frontier-themed dance hall frequented by bikers and artists and other jolly modern species of degenerates. It's only six miles northeast of their new home and burns like a Roman candle against the immensity of the Mojave. Through surveying expeditions made in Jerry's truck, Andy has delimited the boundary lines of Angie's tolerance; once they move beyond a certain radius, she says that her head feels "green" and her bones begin to ache. Pain holds her here—that's their shared impression. So when Andy parks the truck, they are both relieved to discover that she is smiling.

The Joshua tree discovers that it *loves* to dance! Better even than church is the soft glow of the uneven dance floor. Swung around in strangers' arms, Andy and Angie let themselves dance until they are sick, at the edge of the universe. Andy lets Angie buy him three shots of rum. A weather seizes them and blows them around—a weather you can order for a quarter, the jukebox song.

It is a good night. Outside the dance hall, the parking lot is full of cars and trucks, empty of humans. The wind pushes into them, as hot as the blasts of air from a hand dryer.

Angie draws Andy's attention to the claret cup of the moon. "It looks red," she says. And it does. Sitting on a stranger's fender, listening to the dying strains of a pop song they both despise, Andy asks her softly, "What's changed, Angie?"

And when she doesn't or can't answer, he asks, "What's changing now?"

A question they like better, because at least its tense sounds more hopeful.

The Joshua tree leafs out in her mind. Heat blankets her; for a moment she is sure she will faint. Her vision clears. "Bamboleo" plays inside the dance hall. Through the illuminated squares of its windows, they can see the waving wheat of the dancers' upper bodies. Mouths gape in angry shock behind the frosted glass; they are only singing along to the music, Angie knows. Outside, the boy presses his mouth against hers. Now he is pressing every part of himself against the girl; inside her, his competitor presses back.

"Let's go. Let's go. Let's get the fuck out of here."

"Let's go back inside."

In the end, the three of them settle on a compromise: they dance in the empty parking lot, under stars that shoot eastward like lateral rain.

For a second, the Joshua tree can feel its grip on the host weakening. The present threatens its existence: the couple's roaring happiness might dislodge the ghostly tree. So it renews its purchase on the girl, roots into her memory.

"Remember our first day, Andy? The hike through Joshua Tree?"

Compared with that, Angie thinks, *what is there for us in the present?* "Nostalgia," we are apt to label this phenomenon.

It is the success of the invading plant, which seeks only to anchor itself in the past. Why move forward? Why move at all?

"Is this the spot? Are you sure?"

Andy spreads out the blanket. A soft aura surrounds the low moon, as if the moon itself were dreaming. The red halo reminds him of a miner's carbide lantern.

At first, when the girl suggested that they drive out to the park, he felt annoyed, then scared; the light was in her eyes again, eclipsing the girl she'd been only seconds earlier. But once he'd yielded to her plan, the night had organized itself into a series of surprises, the first of which was his own sharp joy; now he finds he's thrilled to be back inside the Black Rock Canyon campground with her. (The Joshua is also pleased, smiling up through Angie's eyes.) It is her idea to retrace the steps of their first hike to Warren Peak. "For our anniversary," she says coolly, although this rationale rings hollow, reminds Andy of his own bullshit justifications for taking out a lease on a desert "bungalow." He does not guess the truth, of course, which is that, slyly, the Joshua tree is proliferating inside Angie, each of its six arms forking and flowering throughout her in the densest multiplication of desire. *Leap, Leap, Leap.* For months it has been trying to drive the couple back to this spot. Its vast root brain awaits it, forty feet below the soil.

Angie has no difficulty navigating down the dark path; the little flashlight around her neck is bouncing like a leashed green sun. Her smile, when she turns to find Andy, is so huge that he wonders if he wasn't the one to suggest this night hike to her. Something unexpected happens then, for all of them: they reenter the romance of the past.

Why didn't we then . . . , all three think as one.

Quickly that sentiment jumps tenses, becomes:

Why don't we now . . .

When they reach the water tank, which is two hundred yards from the site of the Leap, Angie asks Andy to shake out the blanket. She sucks on the finger she pricked.

Around the blanket, tree branches divide and braid. They look mutinous in their stillness. Andy can see the movie scene: Bruce Willis attacking an army of Joshuas. He is imagining this, the trees swimming across the land like sand octopuses, flailing their spastic arms, when the girl catches his wrist in her fingers.

"Can we . . ."

"Why not?"

Why didn't we, Andy wonders, *back then?* The first time they walked this loop, they were preparing to do plenty. Andy unzips his jeans, shakes the caked-black denim off like solid dust. Angie is wearing a dress. Their naked legs tangle together in a pale, fleshy echo of the static contortionists that surround their blanket. Now the Joshua tree loves her. It grows and it flowers.

Angie will later wonder how exactly she came to be in possession of Andy's knife. Its bare blade holds the red moon inside it. She watches it glimmer there, poised just above Andy's right shoulder. The ground underneath the blanket seems to undulate; the fabric of the desert is wrinkling and flowing all around them. Even the Joshua trees, sham dead, now begin to move; or so it seems to the girl, whose blinded eyes keep stuttering.

The boy's mouth is at the hollow of the girl's throat, then lower; she moans as the invader's leaves and roots go spearing through her, and still he is unaware that he's in any danger.

I can Leap back, the plant thinks.

Angie can no longer see what she is doing. Her eyes are shut; her thoughts have stopped. One small hand rests on Andy's neck; the other fist withdraws until the knife points earthward. *Down, down, down,* the invader demands. Something sighs sharply, and it might be Andy or it might be the entire forest.

Leap, Leap, Leap, the Joshua implores.

———

What saves the boy is such a simple thing. Andy props himself up on an elbow, pausing to steady his breath. He missed the moment when she slid the knife from the crumpled heap of his clothing; he has no idea that its blade is sparkling inches from his neck. Staring at Angie's waxy, serious face, he is overcome by a flood of memories.

"Hey, Angie?" he asks, stroking the fine dark hairs along her arm. "Remember how we met?"

One of the extraordinary adaptive powers of our species is its ability to transmute a stray encounter into a first chapter.

Angie has never had sticking power. She dropped out of high school; she walked out of the GED exam. Her longest relationship, prior to falling for Andy, was seven months. But then they'd met (no epic tale there—the game was on at a hometown bar), and something in her character was spontaneously altered.

He remembers the song that was playing. He remembers ordering another round he could not afford—a freezing Yuengling for himself, ginger ale for her. They were sitting on the same wooden stools, battered tripods, that had supported the plans and commitments of the young in that town for generations.

The Joshua tree flexes its roots. Desperately, it tries to fix its life to her life. In the human mind, a Joshua's spirit can be destroyed by the wind and radiation fluxes of memory. Casting its spectral roots around, the plant furiously reddens with a very human feeling: humiliation.

What a thing to be undone by—golden hops and gingerroot, the clay shales of Pennsylvania!

It loses its grip on her arm; the strength runs out of her tensed biceps.

The girl's fingers loosen; the knife falls, unnoticed, to the sand.

The green invader is displaced by the swelling heat of their earliest happiness. Banished to the outermost reaches of Angie's consciousness, the Joshua tree now hovers in agony, half forgotten, half dissolving, losing its purchase on her awareness and so on its own reality.

"What a perfect night!" the couple agrees.

Angie stands and brushes sand from her dress. Andy frowns at the knife, picks it up.

"Happy anniversary," he says.

It is not their anniversary, but doesn't it make sense for them to celebrate the beginning here? This desert hike marked the last point in space where they'd both wanted the same future. What they are nostalgic for is the old plan, the first one. Their antique horizon.

Down the trail, up and down through time, the couple walks back toward the campground parking lot. Making plans again, each of them babbling excitedly over the other. Maybe Reno. Maybe Juneau.

Andy jogs ahead to their loaner getaway vehicle.

The Black Rock Canyon campground is one of the few places in the park where visitors can sleep amid the Joshua trees, soaking up the starlight from those complex crystals that have formed over millennia in the desert sky. Few of these campers are still outside their tents and RVs, but there is one familiar silhouette: it's the ranger, who is warming his enormous feet, bony and perfectly white, by the firepit. Shag covers the five-foot cactus behind him, which makes it look like a giant's mummified thumb.

"You lovebirds again!" he crows, waving them over.

Reluctantly, Andy doubles back. Angie is pleased, and frightened, that he remembers them.

"Ha! Guess you liked the hike."

For a few surreal minutes, standing before the leaping flames, they talk about the hike, the moths, the Joshua woodland. Andy is itching to be gone; already he is imagining giving notice at the saloon, packing up their house, getting back on the endlessly branching interstate. But Angie is curious. Andy is a little embarrassed, in fact, by the urgent tone of her questions. She wants to hear more about the marriage of the yucca moth and the Joshua—is theirs a doomed romance? Can't the two species untwine, separate their fortunes?

Andy leaves to get the truck.

And the pulse event? Have the moths all flown? Will the Joshua tree die out, go extinct in the park?

A key turns in the ignition. At the entrance to Black Rock Canyon, Andy leans forward against the wheel, squinting through the windshield. He is waiting for the girl to emerge from the shadows, certain that she will do so; and then a little less sure.

"Oh, it's a hardy species," the ranger says. His whiskers are clear tubes that hold the red firelight. "Those roots go deep. I wouldn't count a tree like that out."

Bog Girl: A Romance

The young turf cutter fell hard for his first girlfriend while operating heavy machinery in the peatlands. His name was Cillian Eddowis, he was fifteen years old, and he was illegally employed by Bos Ardee. He had celery-green eyes and a stutter that had been corrected at the state's expense; it resurfaced whenever he got nervous. "Th-th-th," he'd said, accepting the job. How did Cillian persuade Bos Ardee to hire him? The boy had lyingly laid claim to many qualities: strength, maturity, experience. When that didn't work, he pointed to his bedroom window, a quarter mile away, on the misty periphery of the cutaway bog, where the undrained water still sparkled between the larch trees. The intimation was clear: what the thin, strange boy lacked in muscle power he made up for in proximity to the work site.

Peat is harvested from bogs, watery mires where the earth yawns open. The bottom is a breathless place—cold, acidic, anaerobic—with no oxygen to decompose the willow branches or the small, still faces of the foxes interred there. Sphagnum mosses wrap around fur, wood, skin, casting their spell of chemical protection, preserving them whole. Growth is impossible, and Death cannot complete her lean work. Once cut, the peat becomes turf, and many locals on this green island off the coast of northern Europe still heat their homes with this peculiar energy source. Nobody gives much thought to the fuel's mortuary origins. Cillian, his mother, and several thousand others lived on the island, part of the archipelago known to older generations as the Four Horsemen. It's unlikely that you've ever visited. It's not really on the circuit.

Neolithic farmers were the first to clear the island's woods. Two thousand years later, peat had swallowed the remains of their pastures. Bogs blanketed the hills. In the Iron Age, these bogs were portals to distant worlds, wilder realms. Gods traveled the bogs. Gods wore crowns of starry asphodels, floating above the purple heather.

Now industrial harvesters rode over the drained bogs, combing the earth into even geometries. On the summer morning that Cillian found the Bog Girl, he was driving the Peatmax toward a copse of trees at the bog's western edge, pushing the dried peat into black ridges. True, it looked as if he was pleating shit, but Cill had a higher purpose. He was saving to buy his neighbor Pogo's white hatchback. Once he had a car, it would be no great challenge to sleep with a girl or a woman. Cillian was open to either experience. Or both. But he was far too shy to have an eye-level crush on anyone in his grade. Not Deedee, not Stacia, not Vicki, not Yvonne. He had a crush, taboo and distressing, on his aunt Cathy's ankles in socks. He had a crush on the anonymous shoulders of a shampoo model.

He had just driven into the western cutaway bog when he looked over the side of the Peatmax and screamed. A hand was sticking out of the mud. Cillian's first word to the Bog Girl required all the air in his lungs: "Ahhhhhhfuuuuuck!"

Here was a secret, flagging him down. A secret the world had kept for two thousand years and been unable to keep for two seconds longer. The bog had confessed her.

When the other men arrived, Cillian was on his knees, scratching up peat like a dog. Already he had dug out her head. She was whole and intact, cocooned in peat, curled like a sleeping child, with her head turned west of her pelvis. Thick, lustrous hair fanned over the tarp, the wild red-orange of an orangutan's fur, dyed by the bog acids. Moving clouds caused her colors to change continuously; now they were a tawny bronze, now a mineral blue. It was a very young face.

Cradling her head, Cillian lost all feeling in his legs. A light rain began to fall, but he would not relinquish his position. Every man gathered was staring at them. Ordinarily, their pronged attention encircled him like a crown of thorns, making him self-conscious, causing red fear to leak into his inner vision. Today, he didn't give a damn about the judgments of the mouth breathers above him. Who had ever seen a face so beautiful, so perfectly serene?

"Mother of God!" one of the men screamed. He pointed to the noose. A rope, nearly black with peat, ran down the length of her back.

Murder. That was the men's consensus. Bos Ardee called the police.

But Cillian barely heard the talk above him. If you saw the Bog Girl from one angle only, you would assume that she was a cherished daughter, laid to rest by hands that loved her. But she had been killed, and now her smile seemed even more impressive to him, and he wanted only to protect her from future harm. The men kept calling her "the body," which baffled Cillian—the word seemed to blind them to the deep and flowing dream life behind her smile. "There is so much more to you than what they see," he reassured her in a whisper. "I am so sorry about what happened to you. I am going to keep you safe now."

After this secret conversation, Cill fell rapidly in love.

Cillian was lucky that he met his girlfriend on such a remote island. When these bodies are discovered in Ireland, for example, or in the humid Florida bogs sprinkled between Disney World and Cape Canaveral, things proceed differently. The area is cordoned off. Teams of experts arrive to excavate the site. Then the bog people are carefully removed to laboratories, museums, where gloveless hands never touch them.

Cillian touched her hair, touched the rope. He was holding the reins of her life. Three policemen had arrived, and they conferred above Cillian, their black boots squeezing mud around the bog cotton. Once it had been determined that the girl was not a recent murder victim, the policemen relaxed. The chief asked Cillian a single question: "You're going to keep her, then?"

Gillian Eddowis was on a party line with her three sisters. She tucked the phone under her chin and took the ruby kettle off the range, opening a window to shoo the blue steam free. In the living room, roars of studio laughter erupted from the television; Cillian and the Bog Girl were watching a sitcom about a Canadian trailer park. Their long silences unnerved her; surely they weren't getting into trouble, ten feet away from her? She had never had cause to discipline her son. She wouldn't know where to begin. He was so kind, so intelligent, so unusual, so sensitive—such an outlier in the Eddowis family that his aunts had paid him the modern compliment of assuming that he was gay.

Voices sieved into Gillian's left ear:

"You want to warn them," Sister Abby said.

"But, Virgin Mother, there is no way to warn them!" Sister Patty finished.

"We were all sixteen once," Cathy growled. "We all survived it."

"Cillian is *fifteen*," Gillian corrected. "And the girlfriend is two thousand."

Abby, who had seen a picture of the Bog Girl in the local newspaper, suggested that *somebody* was rounding down.

A university man had also read the story of the Bog Girl's discovery. He'd taken a train and a ferry to find them. "I've come to make an Urgent Solicitation on Behalf of History," he said. He wanted to acquire the Bog Girl for the national museum. The sum he offered them was half of Gillian's salary at the post office.

In the end, what had happened? Christian feeling had muzzled her. How could she sell a girl to a stranger? Or pretend that she had any claim to her, this orphan from the Iron Age? Gillian told the university man that the Bog Girl was their houseguest and would be living with them until social services could locate her next of kin. At this, all the purple veins in the man's neck stood out. His tone sank into petulant defeat. "Mark my words, you people do not have the knowledge to properly care for her," he said. "She'll fall apart on you." The Bog Girl, propped up next to the ironing board, watched them argue with an implacable smile. The university man left empty-handed, and for a night and a day Gillian was a hero to her son.

"So she's just freeloading, then? Living off your coin?" Cathy asked.

"Oh, yes. She's quite shameless about it."

How could she explain to her sisters what she could barely admit to herself? The boy was in love. It was a monstrous, misdirected love; nevertheless, it commanded her respect.

"The Bog Girl is a bad influence on him," she told her sisters. "She doesn't work, she doesn't help. All day she lazes about the house."

Patty coughed and said, "If you feel that way, then why—"

Cathy screamed, "Gillian! She cannot *stay* with you!"

It was gentle Abby who formulated the solution: "Put her back in the bog."

"Gillian. *Do it tonight.*"

"Who's going to miss her?"

"I can't put her back in the bog. It would be . . ."

Silence drilled into her ears. Her family had a talent for emitting judgment without articulating words. When she was in high school and five months pregnant, everyone had quietly made clear that she was sacrificing her future. She'd run away to be with Cillian's father, then returned to the boglands alone with a bug-eyed toddler.

"I'm afraid," she confessed to her sisters. "If I put her out of the house, he'll leave with her."

"Oh!" they cried in unison. As if a needle had infected them all with her fear.

"Do something crazy, stupid . . ."

Silently adding, *Like we did.*

———

"Now, be honest, you little rat turd. You know *nothing* about her." His uncle put a finger into his peach iced tea, stirred. They were seated on a swing in the darkest part of Cillian's porch. Uncle Sean was as blandly ugly as a big toenail. Egg-bald and cheerfully unemployed, a third-helpings kind of guy. Once, Cillian had watched him eat the sticker on a green apple rather than peel it off. Sean was always over at the cottage, using Gillian's computer to play Poker 3000. He smeared himself throughout their house, his beer rings ghosting over surfaces like fat thumbs on a photograph. His words hung around, too, leaving their brain stain on the air. Uncle Sean took a proprietary interest in anything loved by Cillian. It was no surprise, then, that he was infatuated with the Bog Girl.

"I know that I love her," Cill said warily. He hated to be baited.

Uncle Sean was packing his brown, shaky weed into the rosy crotch of a glass mermaid. He passed his nephew the pipe. "Already, eh? You love her and you don't know the first thing about her?"

What did he know about her?

What did he love about her?

Cillian shrugged, his body crowding with feelings. "And I know that she loves me," he added, somewhat hastily.

Uncle Sean's pink smirk seemed to paste him to the back of the wicker seat. "Oh?" His grin widened. "And how old is she?"

"Two thousand. But she was my age when they put her in the bog."

"Most women *I* know lie freely about their age," Uncle Sean warned. "She may well be eleven. Then again, she could be *three* thousand."

Gillian, plump and starlit, appeared on the porch. A pleasant oniony smell followed her, mixing with the damp odor of Sean's pot.

"Are you smoking?"

"No," they lied in unison.

"Tell your . . . your *friend* that she is welcome to eat with us." With a martyred air, Gillian lifted her kitten-print pot holders to the heavens. Cill smiled; the pot holders made it look as if she approved of the situation—two big thumbs-up! His poor mom. She was so nervous around new people, and the Bog Girl's silence only intimidated her further. She was insecure about her cooking, and he knew she was going to take it very personally when the Bog Girl did not touch it.

Dinner was meat loaf with onions and, for Sean, a thousand beers. It was not a comfortable meal.

Gillian, stirring butter into the lima beans, beamed threats at her son's new girlfriend: *You little bitch. Crawl back into your hole. Stay away from my son.*

"Biscuit?" Gillian asked. "Does she like biscuits, Cill?"

The Bog Girl smiled her gentle smile at the wall, her face reflected in the oval door of the washer-dryer. Against that sudsy turbulence, she looked especially still.

Three drinks in, Uncle Sean slung an arm around the Bog Girl's thin blue shoulder, welcoming her into the family. "I'm proud of my nephew for going after an older woman, a *mature* woman . . . a cougar!"

Cillian fixed his uncle with a homicidal stare. Under the table, he touched his girlfriend's foot with his foot; his eyebrows lifted in apology. His mother shot up with her steaming cauldron of beans, giving everyone another punitive lima ladle and removing the beer from the table. Their dog, returning from her dusk mouse hunt, came berserking into the kitchen, barking at a deranged pitch. She wanted to play tug-of-war with the Bog Girl's noose. "Puddles—no!" Cillian's vision was swimming, his whole body overheating with shame. He relaxed when he stared into the Bog Girl's face, which was void of all judgment, smiling at him with its mysterious kindness. Once again, his embarrassment was soothed by her infinite calm. His eyes lowered from her smile to the noose. *Of course, she's seen far worse than us,* he thought. Outside the window, insects millioned around the porch light. The bog crickets were doing a raspy ventriloquy of the stars;

perhaps she recognized their tiny voices. Soon Uncle Sean was snoring lightly beside the pooling gravy, face down in his big arms. Cill sat slablike in the moonlight. The Bog Girl smiled blindly on.

———

For the first two weeks, the Bog Girl slept on the sofa, the television light flickering gently over her. That was fine by Gillian. She wasn't about to turn an orphan from the Iron Age out on the street.

Then, on a rainy Monday night, without warning or apology, Cillian picked up the Bog Girl. He cradled her like a child, her frondy feet dangling in the air. Gillian, doing a jigsaw puzzle of a horse and colt in the kitchen, looked up in time to see them disappearing. She felt a purple welt rising in her mind, the revelatory pain called wonder. Underneath the shock, other feelings began to flow, among them a disturbed pride. Because hadn't he looked *exactly* like his father? Confident, possessed. He didn't ask for his mother's permission. He did not lie to her about what he was doing, or hide it, or explain it. He simply rose with the Bog Girl in his arms, nuzzling her blue neck. The door shut, and he was gone from sight. Another milestone: she heard the click of the lock.

"Good night, Son!" she cried after them, panicked.

She could not reconcile her knowledge of her sweet, awkward boy with this wayward, brazen person. Was she supposed to go up there now? Pound on the door? Oh, who could she call? Nobody, not even her sisters, would take a call about *this* problem, she felt quite certain. Abby's son, Kevin, met his girlfriend in church. Cathy's son, Patrick, had a lovely fiancée who taught kindergarten. Murry's girlfriend was in jail for vehicular manslaughter—but at least she was alive!

In the morning, she watched the mute, hitching muscles of his back as he fumbled with the coffeepot. So he was a coffee drinker now. News to her. He kissed his mother's forehead as he left for work, but he was whistling to himself, oblivious of her sadness, her fear, completely self-enclosed in his new happiness. *It's too soon for this,* she thought. And: *Not you, too. Please, please, please,* she prayed, the incomplete prayer of mothers everywhere who cannot conceive of a solution.

That evening, she announced a new rule: "Everyone has to wear clothes. And no more locked doors."

One chilly Saturday, Cillian took the ferry three hours to a mainland museum. Twelve bog bodies were on display, part of a traveling exhibition called *Kings of the Iron Age.* The Bog Girl had met his family—the least he could do was return the favor. Cill sneaked into a tour in progress, following a docent from sepulchre to sepulchre. Under the glass, the kings of the Iron Age lay like chewed taffy. One man was naked except for a fox-fur armband. Another was a giant. Another had two sets of thumbs.

Cillian learned that the bogs of the islands in the cold Atlantic were particularly acidic. Pickled bodies from the Iron Age had emerged from these deep vats. Their fetally scrolled bodies often doubled as the crumpled maps of murders. They might have been human sacrifices, the docent said. Left in the bog water for the harvest god. Kings, queens, scapegoats, victims—they might have been any of these things.

"From the contents of his stomach, we can surmise that he last dined on oat gruel . . .

"From the forensic analyses, we can surmise that she was killed by an arrow . . .

"From the ornaments on this belt buckle, we can surmise that these were a wealthy people . . ."

What? No more than this could be surmised?

The docent pointed out the dots and stripes on the potsherds. Charcoal smudges that might be stars or animals. Evidence, she said, of "a robust culture." Cillian took notes:

THEY HAD TIME TO KILL. THEY LIKED ART, TOO.

Back on the ferry, he could admit to his relief: none of the other bog bodies stirred any feeling in him. He loved one specific person. He could see things about the Bog Girl to which this batty docent would be totally blind—for example, the secret depths her smile concealed. How badly misunderstood she had been by her own people. She was an alien from a planet that nobody alive could visit—the planet Earth, in the first century A.D. She felt soft in his arms, bonelessly soft, but she also seemed indestructible. According to the experts, a bog body should begin to decompose rapidly when exposed to air. Curiously enough, this Bog Girl had not. He told no one his theory but polished it inside his mind like an amulet: it was his love that was protecting her.

By August, their rapport had deepened immeasurably. They didn't need to say a word, Cill was discovering, to perfectly understand each other. Falling in love with the Bog Girl was a wonderful thing—it was permission to ignore everyone else. When school started, in September, he made a bespoke sling and brought her with him. His girlfriend, propped like a broomstick against the rows of lockers, waited for him during Biology and Music II, as cool and impassive as the most popular girl the world has ever known.

Nobody in the school administration objected to the presence of the Bog Girl. Ancestral superstitions still hovered over the islanders' minds, exerting their quiet influence, and nobody wanted to be the person responsible for angering a visitor from the past. Soon she was permitted to audit all of Cillian's classes, smiling patiently at the flustered, frightened teachers.

One afternoon, the vice-principal called her into his office and presented her with a red-and-gold badge to wear in the halls: VISITING STUDENT.

"I don't think that's really accurate, sir," Cillian said.

"Oh, no?"

"She's not a visitor. She was born here." In fact, the Bog Girl was the island's oldest resident, by at least nineteen hundred years. Cillian paused. "Also, her eyes are shut, you see. So I don't think she can really, ah, study . . ."

"Well!" The vice-principal clapped his hands. He had a school to run, quotas to fulfill. "We will be studying *her,* then. She will give us all an exciting new perspective on our modern life and times—oh my! Oh dear." The Bog Girl had slumped into his aloe planter.

Cillian put the badge on her polyester blouse, a loaner from his mother that was vintage cool. Cillian—who never gave a thought to his own clothing—enjoyed dressing the Bog Girl for school in the morning. He raided his mother's closet, resurrecting her baby-doll dresses. The eleventh-grade girls organized a clothing drive for the Bog Girl, collecting many shoplifted donations of fall tunics and on-trend boots.

Rumorsprawl. Word got around that the Bog Girl was actually a princess. A princess, or possibly a witch. Within a week, she was eating at the popular girls' table. They'd kidnapped her from where Cillian had positioned her on a bench, propped between two book bags, and taken her to lunch. Already they had restyled her hair with rhinestone barrettes.

"You stole my girlfriend," Cillian said.

"Something *awful* happened to her," Vicki said reverently.

"So bad," Georgette echoed.

"She doesn't like to talk about it," Priscilla said, looping a protective arm around the Bog Girl. The girls had matching lunches: lettuce salads, diet candy bars, diet shakes. They were all jealous of how little she ate.

How had Cill not foreseen this turn of events? The Bog Girl was diminutive, wounded, mysterious, a redhead. Best of all, she could never contradict any rumor the living girls distributed about her.

"She was too beautiful to live!" Priscilla gasped. "They killed her for her beauty."

"I don't th-th-think," Cill said, "that it happened quite like that."

The popular girls adjusted their leggings, annoyed. "No?"

Cillian was dimly aware that other tables were listening in, but the density of the attention in no way affected him. "I am hers, and she is mine," he announced. "I have dedicated myself to learning everything about her."

A sighing spasm of envy moved down the popular girls' table—what boy alive would say this about them? A miracle: nobody mocked Cillian Eddowis. They were all starving to be loved like this. The popular girls watched him avidly as he ate a grilled cheese and waffle fries, his green irises burning. Between bites, his left hand rose to touch the Bog Girl's red braid, tousling it like the pull-chain of a lamp.

Gillian couldn't help it: she was heartbroken. The past that was most precious to her had filtered right through her son. The songs she'd sung to him when he was nursing? The care with which she'd cut the tiny moons of his fingernails? Their 4 a.m. feedings? Erased! Her son had matured into amnesia about his earliest years. Now her body was the only place where the memories were preserved. Cillian, like all sons, was blithe about this betrayal.

"There is so much about yourself that you do not recall," Gillian accused him after dinner one night. Cillian, writing a paper about igneous rocks at the kitchen table, did not look up.

"When you were my boy, just a wee boy," Gillian said in a

voice of true agony, "you used to be terrified of the vacuum cleaner. You loved your froggy pajamas. You used so much glue on your art projects that your teachers—"

"Quit it with these dumb stories, Ma!"

"Oh, you find them dumb, do you? The stories about how I had to raise you alone, without a penny from your father—"

"You're just trying to *embarrass* me in front of her!"

The Bog Girl smiled at them from the amber armchair. Her leather skirt was outrageously short, a donation from tall Bianca. Decorously, Cillian had draped the cable guide over her lap. Bugs spun in her water glass; mosquitoes and dragonflies were always diving into the Bog Girl's food and drink, as if in strange solidarity with her.

Cillian drew himself up triumphantly, a foot taller than his mother. "You don't want me to grow up."

"What? Of course I do!"

But Cill was ready with his rebuttal: "You gave us rhyming names, Ma!"

This was true. Gillian and Cillian. She'd come up with that plan when she was a teenager herself, and pregnant with a nameless otter, some gyring little animal. A rhyming name had seemed just right then; she couldn't have said why, at seventeen. Had Cillian been a girl, she would have named her Lillian.

"You're so young, you can't know . . ." But what did she want to tell him?

Her body seemed to cave in on itself then, becoming smaller and smaller, so that even Cillian, fortressed behind the wall of his love, noticed and became alarmed. "Ma? What's wrong?"

"It's changing all the time," she murmured ominously.

"Just, please, wait, my love. Don't . . . *settle*." What a word! She pictured her son sinking up to his neck in the reddish bog water.

She was hiccuping now, unable to name her own feelings. Without thinking, she picked up the murky water glass, drank from it. "Your potential . . . all the teachers tell me you have great potential."

Just come out and say it. "I don't want you to throw your *life* away on some Bog Girl!"

"Oh, Ma." Cill patted her back until the hiccups stopped. Her face looked crumpled and blue in the unlit room, hovering above the seated Bog Girl. For a second, they might have been sisters.

The Bog Girl floated, thin as a dress, on the mattress. Barrettes, pink and purple, were scattered all over the pillow. She smiled at Cillian, or beyond him, with her desiccated calm. Downstairs, Gillian was making breakfast, the buttery smells threading through his nostrils like an ox ring, tugging him toward them. But when she called up for him he was barely in the room. He was digging and digging into the peat-moss bog again, smoothing her blue cheeks with both hands, spading down into the kingdom that she came from.

"Cillian! The bus is coming!" It should have taken him twenty seconds to put on pants. What was he doing in there? Probably jacking off to a "meme," whatever that was, or buying perfume for the Bog Girl on her credit cards.

"Coming, Ma!"

Cillian was always learning new things about his girl-friend. The longer he looked at her, the more he saw. Her face grew silty with personality. Although she was young when she disappeared into the bog, her face was plowed with tiny wrinklings. Some dream or mood had recurred frequently enough to hammer lines across her brow. Here were the ridges and the gullies her mental weathers had worked into her skin.

Cill studied the inflorescences on her cheeks. Her brain is in there, the university man had said. Her brain is intact, preserved by the bog acids. Cillian spent hours doing this forensic palmistry, trying to read her mind.

———

On the weekends, Cillian still drove the Peatmax in the bog-lands. They needed the money. On the radio one Saturday morning, he was surprised to find two men debating whether or not turf cutting was evil.

"Turf is a fuel that's dirtier than coal," said a representative from Friends of the Island.

"Europe can't tell us what to do with our bogs. We've been working in the bogs for a thousand years . . ."

Cill switched off the radio. It was strange to hear the very verb he was performing so vehemently condemned. Stranger still that he could feel so perfectly indifferent to the debate, even seated in the cab of the world-killing machine. Right or wrong? Right or wrong? The Peatmax had already been in gear when he started listening to the program. Love had com-pletely insulated him from all fear of the future. A hundred times a day, a thousand times a day, he pictured her blue hand reaching up for him. *People waste a lot of time trying to make it one or the other,* thought Cillian. It was right *and* wrong to be with her.

———

"Will you have a talk with him?" Gillian begged Sean. "Something is going really, really wrong with him!"

"First love, first love," Sean murmured sadly, scratching his bubonic nose. "Who are we to intervene, eh? It will die of natural causes."

"Natural causes!"

She was thinking that the poor girl had been garroted. Her bright-red hair racing the tail of the noose down her spine. You could not survive your death, could you? It survived with you.

———

In mid-October, a stretch limousine pulled up to the cottage to take Cillian and the Bog Girl to the annual school dance. A techno-reggae song called "Bump de Ass!" filled the back seat, where half a dozen teenagers sat in churchlike silence. The Bog Girl's reticence was contagious. Ambulance lights sparkled through the tinted windows, causing everyone to jump, with one exception: Cillian Eddowis's date, the glamorous foreigner, or native—nobody was sure how to regard her.

Since acquiring his far-older girlfriend, Cill had begun

speaking to his classmates in the voice of a bachelor who merely tolerates children. "Carla," he said, clearing his throat. "Would you mind exhaling a little closer to the window? Your smoke is blowing on us."

Two girls started debating whether or not a friend should lose her virginity in a BMW that evening. What was the interior of the car like? This was a very important question. The girl's boyfriend was a twenty-six-year-old cocaine dealer. Prior to the Bog Girl's arrival on the scene, everyone had found his age very impressive. The dealer boyfriend had been unable to accompany the girl to the school dance, so she had taken poor Eoin, her sophomore cousin, who looked near fatally compressed by his green cummerbund. The twenty-six-year-old would be waiting for her in the BMW, post-festivities. Should she deflower him?

"Wait. Uh. I think he's deflowering you, right? Or maybe you're deflowering each other? Who's got the flower?"

"Just do it, and then lie about it." Carla shrugged. "That's what I did."

"My advice," Cillian said, in the unfamiliar voice, "my advice is wait. Wait until you find the person with whom you want to spend all your earthly time." The Bog Girl leaned against his shoulder, aloof in her sparkly tiara. "Or until that person finds you. If that's this guy, well, kudos. But, if not, wait. You will meet your soul mate. And you will want to give that person every molecule of your life."

The attempted conversion of the high-school gymnasium into an Arabian-themed wonderland had not been a success. Cill and the Bog Girl stood under a palm tree that looked like an enormous toilet brush, made of cellophane and cardboard tubes. Three girls from the limo came up and asked to dance with Cillian, but he explained that his girlfriend hated to be left alone. All were sulkily respectful of her claim on him.

The after-party was held in an old car-parts warehouse on the west side of the island, where everything was shut or abandoned; the population of the island had been declining steadily for three decades. The music sounded like fists beating at the wall, and the floor was so sticky that Cillian had to lift and cradle the Bog Girl, looping her silver dress around one arm. Cillian had never attended an after-party before. Or a party, for that matter. He surveyed his former tormentors, the seniors, with their piggish faces and their plastic cups. Some were single, some had girlfriends, some were virgins, some were not, but not one of them, Cillian felt very certain, knew the first thing about love.

Eoin the sophomore came over, his date nowhere to be seen. He was breathless in the cummerbund, in visible danger of puking up Bacardi. He rolled a bloodshot eye in Cill's direction, smiling wistfully.

"So," he said, "I'm just wondering. Do you guys—"

Cillian preempted the question: "A gentleman never tells."

It was a phrase he'd once read in a men's magazine while waiting to get a root canal. In fact, his mother needn't have lost so much sleep to this particular fear. At night, Cillian lay beside the Bog Girl, barely touching her. A steady, happy calm radiated from her, which filled him with a parallel euphoria.

Cillian carried the Bog Girl onto the dance floor, her braided noose flung over his shoulder. And even Eoin, minutes from unconsciousness, could see exactly who the older boy believed himself to be in this story: Cillian the Rescuer.

"Oh, damn! Wise up! She'll make you wait forever, man!" The lonely laugh of Eoin died a terrible death, like a bird impaled on a spike.

———

At 3 a.m., the lights were still on. *Uh-oh,* Cill thought. *Mom got into the gin again.*

Drinking made her silences bubble volubly. He almost got the hiccups himself, listening to her silences. Oh, God. There was so much pain inside her, so much she wanted to share with him. Cillian and the Bog Girl tried to tiptoe past her to the staircase, but she sprang up like a jack-in-the-box.

"Cillian?" She looked child-small in the dark. Her voice was tremulous and young, and her slurring reminded him of his own stutter, that undead vestige of his early years. His mother sounded like a sleepy girl, four or five years old. Her feet were bare, and she rose onto her stubby toes to grip his arm. "Where are you coming from?"

"Nowhere. The dance. It was fun."

"Where are you going?"

"Aw, Mom. Where do you th-th-think?"

"Good night!" she called after him desperately. "I hope you had a good time! You look so handsome! So grown up!"

———

By early winter, the Bog Girl's stillness had begun to provoke a restlessness in Cillian, a squeezed and throbbing feeling. He was failing three subjects. His mother had threatened to send him to live with Aunt Cathy until he "straightened out." He didn't care. Waiting for the bus in the freezing rain, he no longer dreamed about owning a car. He knew what he would do with the summer money he'd earned from Bos Ardee: run away with her.

He'd flunk out of school and take the Bog Girl with him to the mainland. She'd be homesick at first, maybe, but they'd go on trips to urban parks. It was the burr of peace, the burr of happiness, goading him on to new movement. Oh, he was frightened, too.

In his fantasy life, Cillian drew the noose tighter and tighter. He imagined, with a strange joy, the narrow life they would lead. No children, no sex, no messy nights vomiting outside bars, no unintended pregnancies, no fights in the street, no betrayals, no surprises, no broken promises, no promises.

Was the Bog Girl a cosigner to this fantasy? Cillian had every reason to believe so. When he described his plans to her, the smile never left her face. Was their love one-sided, as the concerned and unimaginative adults in his life kept insisting? No—but the proof of this surprised no one more terribly than Cillian.

One night in mid-December, lying in bed, he felt a cobwebby softness on his left cheek. It was her eyelashes, flicking over him. They glowed radish red in the moonlight. Cillian swatted at his face, his own eyes never opening. Still sunk in his dreaming, he grunted and rolled over.

Cillian.

Cillian.

The Bog Girl sat up.

With fluttering effort, the muscles of her blue jaw yawned. One eye opened. It studied itself in the dresser mirror for a long instant, then turned calmly back toward Cillian. Very slowly, her left arm unhinged itself and dropped to the plaid bedspread. The fingers curled around the blanket's edge and drew it down. A blush of primal satisfaction colored the Bog Girl's cheeks as the fabric moved. She tugged more forcefully, revealing Cillian curled on his side in his white undershirt. Groaning in his sleep, he jerked the covers back up.

"Cillian," she said aloud.

Now Cillian was awake—he was irreversibly awake. He blinked up at her face, which was staring down at him. When they locked eyes, her frozen smile widened.

"Mom!" he couldn't help screaming. "Help!"

The Bog Girl, imitating him, began to scream and scream. And he could see, radiating from her gaze, the same blind tenderness that he had directed at her. Now he was its object. Something truly terrifying had happened: she loved him back.

For months, Cillian had been decoding the Bog Girl's silences. He'd tried to translate her dreams, her fears, her innermost thoughts. But her real voice was nothing like the voice that he'd imagined for her—a cross between Vicki Gilvarry and Patti LaBelle. Its high-pitched ululations hailed over him. In the kitchen, the dog began to bark. The language that she spoke was no longer spoken anywhere on earth.

He stumbled up, tugging at his boxers. The Bog Girl stood, too. The past, with its monstrous depth and span, reached toward him, demanding an understanding that he simply could not give it. His mind was too young and too narrow to withstand the onrush of her life. An invisible woods was in the bedroom with them, the scent of trees multiplying. Some mental earthquake inside the Bog Girl was casting up a world, green and unknown to him, or to anyone living: her homeland. Her gaze drove inward, carrying Cillian with it. For an instant, he thought he glimpsed her parents. Her brothers, her sisters, a nation of people. Their cheeks now beginning to brighten, every one of them alive again inside her village. Pines rippling seaward. Gods, horned and faceless, walking the lakes that once covered Cillian's home. Cillian was buried in water, in liquid images of her; he had to push through so many strata of her memories to reach the surface of her mind. Most of what he saw he shrank away from. His mind felt like a burned tongue, numbly touching her reality.

"W-w-who are you?"

Heartbreak is the universal diagnosis for the pain that accompanies the end of love. But this was an unusual breakup, in that Cillian's mind shattered first. The fantasy that had protected him began to fall away. Piece after piece of it clattered from his chest, an armor rusting off him. *What are you?*

The Bog Girl lurched toward him, her arms open. First she moved like a hopping chick, with an unexpected buoyancy. Then she seemed to remember how to step, heel to toe. She came for him like an astronaut, bouncing on the gray carpet. The only English word she knew was his name.

Almost weightlessly, she reached for him. For wasn't she equally terrified? There was no buoy other than this boy, who had gripped her with his thin, freckled arms, bellying her out of the peat bog and into time.

Cillian hid behind the dresser.

Her fingers found his hand, threaded through his fingers.

He screamed again, even as he squeezed the hand back.

Her words rushed together, a thawing waterfall, moving intricately between octaves; still the only word he understood was his name. Perhaps nothing he had said to her, in their six months as a couple, had been comprehended. Cillian worked the levers in his brain, desperately trying to find the words that would release him.

"Unlock the door," his mother's beautiful voice called.

Cillian was frozen in the Bog Girl's grip, unable even to call out. But a moment later he heard the key turning in the lock. Gillian stood in the doorway in her yellow pajamas. With a panoramic comprehension, she took in what had happened. She knew, too, what must now be done. If she could have freed these two from the embrace herself, she would have done so; but now she understood the challenge. The boy would have to make his own way out. "Take her home, Cillian. Make sure that she gets home safely."

Cillian, his eyes round with panic, only nodded.

Gillian went to the Bog Girl, helping her into a sweater. "Put a hat on. And pants."

His mother shepherded them downstairs and onto the porch, switching on every yellow bulb as they moved through the cottage. It was the warmest December on record, rain falling instead of snow, the drops disappearing into the rotted wood. Cillian carried the Bog Girl to the edge of the light before he understood that his mother was not coming with him.

"Let her down gently, son!" his mother called after them.

Well, she could do this for him, at least: she held a lantern steady across the rainy lawn, creating a gangplank of light that reached almost to the larches. She watched them moving toward the inky water. The Bog Girl was howling in her foreign tongue; at this distance, Gillian felt she could almost understand it.

Oh, she hoped their breakup would stick. She had divorced Cillian's father, then briefly moved into his new house; it had taken years before their affair was truly over. You had to really cultivate an ending. To get it to last, you had to kneel and tend to the burial ground, continuously firming your resolution.

This was a bad breakup. A quarter mile from the cottage, under a bright moon, Cillian and the Bog Girl were rolling in the mud, each screaming in a different language. Their screams twined together, their hands reaching for each other; it was during this undoing that they were, at last, truly united as a couple. His flashlight rolled with them, plucking amphibious red and yellow eyes out of the reeds. "It's over. It's over. It's over," he kept babbling optimistically, out of his mind with fear. Her throat was vibrating against his skin. He could feel the echo of his own terror and sorrow, and again his mind felt overrun by the lapping waves of time. She clutched at the neck of his T-shirt, her body covered in dark mud and cracked stems of bog cotton, blue lichen. At last he felt her grip on him loosen. Her eyes, opaquely glinting in the moonlight, liquid and enormous, far larger than anyone could have guessed before their unlidding, regarded him with what he imagined was a soft surprise, and disappointment. He was not who she'd expected to find when she opened her eyes, either. Now neither teenager needed to tell the other that it was over. It simply was—and, without another sound, the Bog Girl let go of Cillian and slipped backward into the bog water. Did she sink? It looked almost as if the water were rising to cover her. Her cranberry hair waved away from her scalp. As he watched, her body itself began to break up.

Straightening from where he was kneeling on the ledge of mud, he brushed peat from his pants. His arms tingled where her grip had suddenly relaxed. The clear rain drenched his clothing. The bog was still bubbling, pieces of her sinking back into the black peat, when he turned on his heel and ran. For the next few days, he would be quaky with relief; he'd felt certain, watching her sink away, that he would never see the Bog Girl again in this life.

But here he was mistaken. In the weeks and years to come, Cillian would find himself alone with her memory, struggling to pay attention to his droning contemporaries in the cramped classroom. How often would he retrace his steps, wandering right back to the lip of the bog, peering in? Each dusk, with their primitive eloquence, the air-galloping insects continue to speak the million syllables of her name.

"Ma! Ma! Ma!" That night, Cillian came roaring out of the dark, pistoning his knees as he ran for the light, for his home at the edge of the boglands. "Who was that?"

Madame Bovary's Greyhound

I. FIRST LOVE

They took walks to the beech grove at Banneville, near the abandoned pavilion. Foxglove and gillyflowers, beige lichen growing in one thick, crawling curtain around the socketed windows. Moths blinked wings at them, crescents of blue and red and tiger yellow, like eyes caught in a net.

Emma sat and poked at the grass with the skeletal end of her parasol, as if she were trying to blind each blade.

"Oh, *why* did I ever get married?" she moaned aloud, again and again.

The greyhound whined with her, distressed by her distress. Sometimes, in a traitorous fugue, the dog forgot to be unhappy and ran off to chase purple butterflies or murder shrew mice, or to piss a joyful stream onto the topiaries. But generally, if her mistress was crying, so was the puppy. Her name was Djali, and she had been a gift from the young woman's husband, Dr. Charles Bovary.

Emma wept harder as the year grew older and the temperature dropped, folding herself into the white monotony of trees, leaning farther and farther into the bare trunks. The dog would stand on her hind legs and lick at the snow that fused Emma's shoulders to the coarse wood, as if trying to loosen a hardening glue, and the whole forest would quiver and groan together in sympathy with the woman, and her phantom lovers, and Djali.

At Banneville the wind came directly from the sea and covered the couple in a blue-salt caul. The greyhound loved most when she and Emma were outside like this, bound by the membrane of a gale. Yet as sunset fell, Djali became infected again by her woman's nameless terrors. Orange and red, they seemed to sweat out of the wood. The dog smelled nothing alarming, but love stripped her immunity to the internal weathers of Emma Bovary.

The bloodred haze switched to a silvery-blue light, and Emma shuddered all at once, as if in response to some thicketed danger. They returned to Tostes along the highway.

The greyhound was ignorant of many things. She had no idea, for example, that she was a greyhound. She didn't know that her breed had originated in southern Italy, an ancient pet in Pompeii, a favorite of the thin-nosed English lords and ladies, or that she was perceived to be affectionate, intelligent, and loyal. What she did know, with a whole-body thrill, was the music of her woman coming up the walk, the dizzying explosion of perfume as the door swung wide. She knew when her mistress was pleased with her, and that approval was the fulcrum of her happiness.

"Viscount! Viscount!" Emma whimpered in her sleep. (Rodolphe would come onto the scene later, after the greyhound's flight, and poor Charlie B. never once featured in his wife's unconscious theater.) Then Djali would stand and pace stiff-legged through the cracked bowl of the cold room into which her mistress's dreams were leaking, peering with pricked ears into shadows. It was a strange accordion that linked the woman and the dog: Vaporous drafts caused their pink and gray bellies to clutch inward at the same instant. Moods blew from one mind to the other, delight and melancholy. In the blue atmosphere of the bedroom, the two were very nearly (but never quite) one creature.

Even asleep, the little greyhound trailed after her madame, through a weave of green stars and gas lamps, along the boulevards of Paris. It was a conjured city that no native would recognize—Emma Bovary's head on the pillow, its architect. Her Paris was assembled from a guidebook with an out-of-date map, and from the novels of Balzac and Sand, and from her vividly disordered recollections of the viscount's ball at La Vaubyessard, with its odor of dying flowers, burning flambeaux, and truffles. (Many neighborhoods within the city's quivering boundaries, curiously enough, smelled identical to the viscount's dining room.) A rose-and-gold glow obscured the storefront windows, and cathedral bells tolled continuously as they strolled past the same four landmarks: a tremulous bridge over the roaring Seine, a vanilla-white dress shop, the vague façade of the opera house—overlaid in more gold light—and the crude stencil of a theater. All night they walked like that, companions in Emma's phantasmal labyrinth, suspended by her hopeful mists, and each dawn the dog would wake to the second Madame Bovary, the lightly snoring woman on the mattress, her eyes still hidden beneath a peacock sleep mask. Under the coverlet at night, Charles's blocky legs tangled around Emma in an apprehensive pretzel, a doomed attempt to hold her in their marriage bed.

II. A CHANGE OF HEART

Is there any love as tireless as a dog's in search of its master? Whenever Emma was off shopping for nougat in the market, or visiting God in the churchyard, Djali was stricken by the madness of her absence. The dog's futile hunt through the house turned her maniacal, cannibalistic: She scratched her fur until it became wet and dark. She paced the halls, pausing only to gnaw at her front paws. Félicité, the Bovarys' frightened housekeeper, was forced to imprison her in a closet with a water dish.

The dog's change of heart began in September, some weeks after Madame Bovary's return from La Vaubyessard, where she'd dervished around in another man's arms and given up forever on the project of loving Charles. It is tempting to conclude that Emma somehow transmitted her wanderlust to Djali; but perhaps this is a sentimental impulse, a storyteller's desire to sync two flickering hearts.

One day Emma's scents began to stabilize. Her fragrance became musty, ordinary, melting into the house's stale atmosphere until the woman was nearly invisible to the animal. Djali licked almond talc from Emma's finger webbing. She bucked her head under the madame's hand a dozen times, waiting for the old passion to seize her, yet her brain was uninflamed. The hand had become meaningless pressure, damp heat. No joy snowed out of it as Emma mechanically

stroked between Djali's ears, her gold wedding band rubbing
a raw spot into the fur, branding the dog with her distraction.
There in the bedroom, together and alone, they watched the
rain fall.

By late February, at the same time Charles Bovary was
dosing his young wife with valerian, the dog began refus-
ing her mutton chops. Emma stopped checking her gaunt
face in mirrors, let dead flies swim in the blue glass vases.
The dog neglected to bark at her red winged nemesis, the
rooster. Emma quit playing the piano. The dog lost her zest
for woodland homicide. Under glassy bathwater, Emma
let the hours fill her nostrils with the terrible serenity of a
drowned woman, her naked body as still and bright as quartz
in a quarry. Her fingers circled her navel, seeking an escape.
Fleas held wild circuses on Djali's back as she lay motionless
before the fire for the duration of two enormous logs, unable
to summon the energy to spin a hind leg in protest. Her ears
collapsed against her skull.

Charles rubbed his hand greedily between Emma's legs
and she swatted him off; Emma stroked the dog's neck and
Djali went stiff, slid out of reach. Both woman and animal,
according to the baffled Dr. Bovary, seemed bewitched by
sadness.

This strain of virulent misery, this falling out of love,
caused different symptoms, unique disruptions, in dogs and
humans.

The greyhound, for example, shat everywhere.

Whereas Emma shopped for fabrics in the town.

On the fifth week of the dog's fall, Charles lifted the bed
skirt and discovered the greyhound panting up at him with

a dead-eyed calm. He'd been expecting to find his favorite tall socks, blue wool ineptly darned for him by Emma. He screamed.

"Emma! What do you call your little bitch again? There is something the matter with it!"

"Djali," Emma murmured from the mattress. And the dog, helplessly bound to her owner's voice—if no longer in love with Madame Bovary, still indentured to love's ghost—rose and licked the lady's bare feet.

"Good girl," whispered Emma.

The animal's dry tongue lolled out of her mouth. Inside her body, a foreboding was hardening into a fact. There was no halting the transformation of her devotion into a nothing.

III. WHAT IF?

"If you do not stop making poop in the salon," Félicité growled at the puppy, "I will no longer feed you."

In the sixth month of her life in Tostes, the dog lay glumly on the floor, her pink belly tippled orange by the grated flames, fatally bored. Emma entered the bedroom, and the animal lifted her head from between her tiny polished claws, let it drop again.

"If only I could be you," Emma lamented. "There's no trouble or sorrow in *your* life!" And she soothed the dog in a gurgling monotone, as if she were addressing herself.

Dr. Charles Bovary returned home, whistling after another successful day of leeches and bloodletting in the countryside, to a house of malcontent females:

Emma was stacking a pyramid of greengage plums.

The little greyhound was licking her genitals.

Soon the coarse, unchanging weave of the rug in Emma's bedroom became unbearable. The dog's mind filled with smells that had no origin, sounds that arose from no friction. Unreal expanses. She closed her eyes and stepped cautiously through tall purple grass she'd never seen before in her life.

She wondered if there might not have been some other way, through a different set of circumstances, of meeting another woman; and she tried to imagine those events that had not happened, that shadow life. Her owner might have been a bloody-smocked man, a baritone, a butcher with bags of bones always hidden in his pockets. Or perhaps a child, the butcher's daughter, say, a pork chop–scented girl who loved to throw sticks. Djali had observed a flatulent malamute trailing his old man in the park, each animal besotted with the other. Blue poodles, inbred and fat, smugly certain of their women's adoration. She'd seen a balding Pomeranian riding high in a toy wagon, doted on by the son of a king. Not all humans were like Emma Bovary.

Out of habit, she howled her old courtship song at Emma's feet, and Emma reached down distractedly, gave the dog's ears a stiff brushing. She was seated before her bedroom vanity, cross-examining a pimple, very preoccupied, for at four o'clock Monsieur Roualt was coming for biscuits and judgment and jelly.

A dog's love is forever. We expect infidelity from one another; we marvel at this one's ability to hold that one's interest for fifty, sixty years; perhaps some of us feel a secret contempt for monogamy even as we extol it, wishing parole for its weary participants. But dogs do not receive our sympathy or our suspicion—from dogs we presume an eternal adoration.

In the strange case of Madame Bovary's greyhound, however, "forever" was a tensed muscle that began to shake. During the Christmas holidays, she had daily seizures before the fireplace, chattering in the red light like a loose tooth. Loyalty was a posture she could no longer hold.

Meanwhile, Emma had become pregnant.

The Bovarys were preparing to move.

On one of the last of her afternoons in Tostes, the dog ceased trembling and looked around. Beyond the cabbage rows, the green grasses waved endlessly away from her, beckoning her. She stretched her hind legs. A terrible itching spread through her body, and the last threads of love slipped like a noose from her neck. Nothing owned her anymore. Rolling, moaning, belly to the red sun, she dug her spine into the hill.

"Oh, dear," mumbled the coachman, Monsieur Hivert, watching the dog from the yard. "Something seems to be attacking your greyhound, madame. Bees, I'd wager."

"Djali!" chided Emma, embarrassed that a pet of hers should behave so poorly before the gentlemen. "My goodness! You look possessed!"

IV. FREEDOM

On the way to Yonville, the greyhound wandered fifty yards from the Bovarys' stagecoach. Then she broke into a run.

"Djaliiiii!" Emma shrieked, uncorking a spray of champagne-yellow birds from the nearby poplars. *"Stay!"*

Weightlessly the dog entered the forest.

"Stay! Stay! Stay!" the humans called after her, their directives like bullets missing their target. Her former mistress, the screaming woman, was a stranger. And the greyhound lunged forward, riding the shoals of her own green-flecked shadow.

In the late afternoon she paused to drink water from large cups in the mossy roots of unfamiliar trees. She was miles from her old life. Herons sailed over her head, their broad wings flat as palms, stroking her from scalp to tail at an immense distance, and the dog's mind became empty and smooth. Skies rolled through her chest; her small rib cage and her iron-gray pelt enclosed a blue without limit. She was free.

From a hilltop near a riverbank, through an azure mist, she spotted two creatures with sizzling faces clawing into the water. Cats larger than any she'd ever seen, spear-shouldered and casually savage. Lynx, a mated pair. Far north for this season. They were three times the size of the Bovarys' barn cat yet bore the same taunting anatomy. Analogous golden eyes. They feasted on some prey that looked of another world—flat, thrashing lives they swallowed whole.

Gazehound, huntress—the dog began to remember what she'd been before she was born.

Winter was still raking its white talons across the forest; spring was delayed that year. Fleshless fingers for tree branches. Not a blade or bud of green yet. The dog sought shelter, but shelter was stony and cold this far out, always inhuman. Nothing like the soft-bodied sanctuary she'd left behind.

One night the greyhound was caught out in unknown territory, a deep valley many miles from the river. Stars appeared, and she felt a light sprinkling of panic. Now the owls were awake. Pale hunger came shining out of their beaks, looping above their flaming heads like ropes. In Tostes their hooting had sounded like laughter in the trees. But here, with no bedroom rafters to protect her, she watched the boughs blow apart to reveal nocturnal eyes bulging from white faces; she heard hollow mouths emitting strange songs. Death's rattle, old wind without home or origin, rode the frequencies above her.

A concentrated darkness screeched and dove near her head, and then another, and then the dog began to run. Dawn was six hours away.

She pushed from the valley floor toward higher ground, eventually finding a narrow fissure in the limestone cliffs. She trotted into the blackness like a small key entering a tall lock. Once inside she was struck by a familiar smell, which confused and upset her. Backlit by the moon, her flat, pointed skull and tucked abdomen cast a hieroglyphic silhouette against the wavy wall.

The greyhound spent the next few days exploring her new home. The soil here was like a great cold nose—wet, breathing, yielding. To eat, she had to hunt the vast network of hollows for red squirrels, voles. A spiderweb of bone and fur soon wove itself in the cave's shadows, where she dragged her kills. When she'd lived with the Bovarys, in the early days of their courtship, Emma would let the puppy lick yellow yolks and golden sugar from the flat of a soft palm.

Undeliberate, absolved of rue and intent, the dog continued to forget Madame Bovary.

Gnawing on a femur near the river one afternoon, she bristled and turned. A deer's head was watching her thoughtfully from the silver rushes—separated, by some incommunicable misfortune, from its body. Its neck terminated in a chaos of crawling blackflies, a spill of jeweled rot like boiling cranberries. Its tongue hung limp like a flag of surrender. Insects were eating an osseous cap between the buck's yellow ears, a white knob the diameter of a sand dollar. A low, bad feeling drove the dog away.

V. REGRET

Regret, as experienced by the dog, was a frightening disorientation—she turned in circles and doubled back, trying to uncover the scent of her home. Some organ had never stopped its useless secretions, even without an Emma to provoke them. Hearth and leash, harsh voice, mutton chop, affectionate thump—she wanted all this again.

There was a day when she passed near the town of Airaines, a mere nine miles from the Bovarys' new residence in Yonville; and had the winds changed at that particular moment and carried a certain woman's lilac-scented sweat to her, this story might have had a very different ending.

One midnight, just after the late April thaw, the dog woke to the sight of a large wolf standing in the cave mouth, nakedly weighing her as prey. And even under that crushing stare she did not cower; rather, she felt elevated, vibrating with some primitive species of admiration for this more pure being, solitary and wholly itself. The wolf swelled with appetites that were ancient, straightforward—a belly hunger that was satisfied nightly. An old wound hid beneath a brittle scab on its left shoulder, and a young boar's blood ran in torrents from its magnificent jaws. The greyhound's tail began to wag as if cabled to some current; a growl rose midway up her throat. The predator then turned away from her. Panting— *ha-ha-ha*—it licked green slime from the cave wall, crunching the spires of tiny amber snails. The wolf glanced once more around the chasm before springing eastward. Dawn lumbered behind her, through the pointed firs, unholstering the sun; and the wind began to howl, as if in lamentation, calling the beast back.

Caught between two equally invalid ways of life, the greyhound whimpered herself toward sleep, unaware that in Yonville Emma Bovary was drinking vinegar in black stockings and sobbing at the exact same pitch. Each had forgotten entirely about the other, yet they retained the same peculiar vacancies within their bodies and suffered the same dread-filled dreams. Love had returned, and it went spoiling through them with no outlet.

In summer the dog crossed a final frontier, eating the greasy liver of a murdered bear in the wide open. The big female had been gutshot for sport by teenage brothers from Rouen, who'd then been too terrified by the creature's drunken, hauntingly prolonged death throes to wait and watch her ebb out. In a last pitch she'd crashed down a column of saplings, her muzzle frothing with red foam. The greyhound was no scavenger by nature, until nature made her one that afternoon. The three cubs squatted on a log like a felled totem and watched with grave maroon eyes, their orphan hearts pounding in unison.

Still, it would be incorrect to claim that the greyhound was now feral, or fully ingrained in these woods. As a fugitive, the dog was a passable success, but as a dog she was a blown spore, drifting everywhere and nowhere, unable to cure her need for a human, or her terror at the insufficiency of her single body.

"Our destinies are united now, aren't they?" whispered Rodolphe near the evaporating blue lake in a forest outside of Yonville that might as well have been centuries distant. Crows deluged the sky. Emma sat on a rock, flushed red from the long ride, pushing damp wood chips around with her boot toe. The horses munched leaves in a chorus as Rodolphe lifted her skirts, the whole world rustling with hungers.

In the cave, the dog had a strange dream.

A long, lingering, indistinct cry came from one of the hills far beyond the forest; it mingled with Emma's silence like music.

VI. A BREAK

The dog shivered. She'd been shivering ceaselessly for how many days and nights now? All the magic of those early weeks had vanished, replaced by a dreary and devoted pain. Winter rose out of her own cavities. It shivered her.

Troubled by the soreness that had entered her muscles, she trotted out of the cave and toward the muddy escarpment where she'd buried a cache of weasel bones. Rain had eroded the path, and in her eagerness to escape her own failing frame, the mute ruminations of her throbbing skeleton, the dog began to run at full bore. Then she was sliding on the mud, her claws scrabbling uselessly at the smooth surface; unable to recover her balance, the greyhound tumbled into a ravine.

An irony:

She had broken her leg.

All at once Emma Bovary's final command came echoing through her: *Stay.*

Sunset jumped above her, so very far above her twisted body, like a heart skipping beats. Blood ran in her eyes. The trees all around swam. She sank farther into a soggy pile of dead leaves as the squealing voices of the blackflies rose in clouds.

Elsewhere in the world, Rodolphe Boulanger sat at his writing desk under the impressive head of a trophy stag. Two fat candles were guttering down. He let their dying light flatter him into melancholy—a feeling quite literary. The note before him would end his love affair with Emma.

How shall I sign it? "Devotedly"? No . . . "Your friend"?

The moon, dark red and perfectly round, rose over the horizon.

Deep in the trench, nostalgias swamped the greyhound in the form of olfactory hallucinations: snowflakes, rising yeast, scooped pumpkin flesh, shoe polish, horse-lathered leather, roasting venison, the explosion of a woman's perfume.

She was dying.

She buried her nose in the litterfall, stifling these visions until they ebbed and faded.

It just so happened that a game warden was wandering in that part of the woods, hours later or maybe days. Something in the ravine caught his eye—low to the ground, a flash of unexpected silver. He dropped to his knees for a closer look.

"Oh!" he gasped, calloused hands parting the dead leaves.

VII. THE TWO HUBERTS

The greyhound lived with the game warden, in a cottage at the edge of a town. He was not a particularly creative man, and he gave the dog his same name: Hubert. He treated her wounds as those of a human child, with poultices and bandages. She slept curled at the foot of his bed and woke each morning to the new green of a million spring buds erupting out of logs, sky-blue birdsong, minced chlorophyll.

"Bonjour, Hubert!" Hubert would call, sending himself into hysterics, and Hubert the dog would bound into his arms—and their love was like this, a joke that never grew old. And like this they passed five years.

Early one December evening Hubert accompanied Hubert to Yonville, to say a prayer over the grave of his mother. The snow hid the tombstones, and only the most stalwart mourners came out for such a grim treasure hunt. Among them was Emma Bovary. From within her hooded crimson cloak she noticed a shape darting between the snowflakes—a gray ghost trotting with its lips peeled back from black gums.

"Oh!" she cried. "How precious you are! Come here—"

Her whistle pierced the dog's chest, splintering into antipodal desires:

Run.

Stay.

And it was in this struggle that the dog encountered herself, felt a shimmering precursor to consciousness—the same stirring that lifted the iron hairs on her neck whenever she peered into mirrors, or discovered a small, odorless dog inside a lake.

The whistle rose in pitch, and now she *did* remember: Midnight in Tostes. The walks through the ruined pavilion. Crows at dusk. The tug of a leather leash. Piano music. Egg yolk in a perfumed hand. Sad, impatient fingers scratching her ears.

Something bubbled and broke inside the creature's heart.

Emma was walking through the thick snow, toward the oblivious game warden, one dark strand of hair loose and blowing in the twilight.

"Oh, monsieur! I, too, once had a greyhound!" She shut her eyes and sighed longingly, as if straining to call back not only the memory but the dog herself.

And she very nearly succeeded.

The greyhound's tail began helplessly to wag.

"Her name was Deeeaaaa . . . Dahhh . . ."

And then the dog remembered, too, calloused hands brushing dead leaves from her fur, clearing the seams of blackflies from her eyelids and nostrils, lifting her from the trench. Their sturdy fingers clasped firmly around her belly as she flew through evening air. The man's rank, tuberlike scent enveloping her, the firelight in the eyes of her rescuer. Over his shoulder she'd glimpsed the shallow imprint of a dog's body in the mud.

With a lovely, amnesiac smile, Emma Bovary continued

to fail to remember the name of her greyhound. And each soft sound she mouthed tugged the dog deeper into the past.

It was an impossible moment, and the pain the animal experienced—staring from old, rumpled Hubert to the pale, evanescing Emma—did feel very much like an ax falling through her snow-wet fur, splitting down the rail of her tingling spine, fatally dividing her.

"My dog's name is Hubert," Hubert said to Madame Bovary, with his stupid frankness. He glanced fondly at little Hubert, attributing the greyhound's spasms in the cemetery drifts to the usual culprits: giddiness or fleas.

Writhing in an agony, the dog rose to her feet. She closed the small, incredibly cold gulf of snow between herself and her master.

Sit, she then commanded herself, and she obeyed.

The Tornado Auction

You know, there was never any money in it, even back then. If you were a breakeven, you were a success.

I'd been fully retired for nearly fifteen years when I decided, on a whim, to return to the sale barn. Driving home from the pharmacy, passing the shoals of purple corn, I watched the wheel turning in my hands. The barn's howling interior, with its warrens of wind hoses, was as familiar to me as my home, but I recognized almost no one. How young the faces had become! Just about everybody I've ever wanted to impress, I've now outlived.

Baby southerlies whinnied around, shrieking their inhuman sounds. Violet funnels chased one another beneath the shivering ducts. Crocus-blue mists, soft as exhalations, fogged their incubator walls. I felt a growl under my navel as I passed Chute 7—the doorway out of which my own twisters had flown, once upon a time. New lunacies greeted me on either side. What a catalog of weathers my peers were now breeding, dreaming up on their ranchlands. Clouds branded Pink

Cauliflower and Lucifer's Bridal Veil. Clouds almost too
bloated with rain to move. I found plenty to admire, despite
the grim forecasts I'd been reading all year.

Moisture began to clot on my glasses, so I removed them.
Some things, I swear, I see better without correction. Tor-
nadoes, for one. My eyes often snag on irrelevancies when
I'm wearing my glasses; without them, I can take in more.
The panorama, you know, the whole sublime blur. Estelle,
I think, hated the sight of my naked face. *(Jesus, Robert! Do
you know how scary you look, wandering around out there like
Mr. Magoo?)*

The national anthem cranked up, and everyone stood. By
the old custom, one of the local families had donated a runty
funnel, set to manifest at the crowd's off-key crescendo. So
while we sang, hands on hearts, a howler blew out of Chute 1.

"Oh my God," I breathed. And I felt the way I always hope
to feel in church. As the twister kicked and spun around the
arena floor, the howl rose from its center, throbbing without
discrimination into and through each of us, and row by row
we fell helplessly to our knees.

The auction is a quarterly event, and until my retirement
I attended every one. You'll read in the papers that ours is
a "graying community," a defunct way of life. But on auction day, it never feels so. Scattered around the parking lot,
more than a hundred twitching, immature storms dimple
the roofs of their trailers, like pipping chicks testing their
shells. Their wailing surrounds and fills the barn, harmoniz-
ing with the hum of machinery. The viper pit of hoses, the

blue convection modules stuck to every wall like big square dewdrops—the various modern wet nurses that keep a developing storm alive. "Back in the Dark Ages, all we had to work with was liquid propane and the real wind," my old man liked to remind me.

On my way to the sale barn, I'd passed a quintet of freshly weaned storms, all sired by the same cumuliform supercell out of Dalhart. Beautiful orphans, thriving independently. I'd known this line of clouds my whole life; that Dalhart stud cell was famous when I was a kid. Its signature thunder went rolling through this very sale barn, and I smiled to hear it once more. TORNADO ALLEY SUPERCELL: THE FASTEST WINDS ON EARTH. You hear those young clouds rumbling, you get the child-joy, the child-fever. I'll turn seventy-four this March, and it doesn't matter: that joy regresses you.

It's been a bad season for seasons. Not just here in Gosper County but all across the country. After the anthem, we sat while the flag was attacked by the last of the purebred gusts and the cloud danced itself out. Then I saw the one face I'd been counting on seeing, as surely as flipping over a penny to find mournful Lincoln: the Rev.

"I don't care what your politics are," the Rev crooned. "I think it's time we all admit that the weather is changing . . ."

A few boos, though most were nodding, hat bills stabbing at the air like a bunch of dour woodpeckers. Everybody here has been hit by the warming. This year, if you wanted cold, moist air, you had to pipe it in. The dry-line days on which we breeders rely did not come.

Guilt rose from the bleachers like a rippling stink. Relative to the West Texas cloud-seeding corporations, our approach here in southern Nebraska remains pretty Amish. Still, when you're raising weather by artificial means, it's hard to pretend you don't have a hand in the Change.

I feel less culpable than some because I always stayed small—I didn't mess with the supercells or the silver iodide; I never went for broke with the ten-thousand-dollar anemometers, the quarter-million-dollar accelerators. One twister at a time, I raised almost by hand.

And I raised them for demolition. This was the seventies, on the ranchlands of Tornado Alley. You can bring down a city block with a rental tornado, and we had contracts. My twisters have felled fire-damaged silos and bankrupt casinos, foundering Chick-N-Shacks and neglected libraries. So long as you properly configured the chute and programmed the expulsion vents, a tornado would roll toward a condemned building as inexorably as a pregnant lady toward rocky road ice cream, as Estelle used to joke in her joking days, when the girls were still small. Elsewhere, I hear, they rent out beehives to pollinate fruit trees. Nowadays, of course, armies of American litigators have made weather-assisted demolition illegal. I suppose that's progress.

Prices for violent storms have bottomed out, and farmers are downsizing, doing dust devils, doing siroccos. Walls of dust raise themselves, some reaching eight thousand feet under the blazing sun, swallowing the gas flares over the oil wells. The jet stream is not cooperating. Neither, for that matter, is the economy. There was a time when a family could support itself with the sale of one or two tornadoes a year, but those days are long gone. To survive you have to sell out to the rodeos, the monster-truck rallies. We don't suffer alone. Offshore rigs report that waterspouts have all but dried up. Here on the plains, an early frost snuffed every budding funnel cloud.

These days anybody with sense farms winds. Winds are the growth industry. Clean energy. You want to get out ahead of the apocalypse, get into winds.

Supercells, those alpha storms that bulge with precipitation like muscle, cost too much in upkeep and insurance for all but the corporate outfits. Culls deemed unfit for sale are left to spin out in the green canyons, thousands of acres of privately held weather graveyards.

A few family farms are still trying to develop prestige twisters; I saw two in utero while driving into town. Sister funnels, housed in adjacent incubators. They looked lonely out there, spinning on their single toes. Purple monsters, twice the height of the cork-colored barn, yawing up and down, consuming bitter air. What it must be costing to irrigate them all through July, to keep those updrafts tight, I shudder to imagine.

Any storm you see at auction was artificially bred, artificially maintained. Coriolis Farms, our family's outfit, was no exception. Our tornadoes we advertised as "hell in a handbasket"—Estelle's copy. Typically rotating around sixty or seventy miles per hour, rarely more than fifty meters across. EF0, EF1. Compact enough to rage in a corral and strong enough to flip a car.

But even corporate-raised stock is far less powerful than the Act-of-God twisters that destroy whole towns. I've seen mobile homes conscripted into a cosmic game of kick the can, and that cruelty is assigned randomly, by forces unknown. Weather damage is the inverse of a victimless crime—people get robbed of everything, and there is no evildoer to lock in a cage.

If a tornado farmer makes a mistake, all hell breaks loose. Whenever a ground-traveling cloud escapes its enclosure, a vigilante mob shows up at the breeder's ranch. Give people a name to blame for their suffering, and you, too, can expect a flood of furious attention. On the night my storm escaped me, the entire county read the damage swath as my autograph.

Just when I'd reconciled myself to anonymity, Lemon Guyron slid onto my bench with his oldest son beside him. I've known Lemon for decades. His deep froggy laugh and his fortressed smile.

"Can that be Wurman? I almost didn't recognize you!"

"We've got some age on us, I guess. How've you been, Lemon?"

"Never better, never better. Bad year for weather, but that'll pass, of course." A grin spread like a moat around his face. "I got no complaints."

Lemon's son, what was his name?

"Actually, Mr. Wurman," said this forty-year-old boy, who'd inherited his father's bassoon of a voice but not his belligerent cheer, "we've had a helluva time finding a buyer this spring. A lot of the state fairs are moving away from tornado riding. Too much liability, and the kids aren't interested." He smiled with his gums, lifting his mustache into a gloomy rainbow. "Like jai alai and unprotected group sex, it has seen its day." We chuckled our stage chuckles, staring ahead.

"You in the market this year, Wurman?"

"I'm not buying," I said. "Just fantasizing."

"Looks like something's coming down . . ."

Knee to knee, we all craned in, stubby number 2s poised above scratch pads. The clouds were loaded in the pens now, coerced into a temporary calm, like genies in their bottles. Bodiless, they could not paw the earth. But we heard them readying for expulsion, whining for release, behind every steel door.

Chute 2 opened first: out whirled a dust devil, shrubby and meek, gyring in place like a music-box ballerina, already dissipating into the golden afternoon air.

"It would exhaust itself right here," I murmured to Lemon, "if it weren't for those hoses stringing it up like a corset."

"That's what the Ahmad brothers are putting up?"

"I heard they had some trouble with their incubator."

"Looks like bad breath."

The Rev chanted over the gusts: "One thousand, now two, now two, who'll give me two? Two, now three, now three, who'll give me three?"

Last year, the nation's top recorded price for a storm was a quarter-million dollars for an EF4 tornado named Jericho, raised by Gomez & Daughters, one of the last matriarchal weather ranches in Texas, and sold to Franklin Fair & Rodeo. That may sound like a lot of money, but consider what it takes to run an aeolian generator, and redo the math; like I said, if you're a breakeven, you're doing better than ninety percent of breeders. People get desperate, they make strange compromises. Pinky Searle told me that, last May, two producers approached his family about a reality TV show.

Two rows down, a kid with bad razor burn and a bony-white Stetson was saying, "I don't think the market will fall out of bed, but I'm saying the highs are in place."

The Rev called speeds into the clown-nosed mic, singing the praises of the yet-to-be. This one, full grown, was sure to be another "storm of the century." That one, the "future terror of the Great Plains." I can tell you what was happening inside the buyer's mind, as the Rev seeded us with his enthusiasm: a second tornado was building. Bigger, faster, stronger, and immensely profitable, the sort of sublime weather that reduces grown men to bed wetters.

Four plummy funnels were rotating around the corral; mushroomy and odd as she was, I couldn't take my eyes off the white one.

"What's got you pinked up? Not that ugly loaf?"

"Maybe so. Who sired it?"

"Supercell Four. Molly's outfit."

"You don't like it?"

"I don't like the looks of it, no. Everybody knows they ionize with junk from China."

"Molly does?"

"Oh, heck yes. That downdraft look natural to you?"

"I'm not buying, anyhow—"

Molly's cull turned a sluggish circle under the fans, a beautiful light streaking her center, like those shy colors inside a marble. My pencil never touched the scratch pad.

"Three thousand, who'll give me four?"

I lifted my paddle.

"The *hell* are you thinking?"

Lemon turned his stare on me. His wintry eye, assessing.

"You're a fool," he offered. "You want to burn up all your kids' money?"

"The girls are grown. They don't need my money."

He laughed angrily. Scared for me, or maybe of me.

"Find a hobby, Wurman. Raise a puppy."

Another paddle went up, jumping the price a thousand dollars. The boy's powder-blue vest revealed him as a proxy of the biggest Texas weather factory, Cloudsmart Corp.

I lifted my paddle.

"You're mad at the girls, I can see that."

"This has nothing to do with the girls."

"Be angry. You have every right. But this is a mistake."

"*Twelve* thousand, do I have thirteen?"

I lifted my paddle.

The Cloudsmart kid raised, too. It wasn't his money, was it? Possibly he'd decided his duckling pride would be injured, losing a cloud to the likes of me.

I lifted my paddle.

"Fifteen, do I have sixteen?"

"Yep!"

"Jesus, Wurman. You don't have that kind of money."

"Who are you to tell me what I've got?"

"You really want to ruin yourself, go jump in the river— it's quicker."

I lifted my paddle.

"Going, going . . ."

Gone. She was mine.

"It's a bad bet."

"My worst," I happily agreed.

"It may die before you get home. You're aware of that possibility?"

The ranching of storms has come a long way since wranglers drove those silent clouds, black and distended, up the Goodnight Trail, or captured Colorado River mists on horseback. But the sale of a tornado is still very much a handshake business.

"I am aware," I said to the seller's fat-lipped manager.

(*Bobby, what did you expect would happen?* One of my wife's favorite questions, whenever things went sideways for us.)

At the loading chute, I clutched the hauling papers, watching the young storm flatten, straighten. Lemon, bless him, had loaned me his trailer to get the bucking cloud home. Moisture found my tongue, settled there. *This is what she tastes like, then. My storm. Mine to keep spinning, mine to make strong.* Moisture dribbled onto my cheeks, amazingly of my own manufacture. Never when I'm called upon to cry can I wince out a tear. At Estelle's funeral, to my girls' disgust, I was a dry teat. Couldn't plug my eyeballs into what I felt deep below.

The pale funnel pulsed out and contracted, like a star exploring its cosmos. In the sunlight, against the dark walls of the chute, it became a ghostly gramophone needle, leaping and falling, lightly and blindly, searching for the groove.

These days such mishaps are rare, but every rancher knows

that anecdote about the fledgling twister that burst its trailer, escaped onto the highway. In the rearview I saw only the solid metal cylinder. But in my mind's eye I beheld her, a cone of swiftly moving air.

I drove south through successively finer meshes of rainfall. Nobody emerged from the house to scream, *Robert, what have you done?*

––––––

My first thought on waking was *Did she live through the night?*

From the bedroom window, I have a clear view across the parched grass to the tornado shelter. Cottony mist enveloped the steel enclosure. Let's admit it was a dumb-ass move, to buy a sluggish cull on credit, at an age when I cannot realistically expect to raise a cloud to tornadic stature, much less turn a profit. To buy a twister, at this most vulnerable stage in its development, without having set foot in my own shelter in half a decade. An impulse purchase is cinnamon gum, not an unvetted cloud.

Twelve hours ago, I'd pulled up to the shelter to unload and found everything still functional. Incredibly, the silent fans had clicked on. The great air bladders that had been idle for years began swelling and falling again. I got the hoses fretworked to maintain the updraft, tubed in some ice crystals. Checked the vertical vorticity levels: all excellent. Warm winds and cold winds charged into the system—the collision of temperatures that keeps a baby spinning, breathing. The goal is to get that rotation to be self-sustaining. It's an art, no doubt, to calibrate your inputs so that you fight off homeostasis, keeping a young storm in that growth state. A tornado farmer is always in pursuit of a paradox: consistent instability. As Estelle and our girls would tell you, if I have one talent, it's for this: knowing what a developing storm needs to stay angry, to live on.

"She's alive!" I exited the house and breathed a sigh of relief. The chimes that ran from the porch beams to the silver dome of the shelter were hysterically singing, which meant that inside the steel walls, my baby was spinning. I couldn't recall the last time I'd been so happy about anything. In my tone I heard the man I'd been when the girls were young and our farm was operational.

My oldest daughter was four pounds at birth, and her appearance flooded the earth with an infinite number of horrors and perils, a demonic surge of catastrophic possibilities out of all proportion to the tiny mass in my arms. Love unlids Pandora's box. Is that obvious? Before her, I honestly did not know it. What I felt for her was of a wholly different order than what I felt for Estelle. Never before had that heat collided with the icy possibilities of accident, of death. Not at these speeds, not with this intensity, and constantly. They were born at the same moment, twins: our baby daughter and the danger.

Raising a tornado, you're always dreaming of its dying day. That's the breeder's ultimate vision—to build a storm until it can unwind spectacularly, releasing all of its cultivated fury, vanishing before your eyes. Whereas with my daughters, I have to pretend they'll live forever. The alternative is too terrible to contemplate. If there is a life after this one, I'll be dead myself and still pretending. What the girls birthed in me was a fear worse than any feeling I had fought through as a single man.

When I reached the shelter, the funnel was suspended between the floor and ceiling vents, looking more irritable than powerful. The anemometer reported no gain in speed, and the wind girdles showed a fairly consistent circumference. But that sound spiraling out, I'd forgotten how a roar like that can fill you up entirely. Hearing loss is part of aging, I suppose. But I hadn't guessed you could go deaf even to a sound's howling absence. To the absence of all pleasure in your life. Now it seemed absurd that I'd endured so many years without a storm to nurse. How had I survived the peace and quiet? My ears were swamped, until there was no longer any room for thought. I moved, and it was the sound moving me.

Two transparent tunnels run from the shelter to the shining fence line between the birches. Cost a fortune to put them in, and then I got only a decade's use out of them before Estelle delivered her ultimatum. It's a joy to watch the young funnel exercise. I hit the lever that releases the doors, and the cloud burst into view, flying the length of the tunnels, blown up and back by the fans.

Having enough pastureland to run your twisters is essential. That spaciousness, I have in abundance. Beautiful country, covered in wildflowers and yucca blooms when we get enough rain. From a plane you can see the erosion lines where the grasslands become the badlands. "So much land, Bobby," Estelle used to say. "Why don't you try growing something else?"

There's another tornado shelter that we never finished, on the other side of the house. There it sits, accusing me still, with the quiet eloquence of my father's old jalopies rusting in the bunchgrass. (*Robert, would you fix those things or sell them? Please?* Estelle would plead. And I'd tell her, which I thought was a pretty good joke, *I'm forming an artificial reef.*) I used to insist the second shelter was at "an early stage of completion," then it gradually became a "stalled construction"; it was a decade before I used the word "abandoned." Now, thanks to my recent purchase, I was going to die penniless, all good intentions still waiting in the rain.

For some reason, the sight of grass poking between the ruined planks of the foundation filled me with relief. Wind plucked at my shirt, tugging at the sleeves. In a cooperative spirit, I undid the buttons and shrugged it to the ground.

Nobody would find me out here on my hands and knees, crawling around the periphery of the shelter to check its ventilation. Nobody would comment on my slack, hairy belly. Nobody would say a word for or against me, because nobody was watching at all.

Around noon, the good feeling broke into articulation, and I could voice precisely what had been making me so happy. Because I'd finally done it, hadn't I? I'd outlasted my life. The girls were grown; Estelle was gone. There was nobody left for me to hurt.

Live long enough, and your life becomes your own to gamble with again.

———

By Friday of our third week, we were broaching a level of instability that would allow the funnel to double in strength. I was spending twelve, fourteen hours a day by her side, monitoring her growth and cooking the hot wind into her, holding my ear to the throbbing hull of the shelter. Her rising and descending wailing followed me home at night, and into my dreams. Something wonderful had happened to me, and my sleeping and waking lives were now identical, filled with singing storms.

I had so many responsibilities at the shelter that I kept forgetting to take my medicine; one afternoon I woke up on my back, watching the real sky darkening above me. Flat, white clouds glided serenely overhead, so that for a moment I felt like I was at the bottom of a lake, staring up at a hundred floating docks.

My old man returned from Germany at twenty-seven already scoliotic with his freight of nightmares and medals. When I was a kid, I hated him for spending so much time away from us. I'm not angry about this today. The same need lives in me, and I wonder at the mechanisms by which such things are inherited. Memories went darkly leafing through my dad, growths he couldn't control. Of course he had to leave us to be with his storms. He had my ma, three midget sons wearing his face and always chanting his name, glomming on to his knees—there was no respite in the house. I imagine a tornado must have been the only ax that could level the entire Hürtgen Forest inside him—again and again, as often as necessary. When you're so thickly sown with ghosts, it makes no sense to plug your ears against them. Those cries come from within. The solution my father hit on, and taught me young, was to raise storms loud enough to drown out all interior sound.

I was always late for dinner. *Eat without me,* I'd beg my family. Outside every window, they could see our black storms feeding. Some nights we had to scream over their howling: HOW WAS SCHOOL, GIRLS? I'd grip the table with knuckles popping to avoid running right back into it. The howling was a magnet, pulling at my spine. The house was a cardboard box, and nowhere I could be for very long. *Our house,* I had to remind myself, because it was Estelle's domain; I did my living outside. At night we left the windows open so that I could pretend I was amphibian, straddling the inner and the outer worlds. Dawn released me back into the lake of the sky. Springtime meant air filled to brimming with secret moisture, begging to be captured and spun into the dark wombs of my twisters. My daughters' gnatlike little voices, I'm sorry to say, were no match for that howling.

When I was a younger man, I liked naming the storms. Shiva, Smash-N-Grab, Jack B. Limber, Calypso the Queen. My daughters got quiet names, each one as sweet and forgettable as a sugar cube dropped into a teacup. Anna, Megan, Susan. You see how it goes for the Bambis and the Rainbows in this world; I wanted the girls, unlike my tornadoes, to travel anywhere they chose without causing a stir.

Six weeks after the auction, kneeling at the midpoint of the tunnels, I clocked my twister barreling overland at fifty-one miles per hour. My throat was on fire before I realized that I was screaming along with her.

Then the bad moment came, when she blasted through the boundary and into the open air, swelling marvelously in diameter, uprooting the centenarian elm and rooster-tailing a wall of red dust. The force of her exit knocked me into a quivering heap in the dirt; I shook my head clear and stood to find the funnel moving straight for me, swallowing the distance between us like brush-fed fire.

I regained consciousness on the far perimeter of the field, resting my head on a pillowy lump that seemed to be made of my own bruised skin. The cloud was sucking topsoil from every direction, turning a muddled brown as she spun off to the east and kicked my truck onto its side. I did not hear or see the windows shatter—without my glasses, the whole scene before me was one streaming tear.

Had she picked a different day to escape, she'd have been dead already; but as it happened, atmospheric conditions at that moment were ideally suited to support her life. All morning, a thunderstorm had been brewing on the western horizon, moving over the dowdy spires of the grain silos. Major precipitation, cherry-sized hailstones, sporadic lightning. Warm surface winds had been pushing up from the Gulf, and the sky overhead was deep blue for miles; she was glutting on that warmth, pulling it into her whirling body. I found myself thinking, insanely, that my cloud must have realized this and planned her break accordingly.

She was flying for the house. My hands muffed my ears,

came away sticky and red. The sight didn't bother me; it was only my blood, after all. I knew the next sight would be my house splitting apart. People report their entire lives flashing before their eyes on such occasions; I saw sticks, a stack of bills. Why didn't I stand then, and run to save myself? But this part of me has always been the broken one. In boyhood, I remember feeling very charitably toward my fevers.

Good luck is luck I don't deserve, and yet this is simply what happened: the wind changed direction. At the precise instant when all seemed lost, my funnel spun one hundred eighty degrees, pivoting with an arbitrary mercy that I had to fight not to take personally as grace from on high. A rear-flank downdraft from the massing weather system might have turned her; I can offer no worthier explanation for what I saw. With the same howling serenity with which she had targeted my house, she flew back the way she had come, blowing in a clean line. The funnel seemed almost human in her retreat, retracing her steps through the gouged pasture and disappearing into the shelter, sucking the gates shut behind her.

"Good girl." I sighed. It felt as if a spear tip had lodged in my left side. I spit up a muddy pink phlegm and felt proud of my cloud, wondering if she'd broken my ribs.

"I thought I was finished today, Estelle," I spoke into the cave of the house. Sandy air settled on my gumline; I'd taken to leaving the windows and the doors open so that I could hear my storm chiming at all hours. "I thought I was finished, but look at how quickly a man can be resuscitated."

"Unscathed, I wouldn't say that," the doctor said, frowning down at me with his expression of Ivy League constipation. "A cracked rib can easily lead to pneumonia, if you're not careful about your breathing."

"Doc, if you'd seen how fast she was going, believe me, you'd know how lucky I am to be breathing at all."

The doctor removed his glasses, and his blue eyes were unshaded lamps. He was a new doctor, a young doctor. Very telegenic. Definitely looked the part of concerned physician. Color me fooled. Because when I told him I needed some relief, his whole face crumpled like a kite in a tree.

"I'm going to suggest an excellent physical therapist. In the meantime, I'd make sure to keep taking all your current medications."

"I was sort of hoping for some painkillers, to be honest with you." I coughed and winced. "Just a vial or two of tide-me-overs."

In the mirror, I watched my features twist to demo my agony. Old men are never taken seriously; we are no longer the authorities on anything, are we? Not even our pain. I resented having to perform it for a stranger, when there is nothing so genuine.

The doctor's mouth puckered further, the lips tugging into a little heart, and I wondered why his pen wasn't moving.

"Tide-me-overs. I see." He placed the pen on the desk. "What exactly did you have in mind?"

His shining eyes didn't fool me now.

"Do I look like a drug dealer, Doctor?"

The doctor smiled at that. "Do I?"

It got so quiet I could almost hear the gavel rapping inside him.

"Can I be honest with you, Mr. Wurman? You look like a man who's falling on hard times. And I promise you, this is not the cushion you want to land on."

———

Driving home from the doctor's with one hand splinting my ribs, I found myself wondering how Suzie was doing. I don't have a favorite daughter, but Suzie is the one I worry about the most at night. During her senior year in high school, I rode her to Lincoln every Friday for her appointments with a great blur of healers, including Dr. Barbara, the "osteopath," a word that made Estelle and me picture a feathery dinosaur. None of them helped, I guess because Suzie couldn't tell us what had broken. Her spirit, or her heart, or possibly something even more delicate and too fast moving to name, like those polar clouds that transform while you watch them. The X-rays revealed only minor fractures. But I broke it, whatever it was—no mystery there. On that count, we were all in agreement. Two decades later, my guilt is alive and well. For a parent, there is no recovering from such knowledge.

She was sucked into the heart of the storm, spun above the shelter, dropped almost a quarter mile away. The newspapers nicknamed her "Dorothy," and TV cameras swarmed our farm. We felt misused by them. They made her eyeball fodder, filler between commercials. Flowers and cards poured in for about a week, and then months of sidelong glances. To this day, on Suzie's rare visits, folks will whistle at her as if she were up on a parade float—"Hey, Dorothy!"—blind or indifferent to her wincing.

Afterward, Suzie was skittish around me. Whenever I tried to touch her, she gasped as if scalded. She couldn't even get to anger, and I worried about that at night. Some natural progression had stalled out inside my daughter, and I knew what that felt like, one forlorn note repeating itself, your song in a rut.

The deal we struck was this: Estelle wouldn't leave me, but I had to do something else. No more howlers in the shelter. I begged her not to take the girls from me. She said she planned to do just that, unless I quit. I conceded, thinking I wouldn't last a month. How could I live without that roaring? Nobody would disagree that raising storms is a poor choice of employment for a father of three children. The simple fact was that I didn't know how to do anything else.

"So learn," my smart wife suggested.

I got a job at a friend's wind farm, cash-cropping zephyrs. It was hackwork, the semi-luminous. I hated the minutes of my life. I wanted to do what I always had done, better than it had ever been done. I wanted to put my head in an oven. But I kept my promise, and collected my checks, and raised the tame weather. And eventually, I retired.

Suzie is thirty-seven now, a paralegal, and she says her day-to-day is very full. But our daughter, "miraculously uninjured," never really recovered. She started dressing like she had something to hide, in black clothes that were slouchy and ugly, slack at the neck. Even the tailored shirts her mother bought her gave up hope on her hunched body, lost their shape. The skittishness became a permanent trait, sunk deep—though ultimately she did get to anger, a special rage that seems to ignite only in my presence.

"What did it feel like, to fly?" strangers would ask my daughter for years afterward. What Suzie said to these people, I have always felt to be a fine distillation of her character: "I won't remember that." Sometimes her inquisitors corrected her, assuming they'd heard wrong: "You can't?" Then she'd repeat herself without further explanation: "I *won't*."

She was unconscious when I got to her, so she couldn't know that I raced across the pasture to her side. When I set my palm to her cheek, she spasmed, her whole body jerking in the dust. I cried out with her. When people ask, "Who found you out there?" she knows to answer, "My father." But she doesn't remember that I gathered her into my arms and held her.

It was my fault, of course, that the twister got loose. I remembered plenty. And I was helpless against an older memory that found me there, kneeling beside my daughter: the time I'd seen a fish dropped by a Swainson's hawk, thrashing on its long fall through the sky and then clapping itself like one white palm against the rocks.

Nothing shattered for me in those moments while I cradled Suzie and rushed for the house; quite the contrary, all the pieces of my life fused into a mirror, spun at last by this event into a glassy coherence, and I saw, I understood, that in fact I had always been the greatest danger to my family. I was the apex predator. Duly noted. I made the revision. Once the girls made it to adulthood, I thought, I could relax. Guiltily, I began to dream of the day when I'd be alone, my shadow roaming the land, unhindered by the fear of hurting anybody.

One by one they blew off—first Estelle, then each of the girls in turn. Today my daughters are far away, rooted in new lives, and safe from me.

After my injury, I more or less gave up driving into town. I couldn't move fast enough to sidestep the staring people. Their cold glances turned me into Bambi on the ice, slipping and sliding all over. Who can price-shop for soup amid that kind of judgment? I bought about a month's supply of milk and cereal, eggs and canned chili, hamburger meat, buy-one-get-one frozen pizzas. A head of lettuce and some freckly bananas as an afterthought, because the doctor had begged me to eat foods with minerals, rich in whatever.

Wes Jeter netted me on my way out the door. His struggle to smile was almost comical—how upset he looked as he grabbed my free hand, pumped!

"I assume you made out better than the cloud."

I grinned in his direction. "We both survived. I got her back into the shelter. Tell you what, Wes, it was a goddamn miracle. She's there now, fattening up on the hoses. Wind speeds of fifty-five this morning."

"Well, you need to put it down, Robert."

"Excuse me?"

"Robert, you look . . . unwell."

"Unwell?" I laughed. People were mincing words for me now, making me a word puree. As if I didn't have the teeth to bite into the apple.

"I ran into Lemon Guyron a few weeks back. He told me what you bid—"

To my surprise, his eyes began to water.

"I don't know what your endgame is here, but, friend—"

"Wes," I said, "I have not felt so alive in years."

———

Here's how the fury forms:

Towering supercells can reach seventy thousand feet into the atmosphere. These are the storms that breed tornadoes in nature. Countervailing winds roll air into a moving tube. (The "corpus" of the storm, some call this. Though a storm, of course, is bodiless.) Sun-warmed air near the ground begins to rise, updrafts that push into the center of the horizontal vector, causing it to bulge. A spectral mountain develops in the sky, energy sheeting down either side. Condensation releases heat, driving the updrafts higher. Two vortices are born; the weak twin dies; the survivor becomes the heart of a new system, the mesocyclone. A funnel descends, tightens, inhales more of that warm surface air, and accelerates its rotation. When that swirling horn makes contact with the ground, it's officially a tornado.

What kills a tornado? Theories vary. Here's what I've observed firsthand: Eventually, the cold outflow of the downdrafts knuckles around the warm inflow, snuffing the tension that fuels its rotation, that keeps the chaos bounded and mobile. As the rotation slows, the funnel disintegrates. Out like a lamb. A loose wisp, swallowed back into the parent storm.

Black heaven spiraling like a celestial drill bit—this is what you likely know of tornadoes from the movies. What you may not know is that there have been several reported cases in which a hand-raised twister has gotten loose, jumped a fence, and ascended toward a passing supercell. Spiraling *up*, not down, and fusing to the placental, moisture-rich belly of the wild storm. The farmer's funnel becomes part of a jaw-dropping wall of cloud.

To attempt to engineer that kind of miracle by, say, failing to bar the doors of your shelter would be an unspeakably dangerous and selfish act; and whenever rumors circulated around the sale barn of a rogue breeder who'd done just that, I sputtered my reproof along with Lemon and the rest. But inside, I was lit by wonder: suppose you could do it once and be guaranteed no casualties, no catastrophes. Imagine watching the cloud you'd raised embraced by the cumulonimbus, bridging this earth's surface and the heavens. What could be more gratifying to a tornado farmer than standing witness to such an ascension? Can you see it? I can, but I've had a lifetime to practice.

———

I can tolerate cities, the crowds and the sounds of cities, but city people often get deeply spooked when they visit our sandy prairie. They call it empty, which isn't true at all, but an error of perception that must result from the absence of tall buildings, groaning subways, or any clustered trees to wall off sight lines. A vast presence comes swarming at you overland, waving and yellow, airy and blue. A radial horizon. I did fine in New York, where I spent three days when my middle girl got married. I didn't spook. I didn't complain about wading shin deep through trash bags in Times Square or the festival of elbows. You add stuff in, and I can manage; you take stuff out, and a city person is undone.

On their less and less frequent stopovers, the girls all refer to it now—"the emptiness." Anna spent two days here in November and complained the whole while. She could no longer hear the land exhaling all around her. That saddened me; I didn't know a child I'd raised could turn so numb. Ask the crowded stars if they find this country empty. Ask the howling guest behind our house.

I'm an inland man, but I've always loved the dial tone, the salty wash of sound that floods into your ear, like the ocean, I imagine, so round and unstoppable that it rinses your memory clean, too, until eventually you forget that you are listening to anything at all. Midnight is the best time to apply this treatment to your ear. You lift the phone, call no one. It works on me the way the TV did back when the house was full. In the fallow years, after giving up the storms, I needed noise piped into my skull.

The phone is a yellow rotary, a perfectly functional piece of equipment that slyly became an antique on our wall. I hate the newer models, which look like plastic antlers. I don't have that little window that tells you the name of the intruder, the caller ID—which was never a problem when no one called.

But since I'd quit town, the phone had started ringing daily, then hourly, sometimes every ten minutes, the sound fire-working through the kitchen until the tape would finally kick on and transmit one of three shrilly familiar voices:

"I just called Amy at the pharmacy, she says you're not picking up your medicine . . ."

"So you're at it again. I cannot fucking believe this . . ."

"I am not bluffing, Dad, I will board a plane tonight if you don't answer . . ."

"Dad, Daddy, pick up, we're all worried . . ."

I considered picking up and telling them they should have been worried a lot earlier, because as it turned out I'd been depressed for years, and only now was I coming out of it. But I knew that I could, and should, conserve my energy. Save my breath, save my strength. Everything I had on reserve was for my cloud; nobody would suffer for want of my presence except for her.

My daughters seem to hold me accountable for some miserable early life that is entirely their fiction, as adult women. "We were tornado farmers in Nebraska," I've heard them say, "we had no childhood." I'm not sure what the motivation is there. Maybe they're ashamed at how little they actually did suffer, relative to Estelle and me and folks of our generation. Whatever their reasons, our girls have recast their carefree youth into some campfire tale to entertain their city friends, or to chastise me for events long past. I feel outside of every story that they tell about me. "But you were always outside," the middle one, Megan, likes to snap. "Always up, up, and away. We had to scream to get your attention."

Against that last accusation, I won't defend myself. But they forget that I had to scream over the storms, too, at the top of my lungs. And still, they never understood me, did they?

Anna and Megan left five messages apiece. Suzie only called once, on a Tuesday, or a Wednesday or a Thursday or a Sunday—I'll admit I'd lost track—but it was Suzie who finally baited me into answering. I won't let her voice languish inside the machine. I picked up, thinking of the fish's belly on the rocks. Before I could get the receiver to my ear, she was already laying into me:

"Are you insane, Dad?"

"I taught you better manners than that. Want to start with 'hello'?"

"Wes called. He says you're driving without a windshield. And he tells us you bought a tornado, with what money I don't know . . ."

After a moment, I was almost relieved. Old Wes. What a meddlesome prick. He must have really done some detective work, to hunt up Suzie's New York number. Farewell, Wes. One less person to worry about.

"Wes loves you, Dad. He was worried about you."

I could hear her breathing through her mouth, which reminded me that it had been forty minutes since I'd checked my cloud's precipitation levels.

"I gotta go, girl."

"Wes loves you. He loves you. Do you not understand that?"

For a swimmy second, I forgot which daughter I was talking to. It was Suzie, the angry one. Though lately, that was hardly a distinction.

"Megan says you haven't been making your insurance payments."

"How the hell would Megan know that?"

A great pain fanned out behind my eyeballs, and I felt suddenly so very tired.

"Nobody can get hurt this time. Nobody lives out this way. And not that it's any of your business, but the windshield isn't gone, it's just a little broken."

"Can you see through it?"

"I know the roads."

"What you're doing is *selfish,* Dad."

"I don't see how my storm affects anybody but me. But if you want to be upset, that's your choice. This is America."

"America, Home of the Free. Why didn't I think of that? Okay, I choose not to care whether you live or die."

Then we were both exhaling into the receiver. I listened to our breaths collide over the line, my daughter's and mine.

"Goodbye, honey."

"Your friend loves you, okay? That's why he called."

My mind bloated on a single note for a full minute, a pure, consoling sound, before I realized that I'd hung up on her.

I considered calling Wes, to chew his ass out, but the simpler solution, in the end, was to unplug the phone.

Most of the guys I came up with are gone. Who knew that an exit to that hall of mirrors existed? Once, when I was a boy, I ran away from my family. Down the boardwalk, under the pop-eyed red and yellow lights of the carnival, toward the quiet rectangle that waited at the blue edge of the night. I reached that place, and instantly regretted it. The Ferris wheel loomed behind me, a blind monster's eye, and I could hear only the wind sharpening itself against my scalp. I ran too far, didn't I? Out of sight, out of mind. One by one they died, my mother, my father, my brothers, my bosses, my rivals, my storms, my wife, and turned my world into an afterlife. You might discover yourself here one night, and you can tell me then if you find invisibility to be a blessing or a curse.

You know, I have always hated that expression, "a blessing or a curse." As if anything in life were so neatly divisible. Let's try this: a freedom, or something worse.

———

The morning sky was clear and the mercury low, but I knew on waking that rain was coming; and within fifteen minutes the thunderheads rolled in. I switched on the portable to the sirens screaming—a tornado watch, the first of spring: "At ten twenty-eight a.m., National Weather Service Doppler radar detected a severe thunderstorm capable of producing a tornado near Gosper County, Nebraska . . ." And then the patter of a hundred fingers against the kitchen ceiling, when I'd expected the hiss of rainfall. I slid up the sash and looked down to what remained of the wind chimes, scattered about the porch like shell casings, and then over to the shelter, which seemed to convulse before my eyes, the locking bars spinning in their cylinders and the domed roof vibrating; *It will hold,* I thought, just as the steel walls buckled and my twister smashed out. Sucking surface air, she tore a black furrow through the pasture, and within seconds of hitting the atmosphere her pearly color began to mutate as she absorbed the stain of whatever tumbled through her—now she was woodsmoke, now pollen, now gravel, now red dirt.

Crossing into the far meadow, the funnel bloomed and vaulted skyward, reaching into that vast electric field that rolls without boundaries over the West; and as she made contact she started to lift off the ground, howling up and up like a flying top, bumping at the base of the storm. The anvil was already a mile in diameter, easy. The whole purplish wound pushed northeast, self-cauterizing with lightning.

I did a limping sprint to the truck, dropped my keys twice before getting them into the ignition, then watched the needle jump by ten-mile increments as I raced to catch her. A half mile from the shelter, she purled the barbed fencing that separated my farm from Yuri Henao's and began to drill across his flowering gardens. Yuri is a middle-aged man who breeds gentle sun-showers in horseshoe-shaped convection pods, and the guilt I feel today about the devastation to his land was not audible to me then, nor was any real concern for his safety— all swallowed by the high whine of my joy.

As forked light raked the eastern prairie, I tracked the spinning cloud—bouncing down the highway, defining her trajectory, she seemed predatory now, certain of her quarry. She reeled in the galvanic atmosphere, doubling in size while the portable prattled on: "The National Weather Service has issued a tornado watch for Gosper County. A thunderstorm capable of producing a tornado was located over the town of Elwood, moving south at fifty miles per hour. Residents are advised to take caution and begin necessary preparations—"

Next came the infinite moment. Never in my lifetime had I witnessed anything like it.

Two hundred yards ahead of me, the funnel shot across the road, picking up speed and color, turning darker and darker, and then simply levitating. I braked hard, and the truck fishtailed, settling sideways in the empty lane. My hands cramped on the wheel, and muscles I'd forgotten for decades stiffened as my eyes lifted with her: *The gust front could snuff the connection. The downdraft—*

All at once, my mind was serene. Beyond the dusky whirl of my twister, the black mass of the supercell rose, forty thousand feet at least, erasing the horizon, and she went spiraling into its heart. Within seconds, they were one. Wherever the mesocyclone touched down next, nobody would guess that a part of it had been reared on Coriolis Farms; they'd mistake it for an Act of God.

The anvil took on the aspect of a rotting orange, the bruised clouds pierced everywhere by citrus reds and golds. I wasn't thinking then that what I had just done was the equivalent of loading a bullet into a gun. I wasn't thinking at all. My thoughts had merged with the sirens on the radio, as the reports escalated in urgency: The storm now spanned two miles. Winds one hundred forty, one hundred fifty, climbing still. And then the watch was over; the tornado had materialized.

"Flying debris will be life-threatening to those caught out. Mobile homes could be lifted from their foundations, damaged or destroyed. Residents are strongly advised to seek secure shelter immediately—"

I felt no fear, no remorse, my senses rippling out like the

wind through the truck cab. My body was folded into the
driver's seat, but my mind was nowhere at all, floating along
the spiderwebbed windshield and up the ladder of my cloud.
It had become a tornado, a real tornado. At this distance,
perhaps three hundred yards off, it looked like a landlocked
tsunami, a gray wave rearing up and back, dancing foamily
around the empty highway. Belatedly, I felt the prickle of
conscience, but a spiral check showed only the bucking prairie and miles of hard rain. Thank God. It would die out, I
thought, before it could break even one window. Or it would
kill only me.

To my right and left were tractor-access roads, quickly
turning to mud. If I wanted to run, I'd have to make a U-turn.
I cut the engine, pulled the keys from the ignition, settled in.
Rodeo of two. I'd only ever wanted to know what my cloud
could become.

The vortex loomed before me—a colossal door careening
on screaming hinges. Between blinks it seemed to redouble
in power, rocketing overland, belted together by heat. I saw,
quite clearly, my truck smashed against the maw of a concrete
culvert, my body lying in the field beyond, pale as an arma-
dillo. Waiting like a shed skin to be discovered, photographed
by the coroner. Which was perfectly fine by me; I was nothing, or I was breath absorbed into the spinning wind. I would
follow my cloud into the storm's vacant core. I would want
for nothing, feel nothing. I would be spun apart. This mind
of mine, already guttering, clocked its last memory: my old
man pumping air into a dark chamber beneath the moon.

But then the image changed, and it was Suzie—curled in
the red dirt, mouthing my name with bleeding lips, assuring

me that she was happy, that she didn't blame me, that my love had been enough, although we both know this isn't true. I blew on deeper, up and over my still body, into a future where I am past, where my daughters stand beside a gurney, drawing back the white sheet. I wouldn't disappear entirely, would I? Someone would have to identify me. That sight would live inside my girls, twisting, howling.

And then I was back in the truck, and the truck was back on the road—my hands gripping the wheel, turning me away from the only thing I've ever wanted to see. I kept my eyes level with the gray chalk line of the dry horizon. Behind me, I thought I could hear my cloud, orphaned in the screaming air. I imagined the storm disintegrating, pulling apart into brown, scudding dust. Still I never eased off the gas. I couldn't bear to watch her die out, and if she lived, I couldn't risk becoming spellbound again. What a backward way of discovering you are loved—in the damage swath of your death. Anybody watching me flying down the highway that day would have thought I was escaping something, when really I was racing right into the whirlwind. The moment I plugged back in, the yellow phone would start ringing, and I owed my girls some answers. Rain sheeted down the cracked glass as I sped homeward. But let's not mistake this for a happy ending. Nothing destroyed me, and nothing is over.

Black Corfu

The doctor sleeps naked, which is not a widespread practice on the island of Korčula, not even in summer; as if to atone for his bared skin, his wife sleeps in a cakelike tier of bedclothes. Only she is privy to the doctor's secret shamelessness; by daylight, he is the model of propriety. Once upon a time, his wife found this and other bedroom vagaries of the doctor's irresistibly appealing. Tonight he startles awake from his nightmare to find her surfacing from yards and yards of white linen. She rises like a woman clawing out of snow.

I have never lost a patient before . . .

He studies the tiny halved heart of his wife's earlobe. Their room pulses with the moon. He can almost hear the purr of the rumor, yawning awake inside of her, stretching and extending itself. Does she believe it? Is she beginning to believe it? The naked doctor shudders. He imagines a man who resembles him exactly. That man is moving inside of his wife.

What tool can he use, to extract their rumor from her body?

The doctor's costume is hanging on a hook. It is not nearly so frightening as the hooded uniforms worn by physicians during the Great Plague of 1529, the beaky invention of Charles de l'Orme. The doctor's patients are safely buried under consecrated soil before they can pose any risk to him. The doctor wears a simple black smock, black surgical gloves, and his face, when he operates, is bare.

"It is not true," says the doctor in a clear, sober voice.

His wife's face is planked white and blue with moonlight. The one eye that he can see in profile is streaming water. She is like a stony bust granted a single attitude by her sculptor. Silently, the doctor begs her: *Look my way. Crack.*

It is not true.

It is not true.

What can he say, to check the rumor's progress?

"You must promise me that you will put it out of your mind." His voice is still his own. "You betray me by imagining me as that man."

His wife parts her dark hair with the flats of her palm. Does this again and again, like a woman bathing under the river falls. Outside, the moon shines on with its eerie impartiality, illuminating this room, illuminating also the woods of Žrnovo. Where the doctor knows a dozen men are fanning out tonight, hunting for his patient.

"Please. Please. I performed my duty perfectly. I could never make such a mistake."

"I am not even thinking about you. I am listening for the girls."

She says this without turning from the door. Now the doctor hears what must have awoken her. Not his nightmare but their middle daughter's sobbing. Ashamed, he reaches for his robe. "Let me go to her."

The girl sits tall in the bed with white round eyes that seemed to pull in opposite directions, like panicked oxen. Her sleeping sisters bracket her, their faces slack and spit-dewed. The doctor has long suspected that his middle child is his most intelligent.

"Papa, will they punish you? Will you go to prison?"

"Who told you such a thing?"

In fact the punishment would be far worse than that, if it came.

"Nobody told me anything," his daughter says sadly. "But I listen to what they say."

So the rumor has penetrated the walls of his home, the mind of his child. He grows so upset that he forgets to console her and flees the room. In two hours, the dawn bells will begin to ring. Bodies will congregate at the harbor. What if the miasma of the rumor is already changing? Becoming an even-more-toxic, calumnious strain—

I will have to keep the girls indoors from now on, to prevent their further contamination. What will happen to him, if he cannot stop the rumor from spreading? He might be sent to the Venetian garrison. He might be strung up in the dark Aleppo pines before anything so official as a trial. Unofficially, of course, his punishment is well under way. A second death will only be a formality—already, his reputation has been destroyed.

Three days earlier, when this nightmare began, the doc-

tor had never imagined how swiftly his life could be ruined.
Other lives, certainly, but not his own.

———

The doctor had once dreamed of being the sort of doctor
who helps children to walk again; instead, he found himself hobbling them. Children of all ages were carried to him
on stretchers, with blue lips and seamed eyelids. A twisted
plot, without a single author to blame. The disfigurement
of his first dream still causes the doctor excruciating pain.
As a younger man, he'd ventilated the pain through laughter. Sometimes the circumstances of his life struck him as so
unbearably funny that he soared up to a blind height, laughing and laughing until his red eyes shut and spittle flecked
his chin. (*"Open your eyes,"* his wife begged. "My love, you
are frightening us—") But it has been many years now since
such an episode. Only behind the bedroom curtains does the
doctor indulge such wildness today.

His wife is very proud of the doctor's accomplishments.
Because he loves her, he never shares the black joke with her.
Not once does he voice an objection to the injustice of his
fate, or rail against what the island has made of his ambition.
Aboveground, the city physician, the *chirurgo,* practices medicine in his warm salon—performing salubrious bloodlettings,
assisting the pretty young noblewomen with their lactation.
Whereas the doctor must descend into the Neolithic caves
near Žrnovo, under the cold applause of stars.

This doctor is known, more formally, as the Posthumous
Surgeon of Korčula Island. Centuries after his death, he will

be reverenced on Black Corfu as something more and less than a man. Everyone who has lost someone knows the doctor's name. He operates on the dead—these are the only bodies a man of his class is permitted to touch. Before his good name was gutted by his accusers, the doctor had a perfect record. No *vukodlak* had been sighted on the island during his twenty-three-year tenure. Everyone slept more peacefully because of his skill—not only the dead. Whose relief was manifest in the green silence of the woods, in the depths of the cemetery air. Inside that pooling quiet he could hear, unwhispered, *Thank you, Doctor. Bless you, Doctor.*

These islands off the coast of Dalmatia, with their fertile twilights and their thin soils, breed a special kind of monster. A body that continues to walk after its death. Spasming emptily on, mute and blue and alone. Inhabited by air from some other world, or perhaps resuscitated by the devil's breath. Soulless and restless and lost. *Vukodlak, ukodlak,* and *vuk.* These are several of its appellations, designed to distance a grieving family from a terribly familiar face in the woods. The face of a loved one, now bloated and emptied of light.

Korčula is entirely covered by a dark forest, rising out of the mirror-bright Adriatic like a hand gloved in green velvet. It seems to belong to some other world, lush and prehistoric. Trees peer blindly down at the water, black Dalmatian pines and soaring cypress laddering their thousand ruddy arms over the azure sea; below them grows the low macchia, that snarling undergrowth that breaks into sudden shouts of yellow and violet like the singsong joy of the mad. Korčula is the island of shipbuilders and explorers, the fabled birthplace of Marco Polo. That the dead also wander here should perhaps surprise no one. When the Greeks established a colony here in the sixth century B.C., they named the island for its pitch-colored forests. Korkyra Melaina. Corcyra Nigra. Black Corfu. Black Korčula.

The doctor was born during the longest period of Venetian rule over Korčula, a century before the republic would fall to Napoleon. He was the child of the child of a kidnapped child. Human trafficking was outlawed in the kingdom of Venice in the year of our Lord 940. In 1214, the Statute of Korčula Town abolished slavery. The doctor's grandfather was a cook who had escaped from the galley kitchen of a Portuguese ship and oared with seven others through driving winds to reach Black Corfu's shoreline. They lived as freedmen at the base of the cliffs, in the poorest quarter of the stone-walled city, in dwellings that had the fragile tenacity of the red and blue barnacles spiraling out of the rocks. They paid rent to the hereditary counts.

All this was relayed to the doctor by his mother in whispers, like a nightmare half remembered. Because of her skin color and her station, the counts of Korčula and their livid offspring would not touch her; the nobles attended a private Mass in Saint Mark's Cathedral to avoid the threat of such contact. And yet she grew old loving the sight of her face in the mirror. She pushed through the market stalls in a perfume of oblivion, ignoring the catcalling sailors, the curled lips of the upper-class women, whose chins reminded her son of the tiny, hard nipples on lemons. All stares seemed to pass painlessly through his mother, like blades slicing at water. She resented no one, to her son's amazement. However, by the age of seven, trailing her elbow, he'd learned how to gulp back rage. He knew the taste of fury as it sank into the body, that nasal salt of swallowed things.

His mother did not chafe against their lot, or even seem to experience it as a limit. Why not? Why not? *I am smarter than my mother,* this child decided, at an earlier age than most.

Not until he was a father himself did the doctor understand that her docility had been a strategy. Always, she had been protecting him. He'd missed the teeth inside his mother's smile, hadn't he? Now that he was a father, he could guess at the strength it must have taken to raise dark-skinned children on this island, under the flag of an unequal truce—they were accepted as Korčulans so long as they remained in their separate sphere and lived invisibly, beyond rebuke. To survive here required one to take sips of air; the sky belonged to the nobles. From his crabhole in the rocks, the doctor watched the gold and scarlet clouds cluster over the hills. The wide sky was not a birthright he could claim for himself, or for his children.

Although sometimes he sees the early stars and allows himself to feel otherwise. Isn't it possible that a posthumous surgeon might be promoted from his cave to the upper world? Ambroise Paré, a barber's apprentice, became surgeon to the kings of France. He made the ascent by treating battlefield wounds with rosewater and turpentine, instead of scalding wounded men with boiling oil. Perhaps the doctor will be granted a similar opportunity to impress the Council of Ten. To restore the sick to health would have been his preference. But to keep the dead in their coffins is certainly a valuable service to the Republic of Venice—La Serenissima, the "Most Serene."

Why had the doctor grown up expecting something different than his childhood for his own children? What did he ingest as a boy that let him dream up such a life? His mother had died still wondering this. On Black Corfu, there is dispiritingly little friction between the counts and the lower classes. A third of the men are always gone, at sea. Sailors, for all their roistering, defer to the captain's authority. Few Korčulans whose lives overlap with the doctor's remember, or can imagine, an alternative order to the island hierarchies, the birthday assignment of possibilities to bodies.

Her son, the future doctor, was a special case.

———

The new student kept looking backward at the shrinking harbor, where the ship that brought him to Black Corfu that morning was now small as a toy. His legs jerked to a stop, twin animals balking in tandem at the wide cave mouth.

"Few people on the Continent know about the dangers that a body faces *after* death . . ."

The doctor's voice grew ever more sonorous as they moved into the dim, enormous theater. Candles descended with them, leaning out of natural sconces in the rock. Dozens of red hands were ripening along the greenish walls, waving them on.

"Yet a body is at its most defenseless at this time, orphaned in its coffin."

"In Lastovo," the student muttered, "we all know the dangers now. Nobody can escape the knowledge."

Later the doctor recorded his first impression of the student in his log:

January 3, 1620. *What a petulant boy they have sent me. Mere fear of the outbreak infects him, and he counts himself foremost among its victims. How terrible for you, to have your mind occupied by the suffering of others!*

On Lastovo, there had been an outbreak of *vukodlaci*. The first in three generations. The boy described a scene out of the doctor's nightmares. Mass exhumations, emergency surgeries performed in the open. Gravediggers undoing their handiwork, spading up dirt ("They work under the moon, and look like large rabbits digging their warren," said the boy with plainspoken horror). Torches lipping orange syllables over the toppled stones. The only posthumous surgeon in Lastovo was nearing seventy and half blind; in any case, no single surgeon could attend to so many patients at once. And so this boy had been sent here to learn a new trade.

A quarter mile deeper into the caves, the new student introduced himself: his name was Jure da Mosto, and he belonged to one of the most tightly closed aristocracies in all of Europe. Thirteen families have controlled Lastovo for generations. These patricians are identical, in their threatening languor, to those pale island raptors wheeling over the trees, their idle talons tearing at the seafaring clouds.

"A face like yours must irritate your parents, eh?" the doctor offered mildly.

Despite the Italian ancestry he claimed, the boy's face

would always raise suspicions. Who could account for the spiraling colors of the deep past, and where and when they might resurface? Jure da Mosto looked no older than sixteen. He had the stink of some precocious failure on him. The doctor thought: *It would be a joy to be wrong about even one of them.* They'd sent him another reject, perhaps. A dropout from the Ragusa hospital. The family disappointment. Councilmen too often assume that any half-wit can hack away at the dead. Nobody but the posthumous surgeons themselves, a subterranean guild, understand what is required. There is a necessary magic to the practice, in addition to its science. Something ill-expressed in language—a governing instinct that leads one to the right depth when making the first cut. This cannot be taught.

"What do you mean—a face like mine?"

"So . . . overcast. So dark with worry."

The doctor had very little patience for the boy's fear. Even less for his self-pity.

"Once upon a time, I also dreamed of being another sort of man . . ."

The gray-faced student looked startled awake.

"Many of us would have preferred a different life . . ."

The doctor had worked his entire life to ascend to this rank. And yet the pinnacle of his achievement would still be considered, by this boy's people, to be a valley of the shadow. To become a posthumous surgeon is a terrible miscarriage of fortune, for one of their kind.

The boy from Lastovo confessed that he has never been in a cave before.

It looked as if the green stone was lighting the glass walls of the lantern, and not the other way around. Emerald moisture slid down the honeycomb of light. These Korčulan caves have been inhabited since the Ice Age: housing Neolithic tribes, sheltering Illyrian sailors. Since the medieval period, the largest hall has been a medical theater. Rock awning goes sprawling over the posthumous surgeons. Bodies are delivered by runners paid by the families, who take pains to avoid an encounter with the doctor. By some geologic fluke the stalactites here grow to an even length. White calcite, a bright wishbone chandelier over the theater. A patient was waiting quietly on the operating table, a pearl comb glinting in her red hair.

On the last leg of the descent their echoes lapped into one voice:

"What disease does a posthumous doctor treat?"

"Unnatural Life."

All bodies rotting under the moon run the risk of becoming *vukodlaci*. How does a posthumous surgeon protect a corpse from this fate?

By severing the hamstrings. Few think of the humble hamstring as the umbilicus that tethers a corpse to our spinning world. But cut that cord, and no body can be roused to walk the earth. Hamstrung cattle are crippled for life, the doctor reminded Jure. *On the other side of dawn, our patients*

are safely moored in their coffins, protected against every tempta-
tion to rise up.

Language is key, when communicating the risks posed by
the *vukodlaci.* All posthumous surgeons take great care with
their grammar. People need to know that should they cross
paths with a *vukodlak,* this shell is not their beloved. Only
the flesh has been reanimated; the soul, it is presumed, is safe
with God. "An evil wind is blowing Cila's body around" is
a chilling sentence, but far less damaging to the surviving
family than the deranging hope bred by "Cila walks again."

We do this to ensure his rest will be eternal, uninterrupted . . .

We do this by the mandate of the Venetian courts, as a safe-
guard for all living citizenry . . .

We are not injuring your beloved. Your beloved is gone. We are
preventing that old horse thief, the devil, from stealing her form.

As for what the doctor tells his own family?

He is very careful not to frighten them.

"Clipping the birds' wings"—this is his preferred euphe-
mism when speaking to the children about his work.

"Papa does that for humans who have died."

"Why?" his daughters want to know. Touching one another's shoulder blades and giggling, feeling for these secret
wings.

"To free them from their pattern. Otherwise, the song will
not release them. They need to sleep, you know. Just like us."

But the girls are too smart for this; they know their father
does something shameful, something ugly, doesn't he? Otherwise why must he leave at night, in his black robe, for the
distant caves?

"The hamstring extends between the hip and the knee joints."

For the third time, the doctor explained the surgery to Jure da Mosto.

"We first locate the tendons at the back of the knee . . ."

Jure wanted to know: Do the eyes of a cadaver never flutter open? Had there never once been—

Never, said the doctor.

The bug-eyed boy wiped a gloved hand across his mouth, leaving a little spider line of dew. His lips curled, as if he was repulsed by his own interest:

"And in all cases . . . the surgery is a, a success?"

"I understand that these are dark days on Lastovo. You have my every sympathy. But you should know that here on Black Corfu, no such error has ever occurred."

He clapped his hands, as if dismissing a horde of demons from the room.

The surgery of the young woman took a quarter hour and was wholly unremarkable. She was the only daughter of one of the hereditary counts. From this man, the doctor would collect triple his ordinary fee. "The surgeries I perform on the wealthy pay for those for the poor," he explained to young Jure, who was staring at the countess's mouth. Each lip looked like a tiny folded moth. *She is your age, isn't she?* the doctor thought, wondering how many bodies the boy had seen in his short lifetime. Terrible things do happen to the people in the hills, but such cases are viewed as tragedies, aberrations of nature. This poor countess died of a sickness known locally as throat rattle. The same illness had claimed dozens of lives in the doctor's quarter, where the death of children was commonplace.

Midway through the surgery, the student wandered away from the table, his eye caught by the gemstone sparkle in the corner of the theater. It was the doctor's lectern, a naturally occurring pillar. It supported a priceless book, a gift from the Jesuit: a copy of the anatomical sketches of Vesalius. Jure began thumbing through the book with a pouty expression, as if he had already anticipated every flowering organ. "This is the brain, then?" He yawned.

"Come and watch what I am doing," the doctor snapped.

The boy's face went purple in the torchlight, which the doctor took as a hopeful sign. Perhaps young Jure knew enough to feel ashamed of himself.

She had rare red hair, bright as a garnet stone, a comet that resurfaces out of her genetic line once every eight generations. The doctor had never spoken to or touched her in life, but he had seen her scarlet hair moving through the market stalls and known: *the Nikoničić scion. At last,* thought the doctor sadly, making the final cut, *her body will be freed from its earthly orbit;* her soul was already gone, he believed, safely home.

That afternoon, they operated on an old sailor, now at anchor. The doctor drew the boy's fingers down the hairy thigh to the sunken divot of the kneecap. Together their hands flew across a wintry isthmus of skin. They traced the muscles they would handicap. Was the boy attending to the lesson?

The boy's hand stiffened under the doctor's hand.

"Oh, God," he said, jerking back with a shudder. "There has been some bad mistake. I do not belong down here with you. Please, I want to go home."

"Home" being synonymous, for this lucky young man, with the sunlit world above.

Blessed are the living, thought the doctor with his scissors poised, *who can move . . .*

———

Animals, too, can become *vukodlaci.* Almost certainly, some of the birds flocking around Korčula are bloodless, caught in their old orbits. Many Dalmatian sailors have reported seeing the great mixed flocks of living and dead gulls. The undead gulls are easily identifiable. They circle the bay like dragon-flies. They do not flap over the water but have a fixed-wing soar, and their cerulean feathers shine continuously, even on gray afternoons. They sing, and their song is unmistakable, weirding out over the sea.

As a boy, the doctor dedicated himself to tending injured animals. He'd splinted gulls' wings, freed lame foxes from traps to rehabilitate them. He begged his father to tell him stories about the physicians who cured their patients of lameness, madness, blindness, gout. He dreamed of guiding the sick back to the country of health. Physicians seemed more powerful to him than all of the saints. The miracles of saints were original events, contingent on the action of the Holy Ghost, whereas surgery was a human achievement. It could be practiced, perfected, repeated. His father had let the boy believe he would become the city physician, and it was his mother who had at last explained to her son that because of his class and the darkness of his skin, this would never happen.

"Have you ever seen a doctor that looks like us, my son?"

There were two doctors on the island: the city physician, a wealthy old Croat, who, it was whispered, had been unable to cure his own sterility, and the Catholic priest, the former rector of Zagreb's Jesuit college. His skin poured forth a yellow light, and his age was unguessable; he seemed somehow to be simultaneously aglow with health and minutes shy of his death. He refused to treat those who had not first made confession. Unbeknownst to most, the Jesuit had been filling an open post, covertly severing the hamstrings of the island's deceased.

"Where do the doctors live?" the mother had prodded.

"With us, on Korčula."

"No. Be more precise, my son. Think like them. What answer would a doctor give?"

The doctor's mother often spoke to her son as if she were trying to gently jostle fruit from a tree without puncturing its skin. She believed in his extraordinary intelligence and did not want to deform its natural progression.

"They live above the rocks."

"Yes."

Where the hereditary counts of Korčula also resided, those pale rulers with belled chests and short femurs who paced their pink marble balconies in the hills. The island's counts, including families Kanavelić, Izmaeli, Gabrijelić, and

Nikoničić, reported to the Venetian Council of Ten. Together, his mother explained, they determined everything that happened on the island. And no count would permit somebody who looked like her son to treat his family.

Heartbroken, he'd approached the Jesuit doctor to plead his case. Was it just, he asked at age thirteen, that he should be prohibited from his life's vocation—simply because of an accident of birth?

"I am a precocious young man," he'd said, repeating the compliment he'd moments earlier overheard a tutor giving his thin-nosed student in the parish hall. "You can teach me anything, and I will master it."

A year later, he found himself performing surgeries under the ground.

From the young doctor's first log:

Absolute rest, starvation, sedation, and bloodletting. These are remedies for living bodies. What I do is a sanctioned desecration . . .

When he was a petulant student himself, luxuriating in a bath of self-pity, the doctor would heap effervescent salts into the boiling cauldron of his mind. Black grief, red rage, crystals quarried from the deepest wounds in his body. He did this until his eyes were wet and raw and his skin took on the shine of deep mud. At last the Jesuit had become exhausted with him. With a sharp cane rap to his shin, he roused the boy who would become the posthumous surgeon back into the room:

"Enough! You think it is *beneath you* to help the dead? Let me tell you a secret, because you have been too dense to realize it—we treat the living. We treat the fears of the living."

The following morning, the boy from Lastovo appeared in the cave mouth looking half dead. Yellow sun puddled around his boots. Squirming miserably in the bright portal, he called for the doctor.

"You are two hours late."

Already the doctor had cut the hamstrings of two patients.

"I did not sleep. Something was howling and howling. Circling right outside my window!"

The bright-eyed *čagljevi,* explained the doctor.

Jackals.

"In the winter months, when there is no food for *čagljevi,* we hear them howl all night."

"But, sir . . . we have barely passed the vernal equinox . . ."

The doctor felt reasonably certain that the young man was describing a vivid nightmare. He was infected by the sounds of Lastovo.

"Yes, I suppose that's true. Perhaps the hunger has overcome them prematurely."

"I know what I heard. It was no animal."

Jure da Mosto wore a look of such open hatred that the doctor could only laugh.

"Young man, why waste your energy on hating me? I am not responsible for the plague of life on Lastovo. Do you find this work beneath you? Tell me if you regret our time together when the dead come knocking on your door . . ."

He is drafting a letter home, isn't he? Telling his mother how poorly he's been treated here.

Jure said nothing. Now the doctor wondered if he was too embarrassed to admit that he had only been dreaming; and he softened a little, recalling how far the boy had traveled from his home.

"If the howling comes again," he counseled his student, "walk outside, and confront the animal."

It was a terrible morning. *Even his reflexes are lazy,* thought the doctor irritably. Jure da Mosto yawned and left his mouth hanging open. He sneezed like a cannon, his arms limp at his sides. He seemed to forget, for long stretches, to blink. How could a person stare and stare without blinking, and still take in nothing? Only from his dead patients did the doctor expect that sort of lidless inattention.

"Repeat what I just said back to me."

"This block is to assist the . . . the extension of the thigh?"

"Incorrect."

After the last surgery of the day, the doctor dismissed sulky Jure. He sat on the operating table and watched a black-and-orange spider ascend the craggy wall. It moved like a single hand scaling a mountain. At the seam where the wall became a ceiling, it deftly flipped itself and continued to the other side.

"I have risen as far as this world will permit me to go," the doctor told the empty cave. "To travel farther, must I also invert myself entirely?"

Cave fauna had impressed a lesson on the young doctor. He watched the fat blue worms wiggle through minuscule clefts. Tiny bats hooking by the hundreds into the limestone. They held on wherever they could, dark puffs of breath in the glittering fissures. The lesson was this: You fit yourself to your circumstances. Wrapped your wings tightly around your skin and settled into your niche. Go smooth, stay flat. Do your breathing in the shadows. Grow even slightly wider, or wilder, and you risk turning your home into your tomb.

However, sometimes the doctor's pragmatism went belly-up. Convictions, too, could upend themselves. Then the hopeful child inside him wondered: *The lesson is this?* He watched the worms slim and fatten as they moved through the cracks. If only there were other rooms, other worlds, than these. And other ways to reach them.

———

In late December, the doctor and his daughters had walked through the freezing *bura* smack into a funeral procession for the son of a count. A wailing train of mourners moved down the street, women with golden eye shadow and charcoal lips, men in round black hats and scarlet vests, music flung from the gaudy mouths of trumpets.

"Papa," his middle daughter had asked. "Why do so many people come to cry for him? When little brother died, we told no one."

Pneumonia was a frequent visitor to their windswept quarter. When informed that her infant brother had stopped breathing, his seven-year-old daughter had wept silent adult tears, comprehending immediately, with a heartbreaking precocity, that there was nothing against which to struggle.

One vertical mile separates the counts' floating quarries from the hovels of the barnacle people. Their rooms he cannot enter, not even with the lockpick of his imagination. It amazed the doctor that the distance between their houses could be measured in human footsteps. They are neighbors, and yet their breath barely overlaps.

———

At dusk, they come to the doctor's house. Four men from the hills, trailed by the city investigator. Flanking the parade is young Jure.

With his back to the doctor, the boy addresses the *chirurgo* in Venetian.

"What are you doing here?" the doctor asks. Everyone ignores him. He knows only a smattering of Venetian. Each word he catches comes as a cold, discrete surprise, raindrops hitting his head from a high ceiling. They explode into meaning: "yesterday," "mistake."

The doctor hears his own name several times, spoken in a tone that frightens him.

So Jure has found an older nobleman, the snowy Croat— the "real" doctor—with whom to lodge some complaint. What is it?

The *chirurgo,* his trapeze-thin brows knotted in astonishment, translates:

"Your patient, Nediljka Nikoničić, daughter of Peter, has been sighted in the woods behind the western cemetery."

"No!"

"This boy says the procedure was done improperly . . ."

Improperly.

"She is a *vukodlak* now, walking the woods."

"Impossible."

Jure da Mosto does not look up to receive the doctor's stare.

"The mistake is not mine," the doctor insists. Perhaps the famished young visitor has hallucinated a woman in the woods? Or fled the early howling of jackals. The doctor asks what proof the boy can offer for his thesis. Waves of hate are sheeting off his skin in Jure's direction. He keeps his voice low and controlled, aware of the open door. Behind him, a child's voice rises: "Papa?"

"No one," the boy says, "could mistake the color of her hair."

The *chirurgo* smacks his dry lips.

"A bloodred color, known to all of us . . ."

"The committee persists in its inquiry . . ."

Hunters are already mounted, searching the woods.

Without turning, the doctor can feel his wife's shadow behind him. His three daughters are hiding under its awning, listening. His throat closes with panic; what if they *believe* this?

Now Jure da Mosto tugs at the investigator's sleeve, whispering something behind the closed shades of their Venetian. One hand lifts and falls, pantomiming slashing. Locked out of their dialect, he is nevertheless certain that the boy is lying.

"This boy does not know where the hamstring is located. Quiz him, and you shall quickly exhaust his knowledge about the surgery—he has none. Ask him what he believes I did improperly."

A translation comes promptly:

"He remembers seeing your hand slip."

Jure da Mosto has retreated behind a human wall of his fellow noblemen. Still he refuses to look at the doctor. His lips spread into a thin, jammy smile, one eye rolling off into space. He does not look like a malicious genius. He looks sixteen years old and embarrassed by his fright. It runs in circles around his pale eyes like a horse he cannot catch and bridle. Why has the boy invented this story? The doctor imagines the point of his scalpel driving toward the boy's open blue eye, expertly peeling back layer after layer of falsehood until he reveals the true memory of yesterday's surgery.

"On the basis of one troubled boy's testimony, you have summoned the hunters?"

"Other sightings," the *chirurgo* says, "are being reported."

The tense shift makes the doctor shudder. Many people in the hills, it seems, have been waiting for this chance to give form to their fears and to accuse the Moorish doctor of malpractice. The *chirurgo* gargles his words, as if their shared language has become distasteful to him. He switches back to Venetian.

"Papa!" his youngest child cries again, followed by the sound of his wife herding the girls away from him. He swallows the globe in his throat.

"Where is she, then? Where was she last seen? Show me on the map."

A map is unfolded.

"By whom was she seen?" he asks softly.

And so the doctor learns the names of his enemies.

———————

That night, his wife presents to her doctor with no symptoms of the rumor's progress inside her save one: her wounded, streaming eyes. He sweeps her black hair from her scalp to examine them, thinking, *The eyes are so easily bruised.* He is afraid that the injury is done; that her love for him is leaking away.

"Hundreds upon hundreds of deaths," he mutters. "Thousands of successes. Years of my life spent under their earth. Which counts for nothing, it seems—"

"If you made a mistake," his wife tells him softly, "that only means that you are fully human."

She touches the top of his cheekbone, as if feeling for the lever of a secret door.

"Only admit it to them, so we might begin to make amends—"

The doctor is speechless. He hears her accusation. Incredibly, he also hears that she has already forgiven him.

In an act of spontaneous combustion, his wife burns up her image of him as a perfect man, resurrects him, and embraces him.

But that's not me! That's an impostor, flawed, ugly, clumsy, deluded . . .

The doctor recoils from her forgiveness, disgusted. Her eyes pool with love, and it seems to him there is something animal or alien about her ability to forgive him for this thing he has not done. Almost instantly, this occurs. The way a lake recovers its composure after a hailstorm. Blue to the bottom again, even the stitches dissolved. *You are a better surgeon than I am,* he thinks, horrified. It is a ghastly thing to behold. *My death.*

There is suddenly, he feels, no one left to defend—that man has been swallowed up into this forgiveness.

"No. No. I did nothing to deserve this, this—"

This love badly frightens him. He does not want it. If she could believe that he'd failed his patient, and lied to everyone about it—

He watches his hands shoving her away.

"If only you believe me, in all the world, I will live," he promises her.

His wife looks up at him with injured, animal surprise; he has never touched her roughly.

"I myself have made a thousand errors—"

"But if you do not believe me," he says. "If you have become . . . like them . . ."

Her small mouth drops open as she reaches for him. She has the face of someone at the top of a fall, her arms wheeling in space. She grabs for his shoulders, sobbing; the sound seems to come from somewhere else. Her small hands paste themselves to his chest. He thinks of the purple stars embroidered on his ceremonial robe. And when her hands at last fall to her sides, he sees stars plummeting from the night sky.

"They are going to strip me of everything now," he tells her. "They will not stop at my reputation. I'll soon be rotting in the garrison—"

Shadows dart down the hall. Stricken, the doctor lurches after his children.

"The surgery was a success, and no woman wanders the woods. If you cannot believe me," he shouts, "then you are not my family."

Several hours later, he dresses and leaves for the caves, although of course no patients await him; he has been suspended from performing surgeries pending the counts' investigation and decision. To reach these caves requires a briary hour-long climb, where to this day the dark forests of Black Corfu loom in fathomless contrast to the turquoise Adriatic.

At the cave mouth, the doctor pauses. It occurs to him that they might be waiting for him deep below. An ambush. The hunters moving onto new quarry in the morning light.

———

Two nights pass. The doctor is unjailed. His wife and daughters do not leave the house. No hunter has captured or even glimpsed the *vukodlak;* at the same time, her presence on the island is ubiquitous. The wailing women in the harbor chapel see nothing else, kneeling in the candlelight with seamed eyelids like seals.

Another doctor is now caroming around Korčula Town: leering and fiendish and floppy-handed. Apocalyptically incompetent. The doctor's twin, ruining his good name. *Open your eyes. Give me a chance to fight him, the Other Man. The usurper who has replaced me in your memory.*

Those few who do meet the doctor's gaze still fail to see

him. Eyes trawl over his skin, and a monster springs into their nets. His voice shakes, and they presume his guilt.

How can I go on living here, unseen . . . ?

Could a rumor so neatly erase every prior memory of him?

Moving behind the market stalls, the doctor eavesdrops on his own death. Everyone is talking about his mistake. In some variants of the rumor, his crime. He hears his former self writhing and dying on the floors of their minds. Once-familiar voices are corrupted, rusty with fear:

". . . because she was *interfered* with—"

". . . the soil disrupted . . ."

". . . and blood in her mouth!"

The doctor goes to the homes of his friends: Nicolas Grbin, Matthias Grbin, John and Jerome Radovanović. Look at me, he begs them. Could I do these things? Out of love, they overcome their horror. Unshade their eyes to meet the red eyes of the doctor. The terrible transparency of the eyes of his friends reveals this: *Nobody, not even those who still love me, believes me.*

———

Three nights without fresh news. The hunters chase a red-tailed squirrel, but have yet to sight a *vukodlak*. Many reputations are now at stake. Hunters grumble that perhaps the boy misled them, while the *chirurgo* defends the investigation to the Council of Ten. Many people, in the end, have a motivation to help a corpse to move again.

So when the doctor learns that the searchers have dug up

the grave of Nediljka Nikoničić, over the family's protesta-
tions, and discovered an empty coffin, he cannot even be certain that it is Jure da Mosto who has framed him.

"Her body is missing," he tells his wife.

"So I've heard."

Incredibly, she takes his hand.

———————

On the night before his deposition is to be taken, the doctor himself comes down with a case of the rumor. The false
memory feasts on his doubts. Parasitically, it grows stronger,
brighter, more vehemently alive. How to combat it?

*He feasts on me like a worm in mutton. To kill him, I must
simply stop imagining him—*

"My hand did not slip," he practices in the mirror. "Never
once, in a thousand surgeries, has my hand slipped."

The doctor tries to conjure his wife's face, and the faces of
his daughters. He needs a shield composed of those faces who
still love him. Instead, he sees his patient walking between
the pines, her red hair brighter than the moon. She is moving
downhill, toward Korčula Town. Try as he might to chop
down these woods and blank his mind, he continues to watch
her hissing descent. This, he knows, signals the beginning of
the end. How can he convince anyone that he has a steady
hand, when he cannot control even his own fantasizing, the
tremors of his imagination?

"Why do you credit this boy's account?" he shouts at the
mirror. "A visitor who arrived mere days ago? It is clear that

this *vukodlak* is nothing but a figment of the boy's disturbed mind—"

But it's too late. The *vukodlak*'s face has lodged inside him, pillary white. In his mind's eye he watches himself lurching over the operating table, a character in their tale. *Oh, Lord, help me, I have been infected—*

Stunned, the poor doctor begins to believe their story.

———

Now it is not his patient with her flaming hair who haunts him, her bare feet taking crunching steps over the pine cones. It is the Other Man.

For the Other Man is everywhere. Leaping from mind to mind, eclipsing him like the false red lid drawn over the true moon . . . *How can I kill the Other Man?*

Who stole my name and my dignity, who stole the trust of my patients from me . . .

Who strolls from mind to mind, knocking on doors and evicting me . . .

The Other Man.

The monster-twin.

It is impossible to forgive his wife for forgiving him. If she is capable of loving such a creature, what can he ever have meant to her? He cannot face the terrible love pouring his way. It will erase him entirely.

"If you could love *that*—"

In his mind's eye, he sees his hand rising and striking her. He watches her neck snapped back. He funnels these visions through the minds of his friends, imagining them imagining him. That he does none of these things does not, in the end, matter. The doctor thinks: *I am their monster.*

———————

"I can be trusted with any patient."

The tribunal has been assembled since dawn. When the bell comes again, tolling ten times, he stares from face to face to face for the eternity of that deafening gonging. All these men are well known to him. He has operated on many of their grandmothers, mothers, great-uncles, fathers. His voice is hoarse but controlled: "As evidence, I remind the court that I have performed this operation on several of my own children."

But midway through his testimony, his composure breaks; at the worst possible moment, he loses control of his voice. His memory betrays him, sucking him into the past. He sees himself walking through the pinewoods of Žrnovo with the littlest of his children in his arms—the stillborn son who never breathed, who would not take a single step. What risk could such a body run of walking the woods? his wife had asked. "Leave him be, my love. He never crawled. He is in heaven now." But the doctor had insisted on taking the precaution. The infant's face was the doctor's face, a tiny amber cameo. He recognized a larval form of his own lips. The bud of his nose, itself a cartilaginous copy of the nose of his grandfather. In the freezing theater, the doctor bent to kiss the lips of his son. A part of the doctor lives in permanent exile on the white

calcite ceiling of the cave. He floats over his son, in the blank
air above his gloved hands. He sees that this detachment is
necessary, and he hates the necessity. That operation cost him
more than he can admit to anyone, and he shrinks away from
the memory.

"I can be trusted—" He winces to hear the high pitch of his
voice, imploring them to trust him. He has already lost, then.
Tears undam themselves and flow freely down the doctor's
cheeks. With his next breath, he manages to steady his voice:

"My record is perfect and I can be trusted with any patient."

But look at what has happened to their faces!

"On January 3, the hand of our posthumous surgeon slipped
while he performed his paralyzing surgery. It is possible that
this slip was, in fact, deliberate—"

After they read out the accusations leveled against him, he
is returned to his home. No *vukodlak* has yet been discovered
in the woods; nevertheless, the case will be sent on to the
Council of Ten that evening. Even now, the ship containing
the investigator's files is leaving the harbor. Months will pass
before a verdict reaches him. Yet there are many impatient
Korčulans who are certain of his guilt. Others, consumed by
fear, conflate the end of their nightmares with the end of his
life. Writing in his log, the doctor wonders: *What has happened to the elderly surgeon on Lastovo? Has he been strung up
in the pines?*

His hand begins to tremble, knocking the oil lamp from

the table. The doctor looks down at it in horror. His fingers are moving independently of him, pinching at the wick. It is possible that they have never been under his control.

I was a good doctor, and now I am not. It is the rumor that is turning him into a monster; he had not been one before, had he? But even that certainty is dissolving.

In later centuries, new etiologies for diseases like the Black Death will evolve. Germ theory replaces miasmatic superstition. Alexander Fleming fights microorganisms with penicillin. But Fleming does not predict how quickly disease-causing bacteria can mutate. Attempts at treatment breed a genetic resilience into the disease. Only the hardiest survivors spawn. And so the cure teaches the disease how to evade it.

The rumor continues to mutate. One strain has it that the Nikoničić countess had been pregnant with the doctor's child at the time of her death. One strain has it that dozens of his patients are circumambulating the woods. Including a naked infant on all fours. One strain has it that his wife is a *vukodlak,* which he keeps boarded up in his house. With each passing minute, it seems, the rumor grows resistant to the truth. The evening after his trial, the investigator dismounts to share its latest evolution with the doctor.

"The boy remembers more and more of the story."

"Does he?"

"Something else came back to him."

Seagulls scream above the harbor. All over the island, in the minds of his neighbors, the red-haired *vukodlak* is just waking up.

"Tell me, what has returned to young Jure now? What imaginary memory?"

As it turns out, the doctor has badly underestimated Jure da Mosto. The boy has a creative gift that belies the poverty of imagination suggested by his bland seed-hull face. The doctor, after being introduced to another nightmare version of himself, walks stiff-legged to the docks and empties the contents of his stomach into the bay. Tiny red fish rise to nibble at his vomit, and the doctor feels consoled by this alone: the voracious appetite of nature and its yawning indifference to his reflection floating on the water.

That evening, the doctor discovers that his quarantine has failed. He finds his wife seated by the window, watching a pale-green sliver of sea. Despite having followed his orders to barricade herself inside the house, his wife has somehow caught wind of the rumor's darkest variant.

She speaks with a calm that shakes him.

"They say you were in love with her."

"No. That is neither possible nor true."

"They say you did something . . . to her body. And kept it here to do more—"

"Oh, my love."

Because she has already watched him doing these hideous things, hasn't she? She has been entertaining him, the Other Man, all afternoon. He cannot prevent her from seeing whatever the rumor commands her to imagine.

"A woman like that," he explodes, "would never touch me in life! Not even in church! She would not touch *you,* she would not touch our *daughters*—"

"They say," says his wife, "that you touched her."

She sleeps on the outer edge of their bed, like a caterpillar clinging to its leaf. Her back is to the doctor. And yet her palm is flung onto the bed behind her, for him to take if he so desires. Her arm bent backward. He stares at it with horror. She is still reaching for him. *How could you possibly, possibly . . . ,* he wonders, afraid even to finish the thought.

———

The doctor spends the next three days knocking on doors, an uninvited guest. He pleads his case to whoever answers. He cannot rest until his reputation is restored. He begins in the poorest quarter of the walled city, crabbing his way up the sea-slick docks. One night soon, he will reach the counts.

"You are behaving like a guilty man," his wife admonishes. "You are making their case for them. You can't see that?"

He looks at his wife blearily. It does not occur to him that he has become a species of *vukodlak* himself, driven to circle the island streets.

"The rumor has polluted every mind on the island. If I cannot defeat it, I see no possibility of a new beginning for us. I would have to change our names, burn off my skin . . ."

His daughters adopt their mother's pitch, blocking the door frame of the apartment with their tiny bodies: "Stay home with us, Papa!"

The doctor blinks at the four of them as if surprised to find intruders in his home. His thumb covers his lower lip, forming a little crucifix; he is afraid that he might cry, or scream.

"Don't you recognize us? We are your family."

That night, his wife approaches him with a new plan: they will flee the island.

"We can leave."

"Oh? Where can we go?" He is smiling broadly now, as if this were the latest uproarious turn in a long joke. At last, he can whisper the punch line to her:

"I have one skill. And now that is in dispute."

He turns his bony hand in front of her face in the light.

"Nobody believes in me anymore."

"We believe you. We are the ones who believe in you."

The doctor laughs until his eyes water. The Other Man is looking out at him.

"Please. Find a ship."

"You all believe I did it."

———

"I can be trusted with any patient," he says aloud to the watchful rabbit. Her pink nostrils inflate and fall, and he feels a rush of love for her; animals, of course, are immune to the rumor. He enters the cave to prepare the theater for a new patient. For a long time the rabbit sits on the rusty-orange log, peering down the throat of the cave to where the shadows jump.

———

The windows of their fortressed houses leave these rich men surprisingly vulnerable, thinks the doctor.

He is genuflecting in a light dusting of snow, midway up the staircase cut into the limestone cliffside which spirals up to the ivory veranda of Peter Nikoničić. Leagues below him, the dark sea rolls into the coastline, gonging soundlessly on

and on. Here is one dilemma which the counts of Korčula
share with the barnacle people: to admit the rich light of the
moon into one's home, one must also expose one's family to
the stares of outsiders. Any pair of eyes can follow the moon-
beams into one's private rooms. The doctor feels he is exploit-
ing a privilege of the already dead. If nobody believes that he
exists any longer, the good doctor, why shouldn't his ghost
take a long look into the amber dining hall of the Nikoničić
family? The doctor has never before climbed to this elevation;
he grows dizzy staring out at the tall waves crashing down
the length of the island. The main house with its colonnades
and every outlying building are made of white stone quarried
from Vrnik. He admires the unity of the house, the luminous
domed roof, like a moon exhumed from under the earth.
Edging closer, the doctor peers into the interior world of his
accusers. A dozen plates are set on a long black table, with
bouquets of nettles. The table itself is an elegant ungulate,
an Italianate species of furniture, with legs that end in oak
hooves. Perhaps it, too, has been hobbled so that it cannot gal-
lop off with the silver, the golden decanter. The Other Man,
the doctor guesses, has already dined here. Peter Nikoničić
no doubt invited the Other Man into his thoughts a hundred
times a day, to reenact the bungled surgery.

Can we be cured? the doctor wonders. Could the right
words, spoken by the doctor, free both men from the grip of
the rumor?

Roasted meats appear on thin platters. Dried berries
heaped like red plunder and deliquescing vegetables. And
there, seated at the middle of the table, surrounded by half
a dozen healthy children, is the doctor's assassin, Jure da

Mosto. Who has combed his long bangs over his eyebrows, his thin torso swallowed by a scarlet vest. His family on Lastovo would be relieved that he'd found a berth in this castle, wouldn't they? In this house, he looks younger than sixteen. He is eleven, ten, puddled and small. Unwillingly, the doctor feels his hatred relaxing, fist to palm. It is too easy for him to imagine why the boy from Lastovo would move the countess's body. He pictures Jure carrying her from the cemetery. Terrified of a *vukodlak* appearing but more afraid of losing the regard of the living.

Ah, we are in the same predicament, then. You do not want to be a liar, any more than I want to be a monster.

Bones stack up beside the drained chalices. The doctor marvels at the speed at which the meal is consumed. He watches his former student laughing, one hand clapped to the shallow hole of his mouth. On his side of the glass, the doctor is deafened by a roaring wind, but his mind supplies the sound. It is nothing so light as laughter. It is quite terrifying, this noise he hears, or imagines he hears, pouring out of young Jure.

The doctor had intended to stand before the meal's end and stride into their room; yet he merely watches, paralyzed, as the table is cleared by three servants. Hypnotized by the ebb and flow of life and shadow inside the great hall. Unaware of the snowflakes collecting on his crouching back. One by one, Jure da Mosto and every Nikoničić and servant disappear. Soon the room has emptied of people, and still the doctor kneels below the window, addressing himself to the count's empty chairs: *I am an innocent man. As the posthumous surgeon of Korčula Island, my record of service is faultless . . .*

You can become numb to your numbness, a final disavowal of the body, and this is precisely what happens to the doctor, kneeling in the snow. He might be kneeling there still, had he not been discovered on the staircase. A hand claps onto his shoulder, wrenching the doctor to his feet.

"Who are you? You do not belong here."

Craning around, the doctor collides with the Other Man. Who is reflected in the gray, frightened eyes of the man pinning him to the stone wall. A bright quarter moon floats over the harbor, winding stripes of light around their bodies. The doctor fights through an endless moment of vertigo. Staring into the count's eyes, he watches himself dissolve into his double.

"Peter Nikoničić." At last he recovers his voice. "Peter Peter Peter Peter *Nikoničić*! Estimable sir, your lordship, Peter *Nikoničić*."

His voice, when it comes, is barely intelligible.

"Forgive my intrusion, but I have come to, to, to . . ."

The doctor slurs his words. His tongue, that trained slug, will not obey him.

"To defend myself!" he bursts forth.

The doctor is not a drunk, but it occurs to him that he might become one, in the future story of this encounter.

"I do not belong here. That is true." The old laughter threatens to boil over. "You people let me fly to the roof of a cave, and no farther. You have blocked our ascent to the true sky. You call me the Moor, Peter Nikoničić, although my family has lived on Black Corfu for as long as your family."

Giggles escape him, rising into the night. A steam of hysteria that does not seem to originate from his mouth but from the crinkling corners of his red eyes. He gapes up, for a moment confusing the frail sound with a column of snowflakes.

"Oh, you people should have hobbled me long ago! You must have guessed that I would one day climb your hills. But I imagined a different kind of ascent, Peter Nikoničić. A promotion!"

The joke of his life seizes him once more. Doubling over, he is convulsed by silent laughter. "Ah, look," he murmurs. "We have an audience."

Blue light floods through one of the upstairs windows; this would be Jure, the doctor feels somehow certain. Jure in his guest room, looking down on them. Looking down is Jure da Mosto's great talent, isn't it? Quite a feat, for an inbred adolescent.

With great effort, the doctor regains control of himself.

Up goes the lantern, illuminating the count's gaunt face. Dozens of blood vessels sprinkle his eyes, like the red seams in green leaves. The doctor seizes the large man's wrists.

"Peter Nikoničić, I never harmed your daughter. You must believe me."

The Other Man lifts out of the dry eyes of Peter Nikoničić to stare at him.

"Please. Please. Please. Remember who I am," the doctor begs. He leans in until their clammy foreheads touch. "Remember me?"

Loosening his grip on the doctor, the count steps back. Both men are breathing heavily. He lowers the lantern. Now only a slice of him is visible, caught in the gluey light: his large, flaring nostrils, a quivering orange mustache. This is enough to reveal the grief of Peter Nikoničić. The doctor came prepared for anger. He is unprepared to hear the horsey bellows of the big man's sorrow in the dark. Now he quiets, recognizing the rhythm of his own despair, for which he knows no cure.

"That boy in your house is a liar. To protect himself, he has hidden the body somewhere. But the surgery was routine, and your daughter is no *vukodlak*."

"She is gone." Peter Nikoničić's face is no longer visible in the darkness on the hill. "And you must go now, too."

———

Midway down the highway that unwinds into the sea, the doctor becomes aware that he is not traveling alone. Snowfall is unusual on the island. On his way home, retracing his steps in the drifts, the doctor notices that there are two sets of prints.

Who is following me? the doctor screams.

Something is moving out of the thicketed darkness. Pleating the leaves. An almost-human whimpering rises out of the woods, a sound that is unbearably familiar.

In a whisper, the doctor asks the forest: "Nediljka?"

Out of the shadows steps a child he knows. His middle daughter.

"Papa!"

"What are you doing here?" How long has she been hovering a foot away from him in the snow? How lost must he be, to have no awareness of his daughter at his heels?

"I wanted to know where you go when you leave us," she

tells him. Flatly as always, and without apology. "I am very cold, Papa."

It's an agony to feel her shivering in his arms and to have no further protection to offer. He walks as fast as he dares through the falling snow. When the snow deepens, he carries his daughter on his shoulders. They move through a ravine of solid moonlight. In this lunar meadowland, they are not alone. His daughter sights the creature first, and screams.

The thing rears onto its hind legs. Its hair is matted to its heaving sides. The doctor's mind, reaching for a name for the giantess's shadow, can find only "monster." It is his daughter who roars back at her, "Bear!"

Just when he'd thought the joke was done with him, a new surprise. We know this species as the European brown bear, a misnomer in this case, because the bear standing on its hind legs has striking reddish fur.

Here, then, is the answer to one riddle. They are staring at the *vukodlak*. The bear with her bloodred muzzle and coppery fur, standing upright in the woods. For an instant the doctor feels a surge of elation, thinking: *I can explain everything to them, and kill off the Other Man.* But of course that's not true. The rumor has moved into the tower of fact. Of history. It does not want to be evicted.

The doctor has been carrying his daughter on his shoulders. When he turns, his daughter is eye level with the bear. Her snout falls open. He sees long black teeth. A levitating slate tongue. The bear, holding her great shaggy arms before her like tree limbs, lets out a roar that seems to shake the island to its bedrock. The roaring goes on and on. Inside of that sound,

a miracle happens. There is really no other human word for
it. The three stand under some spell of mutual hypnosis. Life
recognizes itself, a beam of light flying around three mirrors.
Life reorganizes itself into something new.

Out of their conjoined attention, a fourth mind rears.
Large enough to encompass all of them—building itself
out of them, as a molecule is born from atoms. Their collision sparks the instant evolution of a special, ephemeral
intelligence. Before its collapse, each creature glimpses itself
through the eyes of another. The girl sees herself small as a
blossom atop her father's shoulders, who is, after all, only a
man; the doctor watches himself falling into the bear's mind,
a shadow on the snow, cleansed of every accusation; as for the
bear, her perception floats outside the net of this language.
The three blink once, twice. Each exists, without past or
future, inside the other.

The spell ends—nothing breaks it—it simply runs its
course. With a second roar, the bear resumes her solitary life.
Dropping onto her paws, she shoulders into the pines.

The doctor is left with only an inky memory of the knowledge that engulfed them a moment ago. There is another
country in which he exists, running parallel to this one.

Just before sunrise they reach another clearing, now a plain
of fresh snow. Birds throb into the sky, startled from their
feeding. Their cries are like thunder from another century,
silvery and faraway. Even skimming the earth, they echo
remotely.

Why do they sound like that, Papa?

They are dead and alive, he explains.

His daughter's skin has a blue cast and her eyes are half lidded. The doctor has put his gloves on her hands. He has wrapped her in his robe. He is terrified that the cold may have already invaded her. By the time they reach Korčula Town, the sun is up, sending ice crashing into the sea. Ships loom like alien beasts, their gunwales transformed by ice into wooden gums with orange and violet fangs. *The world will lose a thousand sets of teeth before noon,* thinks the doctor. His daughter stirs, nuzzling her face into his hair.

In the doctor's home, the freeze is only beginning. With a shriek to rival the morning birds, his wife falls upon him. He begins to explain about the bear, but he is interrupted half a dozen times by their middle daughter's coughing. She blinks up at him, still sleepy from the cold.

"Where have you been? Why on earth did you take her out into this weather—"

"She followed me," he says weakly.

"Tell your mother what you saw," he urges her.

"Nobody."

His wife is looking at the doctor as if he is a stranger. A look that tilts her into a future with her children from which he is barred. Quick as an animal, she swoops in and snatches back her daughter. She strokes the side of the girl's skull that is still damp with snow, her colorless lips. Her own face becomes brighter and brighter with life.

"Get out."

This, she says, she cannot forgive.

The doctor sighs. Now he feels almost happy.

"You did love me."

———

That night, the doctor does not return home. He sleeps on a pallet in one of the sailors' brothels, where even the seven-foot proprietor is afraid to touch him. He wakes at dawn and wanders the herringbone maze of the walled city, watching helplessly as the faces of his neighbors flinch away from him as if stung.

At sunset, light ribbons away from the moored ships. The doctor sits on the toothy rocks near the leaping waves. The wind has chased everyone else inside the walls. These rocks are filled in with pieces of chalky shells, and anyone who sits on them will rise with twin crescents of lunar powder on his trousers. The ordinarily meticulous doctor has not visited the barber in a fortnight, and he would have sat down without awareness in a pool of mud, or blood.

Sunset is a violent spectacle on the island of Korčula. The sun flies as if shot behind the rocks. Once the moon has fully risen, he stands and turns toward the pinewoods of Žrnovo, to look for him, the Other Man. It will be a duel to the finish. Scalpel in hand, the doctor starts up the hill.

———

From the doctor's final log:

> *All believe me to be not only a failed surgeon, but a*
> *corrupter of bodies. Even in my wife's embrace, I have begun*

*to imagine my death. It is a dreadful rehearsal. My hands
end my life, again and again; I see my body lamed in its
coffin, removed to a realm beyond all suspicion.*

*Yet I am coming to see that this plan is the only means
by which I can exonerate myself of those charges brought
against me. With a steady hand, I will pour out my blood,
and so cleanse my name, and the name of my family. First
I will sever my hamstrings. I will complete this surgery
perfectly, while still alive. This will mark the first and only
surgery I perform on a living body. After hobbling myself, I
will cut my throat. Thus will I prove to everyone on Korčula
Island that emotion could never have stayed my hand or
vitiated my efforts on behalf of the dead.*

*Meantime my wife is suffering . . . my daughters . . .
the rumor continues to assail us from within, changing the
contents of our minds.*

These and other excerpts are included in the second
file sent from the counts of Korčula to the Council of Ten,
regarding the exhumations in the cemetery of Žrnovo. From
Korčula these documents traveled to the capital of La Serenissima; from there they were forwarded to the Venetian cen-
tral offices in the city on the lagoon. Today, copies translated
into English, German, Spanish, and Chinese are available for
study in the state archives. The doctor's defense is nearly forty
pages long:

*As a boy, I dreamed of saving lives; I have answered that
calling, in the peculiar and the only way available to me . . .*

In addition to the testimony of the doctor's student, Jure da Mosto, the archive includes two depositions of witnesses, Don Anthony Deševic and Janez Krčelić, confirming under oath that on the sixth of January 1620 the cemetery soil was disrupted and the body of a young countess had vanished.

Yet the grave was closed, and the investigation abandoned; it is unclear from these documents if or how the case of the accused was ever resolved.

———

Something comes whistling out of the cave—not stumbling, not lurching, but running down the hillside. Something becomes someone. On shaky legs, the *vukodlak* stalls between two yellow-mossed boulders. Thoughtfully, he pops a finger into his mouth. It is as cold and as dry as the cave he has just exited, devoid of even a drop of fluid. Plants lisp up around him, dark vines with turbulent blossoms. It was winter when he died, but as a *vukodlak* the doctor has emerged into a new season. The air, which he can still smell, is thick with pine resin and salt. He bends a knee and genuflects, staring up at the towering pines. Thin red scars cover the backs of his thighs. He touches these wonderingly, amazed at the supple angle of his leg unbending itself. From a numb core, he watches as pain explodes around him. He is lifted to his feet. Has the operation been a failure, then? For here he stands.

"Perhaps," the doctor's *vukodlak* admits softly to the thousand whispering pines of Black Corfu, "I made a mistake."

The Gondoliers

---

1. THE CHORUS

D r. Glim was supposed to be my last fare of the evening, but when I am a quarter mile from home I hear a man coughing on South Jetty, and against my better judgment, I am drawn down the foamy water of a side canal toward the rattling sound. Through the keyhole spaces in the mangroves, I can see a tall figure in a long green slicker pacing on the jetty. He cries out when he sees me, flagging me down with his whole body.

The sky is two-toned, fiery pink above the green horizon line. It's too late for a passenger, even a regular, someone trusted and familiar. A happy story ends here; a responsible gondolier poles homeward. I can hear my sisters doing just that. They are singing in a wide canal, three boats pulling into a line. Echoes fly into the birdcage of my sternum. Even miles apart, we are always audible to one another.

When I am twenty feet from the jetty, I raise the pole and wave it slowly at him. Power gathers in my cracked heels and pulses upward. Will I take him to his destination? We are equals in our suspense.

"What luck," cries the man. "Are you going north?"

"Push your hood up. I want to see who's asking."

Sunset is less than an hour away, and he won't find another boat if I refuse him. His fear reaches out to stroke my cheek. It makes me feel tenderly toward the white-faced old man; also, powerful. On the poling platform, I am almost eye level with him. Old, I guess that's always relative. Older than me, I should say. Thirty? Forty? But perhaps I look old to him.

"Thank God you spotted me. Please, I'm in a real jam."

He keeps a finger trained on me, as if at any moment I might disappear.

"The boat I hired never showed."

His voice catches. Now that I am closer, I can hear how deeply this rattle has lodged itself inside his body. Even at sunset, it's eighty degrees, but this stranger is shivering. His desperation perfumes the air, a soaking underarm smell. Under the jutting limestone, as if in secret mimicry of him, a thousand tiny, sharp wavelets jump and fall. He is nervous. I am making him nervous. Power whips through me again, and I almost laugh, it feels so good to be alive on the poling platform. Song gathers under my navel and I make no effort to contain it.

"OoOoOoOo—"

I watch him jump.

"Miss, won't you help me?"

"Miss." I smile. "That's a first."

I have two names: Janelle Picarro and Blister. My mother

gave me the first name, my sisters, the latter. Nobody has ever addressed me so formally.

"Can you take me to the seawall in Bahía Rosa?"

A visitor to New Florida usually wants to see the jungle, the ruins. Locals hire us to pole them to the fishing nets, the floating markets. We take children to the school in the morning, weaving around the shadows of the wrecked cruise liners, helping them up the gangplanks to their classrooms. Nobody asks to go to the seawall. My sisters won't pole within a mile of the black buoys.

"We don't go there."

"We?" The man opens an antique red wallet. "But I'm asking *you*."

Two miles away, behind the tangled red mangroves, home calls to me. My sisters and I live inside the ruins of a seaplane hangar, built out of metal and glass a hundred years ago. By now my sisters will be rinsing the salt water from their gondolas. Only my boat slip will be empty. I can hear the twangy echo of my absence in the hangar, a hollow note that gives me a queer twist of pleasure in my gut.

"Money can make sense out of almost anything, can't it?" I watch his black thumbnail riffle the paper. "It's magic that way. But no amount of money can turn a trip to the seawall into a sane journey."

The seawall was erected by the army corps as a last-ditch attempt to protect the city from getting swallowed. It failed, of course, and thousands drowned. We call the silent bay that surrounds it Bahía Rosa—a pretty name for a rippling nowhere. Once, the green lights used by fishing boats draped the ocean in a miasmic fog, so bright it was visible from outer space. Now reddish blooms of a fish-killing algae cover the entire bay. Bahía Rosa gets blamed for everything from cancer to bad dreams. A desire to go there suggests a highly contaminated assessment of risk, reward. Smugglers supposedly meet at the seawall, a rumor I did not much credit until this moment.

"Please, miss. I am falling behind schedule."

He offers me a stupendous sum of money. More than I make in a month as a gondolier on Bahía del Oro.

"Double that," I tell him.

As we pole away from the jetty, I hear a faint, awful rumbling, but I can't decide if this is the true echo of some future disaster or only my guilt. This man is sick, and he has no supplies, no food. But if my last fare wants me to leave him in the middle of the sea, that's his business; my business is transportation. He didn't hire me to ask questions.

Only a lunatic or a criminal goes to the seawall—that's what Viola would say. Viola is my oldest sister, the most responsible of us and in some ways the most guileless; she wouldn't understand the humming in my body that begins when I hear the words "Bahía Rosa." I have been wanting to make this trip myself, and I'm grateful to have the stranger's money as my alibi. Once I deliver him to the seawall, I'll have hours to myself in the unmappable dark. A part of me is already flying into the future, where I am rid of this person, free and alone, and swimming under the blind moon of Bahía Rosa.

His coughing jolts me back into the boat, and I feel sick myself for a miserable moment, wondering if I should turn back. It's a relief to pull clear of the mangroves and join up with the fast-moving current. We go rushing into the wide bay, where the echoes make my decisions for me.

Two birds, one stone. The old, brutal saying returns to me out of the blue. I can't remember where I first heard it; I house thousands of these fragments. Echoes of unknown origin. Words that went skipping across minds for centuries, apparently, before sinking into mine.

———

The current races us through the ruins of Old City, where a teenage boatman drowned just last week. My sisters and I have a monopoly on this territory. Even locals lose their way here, where the debris rearranges itself in a slowly turning kaleidoscope, the garbage mountains always changing shape. The glare of the sun is intense at six o'clock, splintering around the concrete grottoes. We enter the shade of a domed ceiling, poling around the brass-and-silver letters: MI I PL ET RIUM. Former home of the phony night sky, where hundreds of translucent fish now sway, nibbling at the algae on the auditorium walls. Rows of spongy seats glide just below us, a reef of huge brown scallops. Staircases that move like our singing does, lunging in two directions at once.

"OOOoooOOOooo—"

Middle C to E minor. Orange to pink to blue. The song sweeps in front of the bow. I crutch around the drowned beams that fill the planetarium's lobby, singing at the top of my register. Echoes shower into me. My spine feels ignited by them.

New Florida is composed of grassy water, the bleached

reefs of submerged and abandoned cities, and dozens of floating villages. It's illegal to live here, although thousands of us do. Holdouts and the spawn of holdouts. Old Florida is a glassy figment in the minds of the soon to be deceased. If you think our song is monotonous, you should hear our neighbors reminiscing: *Oh, the highways, the indoor malls! Soil as far as a man could travel. Funerals, remember those? The coffins we planted like seeds in the ground.* That Florida, if it ever existed, has no reality for me.

We go mazing between the toppled condominiums, which loom like dark whelks lying on their sides. Golden awnings bloom on the former city's northern border; the tenanted ruins rise in the west. Generator lights glow in several of the third- and fourth-story windows. My passenger turns on the bow seat and shouts over my singing, "Miss, didn't we just come from that tunnel? Are we going in circles?"

"Yes," I call down, enjoying my height. "It's the only way out."

Satellites have been down for half a century. Even those who navigate with salvaged equipment fail to detect the dangers hidden under the water. Perhaps these vintage technologies work on sleepier seas; I have only ever lived here. My sisters and I navigate these margins with breath and bones. We sing, and we absorb the echoes into our skeletons. A map draws itself inside us, revises us.

Three hard strokes, brake. Sit and paddle around a forest of streetlights. Launching my voice against a wall, I can hear the sunken pylons that mean to kill me, and I swerve, changing the future. This happens hundreds of times a day in New Florida.

"Lean back," I tell my passenger, and he folds himself into the gondola as if it's a casket, crossing his arms against the crinkling slicker. It ripples across him, and it's easy to pretend that I am transporting the sea itself, the wind made flesh. We enter the archway to a vanished city park, now a deep green pool. Smells change as we travel: rotting wood, salt-eaten aluminum. The song boomerangs around a flooded parking garage, once large enough to stable hundreds of cars. I close my eyes as we spin around a stone nautilus. Hiding just ahead of us is the decaying, waterlogged hulk of a poinciana tree blocking the exit. Echoes push its branching shape into my skull, and into the skulls of my sisters in the distant, adjacent hangar. Always, we are this close and this remote. Vibrations unite us. We can hear the golden algae that gloves the underwater city and the long bald stretches of sunlit wall. Spongy sounds and waffled ones. But tonight the map is my own creation, the product of a single looping input. C stroke. J stroke. I brace the pole against my chest. The song hunts for an opening, and water spits us into unbroken sky.

When I open my eyes, the man is staring up at me.

"Ah. I've heard about you." He smiles uncertainly. "You're one of those bat girls. The echolocators."

"What luck." I smile back at him. "I am."

———

We call ourselves the Gondoliers. Four singing sisters, poling the canals of New Florida. There are other boats on the water, but only my sisters and I take passengers through Old City. According to Vi, when our mother was alive, people would count four girls seated behind her on the long skiff and reliably say, "Trying for the boy?" "As a matter of fact," she'd snap, "God has blessed me with daughters. If I could, I'd make a hundred more."

My sisters tell this story all the goddamn time. So often that it *feels* like my memory. She drowned when I was three years old, before the cameras in my mind turned on.

Our regulars suspect there's more to our nasally singing than we let on. For sure they know it's not Italian. "Lady, can I please pay you to shut up?" tourists have begged me. I used to think that we were very special, the best boatwomen in the world, but Viola says no, we are only vessels ourselves: something wants to be born. Perhaps there are many others like us around the bays of New Florida and elsewhere. Women who know enough to be silent about what is developing inside their bodies.

This sensitivity grew in us softly, softly. I can only compare it to seeing in the dark. We sing, and shapes tighten out of an interior darkness. Edges and densities. Objects sing back at us: *Turn hard left to avoid the fallen tree. Pole southwest to miss the gluey hill of floating garbage.* Pillars thin as lampposts push fuzzily into our minds; a heartbeat later they rear out of the bay, fatally real.

Our mother could not echolocate, according to my sisters. When I was a child, I found this frightening and sad. Imagine seeing a thousand colors streaking the sky and realizing that your mother saw only one unbroken gray. But Viola says our mother could hear us crying from impressive distances, and now I wonder if she had some precursor of this ability.

Our gift is not a true clairvoyance, or what I imagine that

to be. There's no time for anything like that. It's more like a muscular intuition of what the water is going to do next. And with our poles flying, rattling the oarlocks, we move to accommodate the future of the river.

———

"You could be my age," I tell my new last fare, "in the right lighting."

"Yes." He doesn't turn, but I hear his smile. "Darkness is a real fountain of youth, isn't it."

We slice under the mangroves, riding high with the outgoing tide. His narrow face looks even leaner inside the slicker, like a spadeful of white clay. Nobody I know is so pale. We live on sunshine here, where the canals are inkwells of blinding light. Leaf freckles cover him and disappear again as we bob into the sun. I like knowing that my arms are the engine of this transformation. Masking and unmasking him.

But then I glimpse the real sea rolling beyond the bay, and I remember with a start: *No, you really don't know anything about him. Only surfaces and angles.*

———

In this neighborhood of Bahía del Oro, pollution tints everything with phosphor. Mosses drop in shimmering clumps from the floating oar. I pole from starboard, my bare feet planted against the cypress boards. Orange plants with soft drunken voices slide around the hull, drawling a beautiful lace behind my eyelids.

"I like your boat. Very pretty."

The man's deep voice startles me and causes the shy plants to fall silent. He raps a fist against the hull. I can hear the solidity of my gondola behind the hollowness of his compliment. "Such an unusual design . . ."

Suck my dick.

You can't say that to a paying customer, chides Viola in my mind.

"Suck my cock," I say instead.

He slams a laugh into my chest.

"I haven't heard that one in decades."

I read it on the wall of the flooded school, which is covered in the vanished teenagers' hieroglyphs. SUCK MY DICK. RIDE MY DICK. LICK MY JUICY PUSSY. Names that are still legible at low tide: PAOLA WAS HERE. GABRIEL WAS HERE. SAY MY NAME. HURT LIKE I DO. KISS ME, SOMEONE. Writing that survives the bodies that produced it is always haunted, I guess. But the underwater graffiti of the lost world feels especially so.

"I don't like false praise," I tell him. "And I see that you have eyes."

My gondola is decorated with crude stars that I knifed into the wood. The end result was less like artwork than an attack my boat survived. My boat looks nothing like my sisters' perfectly lovely gondolas, and that is how I wanted it.

After that, there is a long silence. The sun seems to tarry behind the trees, extending our opportunity to beg it to stay. Bright water ripples around either side of us, and the black mangroves slant off into the distance.

"Do you live on Bahía del Oro, sir? I've never seen you out here."

"No, you haven't. That is certainly by design."

"What a feat. A recluse among recluses."

"You don't like false praise. I don't like false people. I choose my company carefully."

Undeterred, the man taps at the steel ornament fixed to the bow, my birthday bird, welded for me by Luna as a counterbalance to my weight in the stern.

"Your work?"

"My sister Luna made it for me. She's the family artist."

The heron is painted a somber Madonna blue, my only criticism of it. Turquoise would have been my choice, I tell him. "Turquoise is what that blue would look like if she divorced the night and went on a fabulous vacation."

He laughs again, a laugh which I bounce back to him at the same low frequency. Warmth stirs in my belly.

"Do you gondoliers ever take a vacation?"

"Oh, never. I feel like I'm always working, even when I'm sleeping. Our beds are practically floating. Our home sits half in water."

"Home." It sounds like a foreign word, the way he intones it. "Where is home?"

It's taboo to ask this question of a stranger in New Florida, but perhaps he does not know our etiquette. I have a bad thought, staring at his bony face—that I can answer him without fear, because he is very close to the end of his life.

"We live in an old seaplane hangar."

"Almost like a cave. Perfect for a bat girl."

"Water laps inside it. You should see the four of us, rowing home at night. Like horses swimming into a barn stall."

He smiles at me strangely, his eyes crossing a little.

"Horses. Have you ever seen a horse?"

I shake my head, embarrassed. Only in books, with water-logged pictures. Stories fly out of the mouths of my oldest neighbors. But I have never seen a swimming horse myself, it's true.

"Tell me, when were you born?"

I whisper the year to him, and something like awe crosses his face.

"How lucky! So you remember nothing, then—none of the evacuations, none of the flooding. None of the floating bodies . . ."

His face puckers and relaxes, a quick civil war.

"You don't remember any of that."

"I know what my older sisters tell me," I say. "It's almost like a memory."

"And what do they tell you?"

"Very little."

We skirt the cathedral, half hidden behind the shivering leaves of the mangroves. A brass steeple soars over the trees, a canted X on which several anhingas dry their wings. Framed by the sun, their glossy feathers look emerald. Hundreds more roost around the ruins. Snakebirds, the ocean swans. Egrets, pelicans, herons. Someone lives here now, it seems. Rope ladders tumble down the walls. As we glide under the cathedral window, a dog begins to bark.

We are only allowed to stay here, says Viola, because officially, we don't exist. Most mainlanders have forgotten us. New Florida has been declared a "wasteland," which is a hilariously inaccurate term, in my opinion, when the southern marshes are brimming with fish and reptiles and birds.

"A resurrection," say the old-timers. But for me, it's the world as it always has been.

"We're almost there," I keep promising the man. I don't like the way the eastern clouds are rumbling. "Twenty minutes," I say. The standard lie. Like a cracker you can hand people to put off their appetite. Every twenty minutes, you repeat this increment. But his impatience seems to burn off him as soon as we pull away from Old City. He begins to hum along with my singing, a beautiful surprise, like someone walking beside me, taking my hand.

"Look," he says dreamily, and points to where the moon is rising, bright and enormous as the door to another galaxy, on the opposite side of the bay.

OoOoOoOo.

OoOoOoOo.

A whiskery sun flashes between the sunken rooftops, but dark clouds have rolled in from the southeast, a bad surprise. I imagine my sisters pointing up at them, shaking their heads.

"Do you feel that?" His frowning face retreats inside the cowl.

Glimmering threads begin to fall. A hissing starts in the back of my brain. Rain is no good. Rain scatters the echoes. I can feel the massing thunderheads like gloved hands at my back, pushing me to go faster and faster. The current is moving us steadily seaward, at a speed of perhaps fifteen knots.

The clouds racing toward us give me a tingling déjà vu, and I realize it's a sky I've seen in dreams, lowering itself into my home. I wasn't yet born when the ocean rode across the peninsula. The great floods happened before Bahía Rosa was Bahía Rosa, back when everything had a different name. But I can hear the waves rearing back, slamming forward, causing the walls to buckle. The cries of the abandoned families, the ambulance boats with their droning sirens. My older sisters become quite agitated when I describe these dreams. "You have no idea what it was like then," Vi told me. "You never lived a day on land. Quit stealing our stories."

Perhaps the memories filtered into me through our mother's blood? I once suggested to my sisters. Viola, in her most condescending voice, then told me to "leave the grieving to the grown-ups." She still thinks of me as her three-year-old ward. It will shock her, someday, to look up and discover that I am an adult now, with secrets of my own.

"The algae." I hold up the flat of my oar. "You see? It's changing color." Brownish gold to reddish pink. Which means we are drawing very near to the seawall. The worst pollution seems to be concentrated under the blooms.

"Do you ever see mutants out this way?" the man asks me, turtled in his hood. He keeps his voice nonchalant, but I watch him peering into the darkening water.

You hear tales of goliath groupers with multicolored eyes, two-headed manatee calves.

"Never once. Does that disappoint you?"

In fact, when I first entered Bahía Rosa, I found something even stranger. But I don't tell the man this; why burden him with a new fear, when we are finally sitting level on the water?

II. THE BRIDGE

One slow afternoon last May, I found myself in the middle of Bahía Rosa. For two hours I'd been tailing a dolphin through the polluted zone, reasoning that if she could breathe here, so could I. When I reached the outermost limits of our territory, where the black buoys warn boaters to turn back, I pushed onward. By this point, the dolphin had disappeared, but I'd already traveled so far from home that it seemed obligatory to continue exploring. My sisters could feel the growing distance between us, but there was nothing they could do about it; they were working in Old City, two hours behind me.

Long before I saw the seawall, I heard it lifting out of the ocean. At last it appeared, a thick hallucination striping the ruddy bay. I knew the stories, but I'd never seen this fossil for myself. Here it was, rising out of the ocean, a monument to its own failure. This mile-long section was largely intact, with bright moving gaps where the maroon water had eaten through the crumbling stone. First I heard, and then saw, what must have been the seawall's former landside edge. It curled toward me, as if uninformed that the land had pulled away, and it was easy to imagine the whole peninsula slipping out of this relaxed embrace and sinking.

What must have once been solid, unbroken coastline, in our mother's youth, was now a pointillist landscape of small tree islands. Many were less than one acre wide, knuckles of limestone covered in flowering vegetation. I had been hugging their muddy shorelines for the past hour. Now I let the springy echoes from the seawall choreograph my passage into deeper water. As smoothly as a happy thought turns black, I found myself in the middle of Bahía Rosa, where the algae waved in every direction. The absence of birdsong made the sky feel empty and tall. A stinging odor lifted off the water. Almost immediately, I developed a terrible headache.

I found the deadspot, or it found me, just as I poled up to the huge, broken molars of the seawall's northern end. Three hundred yards behind me, the bald mangroves lifted onto their tiptoes, as if they, too, were surprised to find this barrier still standing. I could hear its secret skeleton, the weep holes and the reinforcement rods. I heard, as well, the gargling cracks where the wall had failed at the waterline. Pointy barnacles covered the eroded stone, dissipating my song; it seemed possible that in another hundred years they might fuse together into a single speckled shell. I was poling through a pocket of dense red algae that had collected around the wall's concave edge when something astonishing happened to me. The echoes ceased entirely. My sisters' singing fell away, and I was alone. The suddenness of this silence shocked me more than any detonation could have done. The deep sonority of our chorus vanished, and all I could hear was a single, flattened cry. This, I realized, was my voice—separated from the others. Fear spun me around: What had happened to my sisters? Somehow, it seemed, I had poled out of range; I was floating in a kind of *deadspot*.

I watched the waves collapsing into the limestone wall for miles and miles, a birdless sky stretching above me. Nothing sang back to me. The present seemed to spill eternally around me, and no echoes reached my ears. I removed my clothes and slid into the toxic water. I don't know what possessed me to do this, but it was no accident: I pushed my head below the surface, through the slippery blooms, kicking down.

I'd never felt this far removed from my sisters. Under the water, I stopped hearing even the whoosh of my blood. What happened next, I'll never know, because I sank out of earshot of my thoughts.

I surfaced to a grogginess that exceeded anything I'd ever felt in my waking life. A ruff of pearly-blue sea scum encircled me. The plants floating here seemed to emit their own red glow. A light independent of any moon. The raw throats of cypress trunks scraped the sky. I didn't know who I was, what I was. The face floating on the water was not mine, not yet. It wrinkled and smoothed with a foreign serenity. Nothing remembered me.

The seawater I spit out tasted poisonous. Creaturelike, I watched my limbs moving through it. I could name the colors of the bay before I knew what sort of animal I was. An acrid smell lifted off the water, impossible to ignore at low tide, bringing with it visions of putrefying flesh. A smell that should have been incompatible with my bliss, but somehow was not. *How interesting,* I thought from a great distance, rolling my arms through the rosy water, turning onto my back.

"Sensation returned" conveys none of the extraordinary pain I felt, coming to consciousness. My joints began to pulse. A bad sunburn crackled across the mask of my face. When I heard the waves slapping against my gondola, memories swept through me: I was Janelle Picarro again, one of four gondoliers, afloat in the forbidden waters of Bahía Rosa.

My sisters. Queasily I swam for my gondola. The seawall loomed on the horizon, and once I poled out of the dense algae I could hear them again. Viola. Mila. Luna. Seeping back into my skull, a wailing harmony. Only then did I take the measure of what I had done.

Just this once, I thought. *Once, and never again.* This magic phrase inoculated me against my guilt. I pulled the red weeds from my hair and bailed water from the boat. I didn't know that I was setting a precedent. It felt like coming back from the dead that night, rowing into the seaplane hangar under a full moon. My sisters were very angry with me. They wanted to know where I'd been. Those heavy tones fell into me like lead weights after the freedom of the afternoon.

The lie was spontaneous.

Ordinarily it is very difficult to lie to my sisters. But the deadspot had inspired me. Without thinking, I screamed back at them. Swinging my oar, striking at bedrock. Using tone alone, I changed the night's direction.

"Where were *you?*" I counteraccused. "Why didn't anybody answer me?"

I began to sob. I let them witness the release of so much blackness from my body, recalling the silence that had flooded me while I floated under the wavy ceiling of algae. "I was calling and calling for you. I have never felt so all alone on the water."

The best lies have a fleck of truth folded inside them. All good performers know this. Real gold to bite down on. The ringing truth overrides the hollowness of the lie. I could see from my sisters' horrified expressions that they believed me. The transfer of my guilt into their bodies was a success. I even began to believe myself.

My sisters apologized to me. They blamed the weather,

interference from the scattered raindrops. We embraced. My relief could not have been more sincere.

That night, I lay awake for hours in an itchy reverie, curling my toes on the bed railing. We sleep in cots stanchioned to the walls. Luna's body was a lump in the cot above mine; Mila was snoring down below. Waves lapped into the hangar. *Never again,* I promised my sleeping sisters. I could always return to the deadspot in my memory—it was enough to know that kind of quiet existed. I went to sleep feeling warm and lucky. Grateful for the strange experience, and snug in my conviction that I would never repeat it.

Seven hours later, I was poling back toward the deadspot.

III. THE DEADSPOT

We vowel down the channels. Darkness reaches around the eastern skyscrapers, and then those stalagmites are behind us. A pink line stitches day to night. A few early stars have appeared, but that light tells me nothing about our position. Unless I am singing, I really can't tell south from north after dark. Barking seagulls scatter the echoes, and I get caught in a swirling cul-de-sac of water on the outskirts of Old City.

Crackling into my body, I hear my sisters' voices combing the darkening bay like searchlights:

"AAAaaaaaAAA—"

"UuuUuuuUuu—"

Disappearing can make you feel like your own biographer. You hear the absence of your voice, and the notes you are failing to hit make their own shadow melody. You unlid the spaces ordinarily hidden by your body: a new song comes fluting through them. Whenever I hear my sisters singing without me, I get a flash of my own silhouette.

I bounce back a B-flat at the top of my register. The note quivers there, reassuring them: *I am alive, in Old City.* The songlines connecting us pull tight, relax. I hear a pulsing silence: my sisters listening as I move away from them. When I return, I will pile money on the table. I will give my sisters hundreds of reasons to forgive me. What will Viola say, I wonder, when I tell her I've made more in a night than she makes in a summer month on Bahía del Oro?

My passenger cranes around to stare at me, wearing the oddest look. The slicker lays heavily on top of him, alien as frog skin. It seems to breathe on its own.

"Old MacDonald had a farm. E-I-E-I-O—"

I stare down at him, stirring the gold from the bay.

"You sound like you are calling pigs to the trough," he says, but he is smiling.

I like this man. He fixes me with a lolling curiosity, despite his urgency to reach the seawall. He does not offer to help me to row the gondola, as some of the nervous men do. He does not snap at me when I pause to rest my voice. His eyes are mild. He is turning his palms, catching the fat droplets of rain.

"Were you born with the ability?" he asks. "Or is it something you taught yourself out here?"

I feel the song idling in my belly, changing slyly inside me. "Both, I think."

People talk about heredity as if it's linear and vertical. Dead people passing things "down" to the young. But my sisters and I are evolving together, I tell the man. All day, we swap notes around. We blur our voices into one song. Something grows in the fast-moving channels between us, and it's changing all the time. It moves with us, this thing we are inheriting.

To our left, ivory columns stand guard over a submerged pavilion.

"That was a bank once," I tell him. "Did you see the vault in the middle of the floor?" Ferns are curling around it now. "Can you believe that? People kept their money at a great distance from their body."

"I believe it," he says. "But I'm quite a bit older than you."

"My oldest sister, Viola, says—"

"You youngsters only know the stories."

His tone is wistful, but I hear the scolding note. My sisters and I are no strangers to this attitude. Older passengers often seem dismayed that they have to cede the Earth to creatures like us. They are aghast that we know so little about their world and bewildered by our happiness in this one. *We know more than you can imagine,* I want to tell him. But not as badly as I want my tip.

"I wish that I remembered the land, for what it's worth," I tell the man, watching his pale eyes swim over my face. "I would have loved to know what my mother's yard looked like."

" '*Yaaard.*' " He looks up at me thoughtfully. "What an odd word. I never noticed that before. Don't mind me, miss. You should forget even the stories. Look how lightly you sit on the water, remembering only water . . ."

I picture the healthy eelgrass waving in the limpid shallows of Bahía de las Nubes. "The grass is always greener, I guess."

He laughs at that. "Where did you hear *that* one? I'm surprised that it survived the floods. You know all our corny sayings. You're like a jukebox, miss."

His face reminds me of the wild dogs we see on the tree islands, panting with silent laughter. He speaks in a monotone, so I don't know if I should be complimented or insulted. Perhaps I'm being invited to laugh with him.

"A *jokebox*—"

"A jukebox. It was a machine that played the same stale songs over and over."

Blood rushes into my face. Does he think that's what I'm doing? Repeating myself? Can't he hear my singing changing on the air?

We crane up at the washed-violet sky behind the rotting ceiling. The bank shrinks into the distance. When the stranger turns, his face is as composed as a poem, its symmetries perfectly mysterious. My fantasies don't run in his direction. But fear prickles my neck, and it feels almost like lust.

"Hey. What's your name?" I ask him. "Who are you going to meet in Bahía Rosa, where nobody lives?"

He gapes up at me, his Adam's apple jumping. I feel the oddest déjà vu.

"Make up a name for me. Any name you'd like. Give me a nickname while you're at it. I am always in the market for a new name."

"Let me think on it," I tell him. "Maybe we can borrow a name from the posters."

I say this to make a joke and wind up frightening myself. The MISSING PERSON posters flap against the walls of Old City, most bleached beyond recognition. Men and women and children who disappeared in the floods. There is no way to read them as anything but obituaries today.

"Ah, the posters. Yes. I've seen those. A missing person. How perceptive you are. That's me to a T."

He turns back to the light rain fizzing on the water, his hairy knuckles wrapped around the heron's throat. I've retreated into my own thoughts when he calls back, "All of those faces are my face, why not? All of those names can be me. We are fungible sponges, we missing people."

I can't get my bearings in this conversation—is he joking? Is he really a missing person?

"Were you here for the floods?"

He stares at me for a long moment before answering.

"I'm part of a dying breed, bat girl. An *Old Floridian.* I grew up on a street called Coral Way. In a house with a foundation."

"But you stayed."

"No, miss. We fled. I was in the first wave of evacuations. But I wanted to come home before I died. To see my home again." His laugh becomes the phlegmy cough. "I'd need a scuba suit to find it, I guess. I've been here for three weeks, and I can't find a trace of that life."

It does not surprise me that I have a neighbor whose face I've never seen. Millions of people once lived in the coastal cities; thousands of us remain. SQUATTERS RIGHTS, BRO, someone spray-painted on the tallest standing condominium in Old City. But property disputes are rare on moving, glowing water. You have to live here to discover that the pollution isn't strong enough to kill you.

"Where are you moored?"

216 ORANGE WORLD AND OTHER STORIES

"I've been camping at the university. On the roof of the library, I believe. It's a good retirement home. The twilight zone, for my twilight years."

"Come on. You're not *that* old."

We laugh together, a sound I often draw like a tarpaulin over what I do not understand.

"Down here, the world has already ended. It's very peaceful, in its way."

It always surprises me when visitors treat New Florida as if it's a graveyard. Our home is no afterlife, no wasteland. Not an hour earlier, we poled through a rookery that shook with the hungry sobs of fledgling birds. Wood stork chicks and starry white ibis and little green herons wading around the rooftop sloughs. But if my passenger failed to hear them, I doubt my voice can convince him that our world is newborn.

"Do you have a family, sir? Up north?"

"I did. A wife, two sons. Terrestrials, all."

"They must be worried about you. Do they know where you are?"

"They drowned."

"Oh. I'm so sorry."

"I killed them," he elaborates. "I was one of the marine engineers who designed the seawall."

"I don't blame you," I blurt out.

"You should. People my age are criminals. We ruined the world."

Reminiscing about his guilt seems, perversely, to cheer my passenger. His voice brightens as he describes the scale of the failure. "We built the wall to withstand winds of one hundred fifty miles per hour. Does that sound naïve to you?"

I wonder if he can hear the note of pride inside of what he seems to mean as an apology to me. It's a bloated, underwater sound. He's chosen a funny moment to have this conversation, I think, with the wind picking up all around us and rain slanting between our faces.

"You failed." I nod—it seems to be the line he's written for me to say.

"Our imaginations failed us. Our models failed us."

A smile is still playing at the corners of his mouth. I wonder if he knows he's smiling. There is a profoundly unchaperoned quality to his gaze, now that his mind has traveled back in time. I try to listen to the details of his story, but it's his slack, abandoned face that fascinates me. His eyes roll up to the gray clouds, as if something is dragging him skyward by the roots of his hair.

"We all knew the end was coming. Don't let anybody tell you otherwise."

It would be cruel, I decide, to remind him that life is flourishing in New Florida; that it is our world now, not his any longer; that, actually, he is the one who is dying.

"This used to be paradise. I'm sorry, little bat. We ate up the whole horizon. We left you a ghost town. Not even a town. A toxic slough—"

"This is our home," I tell him. "And we are not ghosts."

I stop poling and stare at him. Water rolls along his slicker, capturing the light. As if the green skin is sweating for him. In his voice I hear a longing for release so close to my own that it is almost unbearable.

"There is a place I like to go," I hear myself say. "To fall silent."

As I describe the deadspot to him, he listens in perfect stillness. Even his blinking slows. Several times, I hear him swallowing his coughs. It feels like a betrayal to entrust my secret to this man, when I've told none of my sisters. But almost anything I say to them provokes a terrible reverb. Whereas the stranger is an open field—no buried stalagmites, no love lost between us, no history, and no expectation of a future. These turn out to be the perfect acoustics for confessing a secret on which I do not actually wish to reflect.

"And you don't think the pollution is damaging you?" he asks at last.

Deranging you, I hear.

"No." The skin under my breasts begins to burn. "Not really."

An odd rash has spread silently over my belly, unnoticed by anyone. Even I forget it's there during the daylight hours. My hands remember it, at night.

"You choose to swim here," he says. "In the world's most toxic waters."

"It hasn't affected us."

"Hasn't it, little bat? It's affecting all of us."

He drums his knuckles on his temple, his smile softening like something boiling at the bottom of a pot. His voice curls inward, so that it seems he is talking mostly to himself.

"The gondoliers. The birds of Chernobyl."

"What's that mean?"

"Nothing. A bad joke."

Algae drags behind us like an old-fashioned wedding train. You have to sweep the lantern over it to arouse the red glow; the unlit bay is entirely black now. Soon I will deposit this person on the seawall, I think with relief. Then I will go night swimming. I imagine the water closing over my head, swallowing me into it. The feeling that this water is gestating me, my secret life. So secret that for whole minutes I know nothing about it.

We drift while I rest my voice. Very gingerly, the man lowers his left arm into the algae. Then he drops his soaking hand into his lap, where it looks like a netted white fish. I watch him frowning down at the hand, as if waiting for it to change before his eyes.

"Tell me something," he asks. "Why do you keep returning to this *deadspot*?"

For some reason, I feel myself blushing. "I'm the youngest in our family. My sister Vi was like a mother to me. At the hour of my death, I'll still be the baby sister to them. It doesn't seem like I can age out of the role . . ."

This is certainly part of why I feel entitled to my lonely hours in the deadspot, I explain to the man. Their entire life before my birth is a secret from me. Whereas everything I've ever done has been visible to them.

"Out here, I float into my own element. When I am silent, when I am alone, I feel free. I don't have to sing along with anybody. Even my thoughts stop."

Under the water. Far from my sisters. Outside the chaos of our breaths. Only then, when I am nothing to anyone, do I feel the great peace.

It's as if I've released something living into the narrow gondola. I picture the secret floating between our faces, a jellyfish emitting its soft violet light, blowing open and shut. I wait for the man to turn it into a joke or to shame me for coming here alone.

"Yes," he says quietly. "That's it exactly. What a discovery."

The man lifts his eyes to mine with naked surprise, and I feel equally astonished. The longer we stare at each other, the louder a pure tone grows inside the gondola. Audible, I think, to both of us. He pushes back the green hood, smoothing the wet leaves of his hair. Gray or brown, there's no telling in this lighting. His wide smile sends all his wrinkles into hiding.

"Who doesn't dream of it? The silence that blots up thought. The silence that frees one from the burden of being oneself."

This smile is like a portal back to the stranger's childhood. Every prior grin I've seen tonight, I realize, was a counterfeit of this one. Understanding someone can make you feel understood in turn, and I smile back at him, to let him know that we have this thirst in common. It occurs to me that I should thank this white-faced man, the marine engineer, along with everyone from the last century who heard the water coming and failed to stop it. The deadspot is their creation.

———

We gondoliers operate by the Golden Rule. You do not take any risk you wouldn't want your sister to take. You don't pole into bad weather or shoot the tunnels at low tide. You refuse any passenger who might overpower you. I would kill my sisters, for example, if they risked their lives to take a fare to Bahía Rosa.

My sisters and I all pretend to live by this code. To prize safety over profit. But I have always felt quietly certain that perfect adherence to the Golden Rule would sink our business. We'd never leave the hangar. When I started breaking this rule routinely, it was easy enough to rationalize. I needed a darkness that would have killed the others, and they needed me to keep it a secret from them. This did not feel treacherous, not at first. It felt like a loving choice.

People will tell you that Bahía Rosa is a fatal place, but for months it was my paradise. The black-walled horizons. The silence that let me ripple out of my body, until at last I felt entirely at peace, whole and unfractured. One with the wildest turnings of the universe.

But at the same time I had begun to wonder, poling home from the deadspot, *How true can this sensation of unity really be if you need to leave everyone you care about to get it?*

───────

We float over a school of pompano, dozens of frozen gray faces skipping in front of the bow light. Something has frightened them; I glimpse a long body saucering beneath the transom. The man beckons me down from my platform. When he asks his question, his words quiver like the fishes.

"Do you and your sisters ever hear the voices of the drowned, in this bay?"

"No, sir. That's not . . . we don't have that kind of range."

"I see." He nods, but I don't think he believes me.

The man helps me by bailing water, leaning carefully forward. His green slicker bunches around the stringy muscles of his shoulders. The humming grows inside me until there is no room for worry. What will it feel like, I wonder, to enter the deadspot with another person? To fall silent with him? He thinks my home is a cemetery, and I want him to hear how wrong he is before we part company. The end of his life is not the end of all life. Something wants to be born.

We pass the line of black buoys. They strain after us on their long tethers, like dogs sniffing at the gondola; just as quickly, they are lost to sight. Their nodding heads push against the back of my mind as I sing.

OoOoOoO . . .

OoOoOoOo . . .

For a long time we see nothing at all, only water and more water. But I reassure the man that I can hear the seawall drawing nearer with each boomeranging note of my song. And then we both see it, the bleached wall, looming like a motionless wave on the dark horizon.

I touch my tongue to the inside of my cheek. For hours I've been waiting for this moment, but now that the end is in sight, I don't see how I'm going to manage the pivot. It's impossible to imagine leaving this sick man alone on the seawall with no supplies, no fresh water. Tantamount to pushing him off a roof, on a night like this. The nausea I felt back at the jetty returns with a force that nearly doubles me over.

We shadow the soft shoulders of the tree islands, where I hear the curly voices of laughing-yellow, snarling-green vegetation. In twenty minutes, I tell the man, we will reach the former land-side edge of his wall.

But when we are perhaps three hundred yards to the northwest of the seawall's rocky edge, the rain begins to fall in earnest. It pounds into my skull, drawing a caul around the gondola. More water splits the sky; in an instant, the map inside me dissolves. If I were home right now, I'd be listening to this storm drumming on the metal roof. Luna would be snoring above me, Mila below me. I'd be drifting off myself under the blankets, at the beginning of a dream. Can my sisters still hear me? I hear nothing but rain. I swing my light across the chop and feel the stirrings of real panic. By sight alone, in such a punishing crosswind, there is no way I can make this passage.

"Violaaaa?"

"Milaaaaa?"

"Lunaaaaaa?"

My voice flies off and does not return. Nothing answers me. Nothing steers me here. I place the pole in its mount and climb down from the platform. Perhaps my poker face is not on straight, because the man gives me a wild look and grabs my wrist.

"Why aren't you singing?"

"Forgive me, sir," I say, avoiding his eyes. "I made a mistake. I thought we could beat this storm. But I'm losing my voice. I can't map the channel. If I miscalculate the passage, we'll capsize."

On a slack tide, I explain to him, I'd shortcut across the bay, but the water is alive with eddies, and I don't want to get smashed against the wall or sucked out to the Gulf.

"Girl," he says slowly. "Take me to the goddamn wall."

His voice shakes with a rage I could not have predicted even a heartbeat earlier.

"I can *see* it. We could *swim* there, practically—"

"No. We can't risk it." His face is almost unrecognizable to me, winched tight with anger. "I won't risk it," I clarify, because it's suddenly clear to me that he is making very different calculations.

"You won't *risk it*. You'll bathe in poison, but this is too dangerous?"

The man tugs me toward him, shouting over the wind.

"Tonight is the anniversary of the storm surge. Do they teach that history in your floating schools?"

I had forgotten the date; it isn't one we celebrate. The night the pumping systems failed. The night the seawall was breached by the towering water. The wailing night that did not kill our mother, who would live for another seven years so that I could be born.

He tightens his grip on my wrist, gazing at the spot beyond the bow light where the angled rain is steadily visible. Horror seeps into me; his or my own, I am no longer certain. Large chunks of darkness lift and fall around my gondola.

"I traveled a thousand miles to die here. I chose this spot, this date. I wanted to walk across my wall on my last night on Earth. That was my wish. To die at home, on the anniversary of my children's deaths."

Beneath the sagging hood, he peers up at my face. Here is a man who has written the last scene of his life, I realize, who is furious that his stage directions are getting eaten by the wind. His voice lowers, and inside of the anger I can hear a grinding disappointment.

"Don't hold out on me, miss. It's cruel to stop here, within sight of our destination. I didn't come this close to the end to turn around."

Our destination. Rain pounds into the hull, water we should be bailing. His feet are bare, I notice—at some point, he must have removed his boots. The toes waggle up at me, as if their good humor is still intact, even as the rest of him seems bent on destroying us.

"When the rain stops, I'm turning around." I let out a shaky breath. "I cannot, in good conscience, take you to your death."

"But, miss!" He laughs angrily, reaching a wet palm to my cheek. "You already have. Look around you. We've arrived." The scolding note reenters his voice. "Now, be honest. You knew where you were taking me. The *deadspot,* you called it." Raindrops go jumping off the green slicker, outlining him in fizzing silver. "Get your pole. Finish the job I hired you to do."

"No." I climb back onto the platform and begin to turn us toward the lee side of the nearest tree island, which I can just make out through the rain. When I look again, the man is standing in the stern. We ride up one swell and down into a deep trough, and I have time to feel amazed that we did not capsize just before the man lunges at me. He must be a better echolocator than I am: when my arms lift, his arms shadow them, a rhyming motion. Quite easily, he wrestles the pole away from me. He gives me a terrible grin, gripping my pole to his chest. *Sisters, I was wrong about my last fare. He is stronger than I am, and he is so much sicker than I imagined.*

"Since you refuse to continue, I'm taking command of this vessel . . ."

Warm liquid seeps through my trousers and I am crying now, I want to go home. OoOoOoOo, I scream. The man releases my arm. For a moment, his eyes shine with some trace of our earlier understanding.

"Poor little bat. You just wanted to disappear for a little while, didn't you? You don't actually want to die."

I don't. I don't, but I had to come a great distance to learn that, Sisters.

"You should stop swimming out here, then." Again I hear the scolding note, but it's much fainter now. He is trying, clumsily, to push off the rocky bottom and turn the gondola toward the seawall. I watch him struggling with the push-pole, its foot now choked with mud. "This whole bay is a stomachful of bile."

Then comes a rippling instant where the scene I am imagining becomes the action I am taking. I watch my hands reach out to grab the pole back, my fingers closing just above his knuckles; he doesn't let go but twists around with a cry. I crawl forward and bite at his hands, missing but causing him to howl. He is still clutching my pole when a strong wave washes over the stern, unbalancing us both; I let go to brace myself, and the man falls backward into the rainy water.

I scream with him as he falls, and I go on screaming after

he splashes into the bay. But I don't jump into the churning water after him, terrified that he will drag me down. I don't reach my pole out to him, because I don't have a pole now; it went overboard with the stranger. I croak at the water: "Sir?" My voice is almost gone. It occurs to me that I don't even know what name to call. It's so dark that I can't see where the man surfaces, but I hear his arms crashing heavily through the algal mats. He is swimming away from me, I realize with relief. He is trying to make the wall. If I were to swivel the lantern, perhaps I would find him bobbing mere feet from the boat: his pale face staring up at me, wreathed in glowing algae. Perhaps I could save him. *Save him,* I command myself. But I don't move from the floor of the gondola. Instead I cover my light, and I wish only for the slapping sounds to stop.

Eventually, my wish is granted: the splashing ceases. Either the man has drowned, or he's swum out of earshot. The new silence is soaked through with his absence. I lie flat on the wet boards, pushing my fists against my stomach. My pole, I imagine, must be riding these same waves into the Gulf or sinking to some depth I cannot hear. And my passenger? He is a true missing person now, I think. A special amphibian. Dead and alive, to anyone who knows him. The last splash he made is a sound that will not leave me. *You killed him,* I try not to think. The moon shines into my eyes; very slowly it occurs to me that the rain has stopped. I have a peculiar, nerveless awareness of the water's trembling surface. Where am I? My mind is like the sky between the stars, void of shapes names facts. But I don't need to sing to guess.

IV. THE CHORUS

I stare up at a busy construction pit. Tiny white spades are tossing huge quantities of darkness around. Stars—these are the stars.

I'm not sure how long I drift like this, trying not to think about the terrible splashing. Without my pole, I'm in bad trouble, but I screamed for so long that I must have blasted all feeling from my body, and it hardly seems to matter that no boats will find me in this distant bay. My bow light plucks at the stringy algae. Perhaps I sailed right through a break in the seawall without realizing it. My song is a pitiful hissing, and it returns no depths or distances to me. When I hear a woman's voice rising out of the darkness, I think it must be my imagination. My light swings in the direction of the singing.

A gondola is arrowing toward me, flat-bottomed and opal white in the powerful beam of my lantern. My good feeling immediately flips into horror. A gondolier stands on the poling platform, her hair blowing loose. The pitch of her singing rises. *God, please, no. God, please, keep us separate. No, no, no. I am not ready to meet her.* OoOoOoO, she sings at me. Can this be possible—am I about to run into my doppelgänger? My double, poling out of the past or the future? Perhaps the man will be seated in her bow, smiling out of his green slicker. Will he be dead, I wonder, or alive?

But it's not my double that draws into view; it's my sister.

Viola glides silently past me, wearing a blindfold with trailing ribbons, her slack face illuminated by the gray orb of her bow light. Her droning song floods into me. I hear the same sound that pours from my throat in the deadspot—an emptying hiss, like grain spilling from a sack.

Her gondola moves much faster than my mind does. Lethargic thoughts chase each other in slow, widening circles: She's come out here to find me. She's put herself in terrible danger, all to find me.

But soon I realize that Vi has no idea that I'm near her. The blindfold is a trick of last resort; tight pressure across the temples can sometimes help us to hear better in bad weather. It doesn't seem to be working. Her hair flies raggedly out behind her. Her singing has the strange, flayed quality of all sounds in the deadspot, shadowless and flat. Now I hear, with excruciating clarity, how much trouble we're in for. Vi didn't come out here to save me. She's lost herself.

"Vi!" I scream. Too hoarse, I'm sure, to be heard.

But Viola unties the red bandage around her eyes, using the blindfold to wipe at her face. Had all the drowned risen up to address me tonight, I could not have been more astonished. Shaking her hair out, she turns and looks right at me: "Blister!"

Fury wheels around our boats, shrieking at such an ear-splitting volume that it's impossible to pinpoint the origin of the feeling.

She poles up to me, our pupils shrinking in the doubled glare of the bow lights. Two voices swing out like hooks, each catching at the other:

"What are you *doing* here?"

The answer floats between us, mocking us. Vi has always seemed to be light-years ahead of me. Perhaps she is as surprised as I am to discover how we overlap.

"Did you come here to find me?" Vi asks me in a stricken voice.

Her face seems to float, unanchored, isolated by the light. I think about lying, then shake my head.

"No. I wanted to come out here, to swim."

"So did I," says my sister, with the ghost of a smile.

Our calamity strikes me, suddenly, as terribly funny. No less astonishing a coincidence, in its way, than being born into the same family.

"How long have you been swimming here?"

"Oh," Vi says pensively, chewing on her thumb pad. "Years."

Years!

One of us asks: "Why didn't you tell me?"

One of us says to the other: "It is *so selfish* to come here."

One of us is burning with shame—is it hers or my own?

One of us shouts: "Who am I hurting?"

And we scream at each other: "Me!"

Silence rips apart down the middle. Silence reveals its tiny serrated fangs. Have we loved each other well? Could we love each other better? I realize that there is so much we have never told one another, and likely never will. Secrets multiply throughout our hangar. A hundred doors that we refuse to test with speech. A hundred others that we pretend are walls. If I were braver, I would fling my voice against them, at the exact pitch to pick the locks. If I were braver, and if I were a better singer.

In a whisper, I tell Viola about my last fare. How I listened, paralyzed, while the moment when I might have saved him flipped into the moment of his death.

To my great surprise, she does not pull away from me. I watch the story fall into her open pupils and prepare myself for Vi's disgust, her anger. But it's love, uninjured, that floats to the surface.

"It's a shame we weren't alive then," Vi murmurs. "We could have told them how to build the seawall. We could have listened for the weak spots."

Over her shoulder, I see a rolling darkness. I have the nauseating thought that the man's green slicker might come floating our way, carrying the glowing algae.

"Can you hear anything out there, Vi?"

"Just you, talking. But let's keep trying."

I crawl into Vi's gondola and hitch my boat to her stern. We try and fail to find a signal. The rain returns, lashing the black water between our boats. Soon she, too, loses her voice. This rain stings wherever it touches our skin. Vi gives up on poling and sits in the stern behind me; I feel the weight of her chin on my left shoulder. She runs the flats of her palms down my curved spine, pressing at the bony knobs. "This is how sisters tune one another," she used to tell me when I was small, to spare my pride when I woke up afraid from a dream and needed her to hold me.

I wonder if we will ever reach the end of the deadspot. It seems to keep spinning us back into it, a hungry red mouth.

"Blister," Vi says, in her flattened voice. "Do you remember the mice?"

We had a single children's book when I was growing up, with a superficially cheerful, apocalyptic plotline. One mouse after another tumbles into a muddy hole, each trying to rescue the others. A family of mice doomed by their clumsiness and by their love, perhaps by a secret wish to save themselves. And saved they must have been, by some tractor pull of grace, because no children's book ends with the death of every protagonist.

But my mind cannot conceive of a way out of our predicament; in fact, my mind has become the hole.

"Are we going to die now?" Vi asks me.

I shake my head, touched that she's sought out my opinion. Another milestone.

"We should never have come here." Vi shudders. "I am sure they are out looking for us."

Mila and Luna. Perhaps we'll hear their voices soon, behind the curtain of rain. I think about the storybook mice, steering a teacup on the high seas. In a family of sisters, everybody gets to play all the parts, the brave ones and the cowards, the doomed ones and the saviors.

We toss our raw voices into the wind. We are rowing sightlessly, possibly in circles, as the keening begins. When the first echo reaches me, I mistake it for a symptom of exhaustion. Another echo returns to me, although my lips are sealed.

"Listen," Vi says, tugging at my elbow.

"I hear it, too. You're not crazy. Or we're both crazy."

Behind me I feel Viola tense. The ocean is breaking into pieces. New pairs of eyes shine up at us below the gunwales: fluorescent, enormous disks, orange and purple and salt white, inlaid in the angular faces of some schooling species I have never seen before. I know the old stories about dolphins saving humans, but these are not dolphins, and they seem wholly oblivious of us, even as their keening penetrates our bones. A humming enters my chest and begins to grow—

a deep, marine roar. Vi wraps her arms around me, and I feel grateful for her heartbeat; I'd go mad in a second if I was hearing this alone. This new song is wrenching my mind wider than it wants to open, faster than I am ready to go. "I'm not ready!" I scream hoarsely, because I can feel myself getting spun into something so much larger than I am, vibrating at a frequency that is not human. Echoes leap into us from dimensions that seem impossibly remote—shivering treetops and submerged walls, the tiny bones of unborn animals. We hear the hollows, the where-to-gos. Spaces in the ruins that cry out with the tides: *This is not the end of the world. This is not the end of the world.*

Without turning, I can feel Vi's lips parting, preparing to sing along. *Vi, Vi,* I want to beg like a child, *please, wait for me.* I had wanted to dissolve on my own terms, and only temporarily; if we go through this door, what will we become? Other singers push into my mind, the gibbering moon and the silver mangroves and the buried coral. I am afraid of the voices lifting out of the dark. I am afraid to join them. But perhaps we will have to, if we want to survive.

Orange World

ABNORMAL RESULT. HIGH RISK.
CLINICAL OUTCOME UNKNOWN.

At night, Rae pulls a pillow between her legs and lets the pain scissor at her. She feels like a gutshot animal lying in the road. Rae was not raised with religion, so when she sees the blood in the toilet she invents her own prayers. After the results from the third set of tests come back, she starts begging anything that might be listening to save her baby.

And then, lo, something does answer.

I can help you. It spoke without speaking, glowing low on the horizon. She had made it over the ledge of 4 a.m. to 5 a.m., what she'd once believed to be a safe hour. The out-of-the-woods hour.

What are you?

The voice tipped out of the red light.

That's the wrong question. What would you like me to do?

————

"Orange World," the New Parents Educator says, "is where most of us live."

She shows a slide: a smiling baby with a magenta birthmark hooping her eye. No—a burn mark. The slides jump back in time, to the irreversible error. Here is the sleepy father, holding a teapot.

Orange World is a nest of tangled electrical cords and open drawers filled with steak knives. It's a baby's fat hand hovering over the blushing coils of a toaster oven. It's a crib purchased used.

"We all make certain compromises, of course. We do things we know to be unsafe. You take a shower with your baby, and suddenly—"

The Educator knocks her fist on the table, to mimic the gavel rap of an infant's skull on marble. Her voice lowers to a whisper, to relate the final crime: "You fall asleep together on the sofa. Only one of you wakes up."

Don't fall asleep, Rae dutifully takes down. *Orange World.*

They have already covered Green World, a fantasy realm of soft corners and infinite attention. Orange World, it seems, is this world, viewed through a spyglass of fire. WELCOME HOME, BABY! says a banner hanging in the classroom's dark corner.

"I want to acknowledge that Green World is the ideal, but Orange World is where most of us live," the Educator repeats.

Next, they watch a parental horror movie in photo stills,

titled *Red World*. The Educator, in her bright Australian accent, encourages them to imagine babies falling down stairwells and elevator chutes. Speared by metal and flung from passenger seats. Drowning in toilet bowls and choking on grapes.

Rae has never made it this far into a pregnancy before. Hers is a geriatric pregnancy. Her husband finds this language hilarious. "Like Sarah in the Bible."

Everybody gets a swaddle and a baby doll. The head comes off of Rae's. While she is jamming the head back on, the swaddle floats to the ground. Picking the swaddle up, she steps on it.

Sneaker bacteria: Orange World. Decapitation: Red World.

"Your head is on backward, love."

The Educator watches as Rae wrenches it around.

"You should go to the New Moms Group," the Educator suggests. "It's a great resource for first-time mothers. Veteran moms show you the ropes."

Rae smiles and thanks her. In this crowded room of cheerful, expectant people, there is no space to say, *I don't know if there will be a baby.*

On the first night that the devil appeared to her, her husband was on a trip to New York to woo new clients. "Woo," what a dumb verb. "Woo!" she screamed, dropping to all fours on the stairs. The pain expanded to fill the empty house. When the pain threatened to take off the roof, she pulled on a wool shirt and stumbled into the moonlit street, a hand spread against her belly. "Help me," Rae begged. The neighboring houses stared down at her like blank-faced jurors. She limped across the road. Strange light brimmed in the gutter that ran along the sidewalk. Its source was unclear. As she advanced, the light changed color, developing a reddish tint. It was a very short step through this mist into the gutter. Wading through ankle-deep water, Rae cried out. Pain folded her knees below her. A taut and fiery string ran from her pelvis to her throat, and it felt as though some secret hand kept plucking at it. This is how the devil woos you, before you know it is the devil. A bodiless, luminous voice rose out of the storm drain.

"Yes," she heard herself promise. "Anything."

———

Three months later, Rae pauses in the bedroom doorway to watch her newborn son breathing. He's got a very mature snore, this baby. His father is also sawing logs. She could listen to their duet all night. Green World. The baby was born on the winter solstice, emerging into a world of lengthening light. He was born healthy, just as the voice in the gutter had promised.

Already, Rae's brain has rewired itself to wake her at 4:35 a.m. Outside, snow pours through the neighbors' leafless birches. The flakes feel wonderful on her upturned face, her fever-freckled chest. Why hadn't she thought to appeal to heaven, Rae wonders now. She took the first deal offered. She'd done a better job negotiating for the Subaru.

Rae kneels in the gutter, on a thick paste of dead leaves. She unbuttons her shirt to the navel. Snow wakes groggily into water, a trickling stream that carries beer tabs and flashing ice into the storm drain. She fishes for the clasp of her bra. Her breasts are straining against the thin lace. On the opposite side of the street, her own home gazes back at her. The windows look like holes that any monster could reach through; the walls seem blue and pregnable. Like clockwork, at 4:44, the devil appears, making itself out of fog and solidifying. Its tone has changed completely since the baby's birth. No longer does it offer any green guarantees, promising safety to her child, her friends, her family. These nights it's all red threat: *Feed me, or else.*

So she does.

The gutter is a cold canoe. Rae lowers onto an elbow, stretching flat. Asphalt pushes at her shoulders, her tailbone. It seems impossible that she hasn't gotten sick yet, in all these weeks of appointments. Perhaps the devil is keeping her well. She tries not to look at it; when she looks at it, her milk dries up. It lays its triangular head on her collarbone, using its thin-fingered paws to squeeze milk from her left breast into its hairy snout. Its tail curls around her waist. Unlike her son, the devil has dozens of irregular teeth, fanged and broken, in three rows; some lie flat against the gums, like bright arrowheads in green mud. Its lips make a cold collar around her nipple. She feels the tugging deep in her groin, a menstrual aching. Milk gushes out of her, more milk than it seems any single body could possibly produce; more milk, she's sure, than her baby ever gets.

Below her, the devil makes a queer gurgling sound.

Tonight it has a long paddlelike tail, erratically needled, like a balding cactus, which lashes at her side; she feels blood racing away from a fresh cut. It drinks. It drinks. More milk floods around its lips, turning its fur shiny and wet.

She hears the devil's swallows slowing, its thorny lashes fluttering against her skin. Its head lolls onto her chest, breath whistling through its teeth. Without thinking, she smooths a raw spot between its ears.

"Goddammit!"

The devil has bitten her; it pushes off her stomach with its clawed feet. It wobbles through the melting snow, its belly swaying beneath it, and vanishes through the bars of the storm drain. She stares at the eerie triple imprint of its teeth, already shrinking from view. The first time, she thought that she'd have to disguise these scratches and bruises, the bloody evidence of their feedings. But, by true dawn, the worst of the wounds had vanished, erased by some bad magic, leaving only a lurid rash. She is back in bed three minutes before her husband stirs on the pillow.

"There you are," he says, smiling. "Our boy slept well, didn't he!"

Rae's mother calls to see how things are going.

Her mother would be here, but she is caring for her own mother on the opposite side of the world, in a hospice facility. Her heart is breaking not to be with her daughter, just as Rae's is breaking not to be with her mother and her grandmother. The breaking is continuous—in the ouroboros of caretaking, guilt and love and fear and love continuously swallow one another.

"I love you," they tell each other frequently on these calls. More truth won't fit through the tiny colander of the telephone receiver.

Rae admits that she is having some difficulties with nursing.

"Oh, God, don't feel guilty!" her mother says. "Give him a bottle, already. You were all formula-fed, and look how you turned out!"

This is not particularly reassuring to Rae, although she appreciates the impulse. There is no natural moment in the conversation to say, *Mother, the devil has me.*

Sixteen weeks into the pregnancy, Rae had received a call from a genetic counselor. Something had gone from being possibly wrong to probably wrong.

In her dream that night, the genetic counselor was picking out nail polish for her. "This black? Or this black? This one?"

In the best of circumstances, a pregnancy was a walk down a gangplank. But theirs were not the best of circumstances, the genetic counselor had told Rae and her husband. It is a scary result, she acknowledged. The numbers kept changing on them: 1/100, 1/50, 1/14. Even early on, when the odds were with them, Rae had feared this outcome.

Somebody has to be the 1.

With a dark egotism, she felt certain that she and the baby would be the raffle winners.

If you believe that, what else do you believe?

But then, a day later, by the train tracks, where pollen floats in a spectral yellow migration to the Willamette River, two deer appear. Fawns, preceding their mother like tiny spotted footmen.

It's a sign.

It's a sign.

All will be well.

And still she hears the calm, dry voice inside her: *If you believe that, what else do you believe?*

———

Even as a girl, Rae was a terrible negotiator. She gave anybody anything they asked of her. She owed the world; the world owned her. She never felt that she could simply take up space; no, one had to earn one's keep here on planet Earth. As a kid, Rae's body soundlessly absorbed the painful things that happened to it, and not even an echo of certain events escaped her lips. Sometimes she thought the problem (the gift, she'd once believed) was anatomical; she didn't seem to have a gag reflex, so none of the secret stuff—the gushy black awful stuff—ever came out. Now it lives inside her, liquefying. Inadmissible, indigestible event. Is that what the devil is drinking?

At 9:09 and 11:32 and 1:19 and 2:04 and 3:22 and 6:12, Rae's son wakes up. They wake together, her eyes flying open just as his wailing rises beside her. Before she knows what she is, she is rolling toward his voice. Night brightens into morning, and they are together for the pivot.

Green World. The wailing is profoundly consolable. It is the question to which she is the answer. The milk satisfies hunger and thirst; it moves softly between their bodies, quieting both of them. Joy has been the great surprise of motherhood. The flood of love for the baby is so fierce that she is always trying to qualify it to herself, to hide it from her own inner sight. Hormones—of course it's all hormones. Hormones? Under her chin, the baby burps. He is wearing pajamas that make him look like a tiny medieval friar. The love winging around the room scares her with its annihilating force. It's loosening the corset strings of her history, the incarcerated fat of "personality." She and the baby are one body again, nourishing itself.

For perhaps the first time in her life, she knows what to do, and she does it.

The New Moms Group meets at the Milk and Honey Co-op, a cheerfully derelict storefront between King of Subs and the weed dispensary, just minutes from Rae's house. One Wednesday, at 10:27 a.m., she puts the baby in his carrier and walks down the hill, kissing his fuzzy head every third step.

"Don't worry, baby," she tells him. "This is just anthropology."

"Did you know," she overhears a woman in line to buy a sack of oats telling her friend, "that breast milk is made from our blood? Isn't the body amazing?"

"That doesn't sound true, Ellen," the friend says, with a blazing lucidity that Rae wants to warm her hands over.

"That's what I thought," Ellen says placatingly. "But Google it. Read the science."

Then she winks at the cashier, Nestor, whom Rae knows because he works a second shift at the gas station where she buys, or bought, cigarettes.

Nestor recognizes Rae and grins. "Hey, what are you doing here?" he asks. "This is a healthy-foods store. No cigarettes."

She stifles the impulse to lie.

"I'm here for the New Moms Group."

When Nestor raises a brow, she laughs and says, "Yes, I know. I'm old. Old women can also be newborn. Anybody can."

The New Moms Group sits in a circle on a faux-fur rug in the homey, dingy back room. Every adult face looks freakishly huge to Rae. The New Moms get pink name tags; the Old Moms, red ones. It's Valentine's Day, a fact that shocks Rae; that's not the kind of time she's been keeping.

Yvette, the group leader, announces that they will "share" around the circle.

"Okay," one of the New Moms says. She's a white woman, wearing sunglasses and overalls and transmitting a definite hostility to being looked at, like a vampire or a vacationing Olsen. "I'll start. My name is Lisette, and I had a baby girl three weeks ago. I'm wearing a diaper right now. I've been finding quarter-size clots of blood in my pants. I piss blood when I sneeze. Okay. Pass."

"Hello. My name is Flore," a hollow-eyed black woman with a newborn gumming her turtleneck says, "and this is Baby Dennis. Baby Dennis wakes up every twenty minutes."

"My name is Halimah. I had a C-section, and I feel like a library where they misshelved all the books."

These women's struggles are identical to Rae's, and yet she has to fight down her distaste, the voice that says, "So what?" and "Shut up" and "You should be ashamed of yourself." *I am a sexist,* she admits to herself. Rae notes the rise of acidity in her body as she listens to the mothers describe their secret torments and night terrors and pelvic agonies.

"My name is Rubecca," a white woman around Rae's age says. She has smile lines and a topless blue mermaid tattooed on her left biceps. Rae envies the mermaid. Gravity is on her side, under the sea.

"Rebecca?" someone hopefully suggests.

"*Ru*becca," Rubecca repeats. For nearly five minutes, she shares about her sciatica. Does she have a baby? It's unclear. What she definitely has is sciatica.

Little babies are yawning all around the circle, held on laps and centered against chests. It's hard not to view the mothers as their large ventriloquist's dummies, yapping away while the babies pull the strings.

When they get to Rae, she freezes.

"Don't be shy," Yvette says. Yvette is a mother of three, or four—Rae didn't catch the exact number. Her children keep running up to her and radiating off again, in an explosion of organic crumbs. She wears her black hair in a high ponytail and looks suspiciously radiant to Rae; she grew up in Miami and works as a choreographer for a dance company; in all her movements, there is a spirited efficiency, a sort of freestyle grace—warm-blooded and unrobotic. She seems to take real

pleasure in helping the bewildered new mothers orient themselves in the postpartum tall grass. But she clearly enjoys her
role as Yvette the veteran, Yvette the alpha mom.

"I'm having a hard time with night feedings," Rae finally
says.

Everyone clucks. Advice rolls over her: Ferber, No-Cry,
weighted blankets, white-noise machines. Has she tried Baby
Merlin's Magic Sleepsuit? Binkys? Loveys? These words
embarrass her. They seem to leach the intelligence from her
body, in the way that the starving devil leaches mineral from
her bones.

At the end of the meeting, Yvette approaches her. They
stand in the bee-products aisle, surrounded by castles of natural laxatives. "I hope that wasn't too overwhelming," Yvette
says. "Really, you just need to experiment and find out what
works for your baby."

"The baby, I love the baby. I love nursing the real baby . . ."

Rae feels dizzy from sleeplessness. She can feel herself
blinking rapidly, water escaping down her cheeks. Oh, God!
For years she was a vault, but now she is a leaky mess. She
can't keep anything inside herself, not the blood ruining her
underwear or her oozing milk or the moisture in her eyes
or the words beading on her tongue: "It's not our baby I was
asking about. Every night since I got home from the hospital,
I've been nursing the devil."

Rae describes the devil in a rush, with a sick satisfaction—
its bulging eyes and the spiny paddle of its tail, the way that
it looks sometimes like a prehistoric porcupine, sometimes
like a sort of mutant red raccoon. Now she watches Yvette's

face and awaits her reassignment, from weary stranger to dangerous lunatic.

Yvette doesn't bat a false eyelash. Indeed, a look of naked exasperation flashes across her carefully made-up face.

"That fucking thing. It's been coming south of Powell?"

The aisle seems to narrow, enclosing them in a daylit tunnel. Is Yvette making fun of her?

"You . . . you've heard of it?"

"Uh-huh. Two winters ago, after my second daughter was born, it came around every night. It moved under my house and never shut up." She shakes her head.

Rae's cheeks are on fire. "Did you . . . did it promise you something, too?"

"Oh," Yvette says, and laughs bitterly. "It certainly tried. I wasn't interested."

Shame nettles over Rae's skull like a tight red cap. "I see. Well, I, ah, I bit? I made a deal with it."

Smoothing her hair back from her temples, Yvette fails to conceal her disappointment. She has long acrylic nails, a chic blue. "Rookie mistake, babe."

Rookie mistake?

Her whole body flushed, Rae leans in to defend herself, which somehow results in an impassioned defense of the very entity that is draining her life: "It saved my child. When he was still inside me—"

"That thing!" Yvette laughs angrily. "That thing can't add a minute to your child's life and it can't take a minute away. It preys. That's all it does. It feasts on blood."

Down the aisle, Yvette's children are drawing on the

freezer door with beeswax lip balm, giggling. As Rae watches, the older boy takes a big bite of wax and swallows.

Rae looks at Yvette with a freezing dread, a melting relief.

"Are you sure? It was pretty convincing. Its eyes, you see . . ."

"Yes, yes, I know," Yvette snaps irritably. "And the voice like a peal of thunder."

Rae nods warily. It feels like sacrilege to be discussing this out loud at noon.

"Whatever you do?" Yvette says. "Don't read anything online. Those message-board bitches are crazy. They'll tell you your baby is going to die and sign off with an angel emoji."

Yvette scribbles her number on a piece of paper and hands it to Rae.

"Here. Call me sometime. You have to break the cycle."

The baby is awake, blinking its dark, innocent eyes. Now Rae worries that Yvette is the lunatic. What is this woman saying? How can she possibly advise breaking a compact with the devil?

"Look, it is not the devil, okay?"

"It's not?"

"It's a devil. Like, one of the little ones. A knockoff Satan."

Rae swallows her shame. "It's not omnipotent. It doesn't claim that. But it is powerful. The things it knows—"

"You really think it's reading your thoughts?" Yvette yawns. "A plant could do that."

"No, you don't understand . . ."

Rae looks down at her son's wispy head, pale as lettuce with intricate blue veins. Veteran mothers seem so smugly certain of everything. Yvette, with her cloth diapers and her homemade yogurt—how does Yvette know for certain what this devil can and cannot do?

"It can't do shit. It's not clairvoyant. It's just a rat fink with a taste for mother's milk."

Yvette's daughter darts between them, a strong, beautiful girl. She sticks her tongue out at Rae.

"Quit feeding it. Cold turkey. You'll see."

———

For a while, Rae is almost euphoric with relief. But as the sun sets, her fear rises. While her husband and her son sleep, Rae reads news stories on her tiny screen, Red World stories. Women in ICE detention centers, separated from their children. Women in Beijing, afraid to breathe the toxic air. She reads and reads until her teeth are vibrating from the sustain pedal of the tragic-news cycle; the horror feels bottomless. She wonders how far afield the devil goes; there are deals to be made all over the globe.

By the time 4 a.m. rolls around, her resolve has evaporated. Rae sees that she has no choice; she has to feed it. To deviate from the pattern she's established would be to risk other deviations.

Even the walk from the front door to the gutter is beset with peril. More snow crystals the trees. A car full of teenagers comes shrieking around the corner, blowing through two stop signs. Only one of the taillights is working. Before giving birth, Rae wouldn't have blinked at any of this. Now she hears the ticking menace latent in the most banal arrangements of weathers and objects and personalities. Orange World. The freezing sky and the night and all the people in it.

Carefully, Rae lowers herself into the gutter. She grips the asphalt, recalling her labor, that earth-splitting pressure. Pain can mean such different things, depending on what you believe is drawing closer to you, pushing into view.

The devil's tongue has a ridge that splits it down the center. Her extraordinary rash, infernally authored, is easy to conceal as an ordinary rash. Nobody wants to look too closely when she nurses, not even her husband. Nobody but Rae is studying her left breast like a painting. Grains of psychedelic color stand out against her skin. A Braille that says THE DEVIL WUZ HERE.

Unlike her son, the devil has no problem latching on. The pain is bearable if she focuses on the nursery window, gleaming on the opposite side of the empty road. Then it starts to chew, and reflex gets the better of her. She shrieks, unthinking, and pulls its snout from her breast. No sooner is she free of the latch than the visions pour into her, a dark flood.

"What are you, really?" she asks.

Standing on its hind legs in the gutter, foaming and bristling, it seems to grow larger and thicker, wilder and sicker, its bright, eggy eyes gleaming with moisture. Oh, God. Is the devil crying?

"You're playing me," she accuses. "You think I don't know the literature?"

The devil bashes its jaw into her collarbone like a shovel. "Ow!"

Feed me, or else, its eyes shine at her.

She sees Yvette's face in the sunny co-op.

"You can't see the future," she says. "You're just plagiarizing my imagination."

How much longer can this continue? A year? Two? Much longer, the devil's ravenous eyes suggest. Starving even while feasting, poor thing. Eating fuels hunger, a devil's full belly flattening as milk stretches her breasts. She watches her hand reach out to smooth its cold, spiny fur.

"See you tomorrow."

Fire is spilling around the distant mountain. Limping home, she can feel the road through the sole of one shoe. She forgot to lock the front door behind her. Her son, awake in his crib, sees her face and begins to cry.

Perhaps this was the wrong strategy, to antagonize the devil. The next night, the creature sinks its fangs into her. Blood sheets down her breast. Now she is infected with new visions. They seep through the porous boundary between her and the creature, whose snout feels as tight as a clothespin against her skin.

This will be your future, the devil's eyes beam up at her. *If you don't obey me.*

What it shows her is so monstrously original that she has to bite her cheeks to keep from screaming and waking her son on the other side of the road. Tonight's special: a made-to-order evil. Her devil has never put this on the table in such precise terms. It must be stealing words from the briny jars in her mind, unspoken and unspeakable—because how could a scaly demon-rat know the verb "predecease"?

That's right. Tits out, bitch.

The devil feasts.

———

Rae's mother is the best woman Rae knows. What would her mother say if she could see Rae, shivering in the gutter, pulling down her modest nursing bra to top off the devil? *A* devil? Yet her son has years and years ahead of him, she hopes, on this earth that can spin from green to orange to red in one nuclear flash.

The bra is new. The devil stares at it thoughtfully, then eats the sale tag.

———

Only once, in all these lonely months of nights, is she spotted. Lying on her side, she is caught in the headlights of a garbage truck. She clutches the devil to her, lacing her fingers through its trembling fingers. Something incredible happens—the driver locks eyes with her, and then goes right on driving. The implacable pace of the truck, huffing mammoth breaths in the street light, makes Rae feel as if she had actually been run over and left for dead. Only as the truck rounds the corner does Rae realize how badly she's been hoping for rescue.

Crawling into bed at dawn, she wakes her husband. Adrenaline hums inside her chest. Once again, she has escaped with her life. Deep in some hell, the devil, swollen with her milk, is beginning to empty again, even as life surges through her. Her husband sighs happily, rolling toward her.

She finds his mouth with her mouth, moves lower. Soon his body is rigid and awake, his mind still trailing dreams. She has almost forgotten that this kind of synchrony is possible, so different from the bad business being transacted in the gutter. Afterward, stroking the healed bruises above her tailbone, he asks, "Were you feeding the baby this whole time? You must be so tired."

"I am. But it feels good to be food."

"What—"

"I said, I feel lucky to know what it means to be food, before I am dead."

———

January 2. Dear Baby: You have been here long enough to accumulate dirt under your fingernails.

Rae stares down at her *Mom's Line-a-Day* journal. At some point, this had sounded like a very manageable goal. One line a day. But she is seriously in the red. The last entry—*You are getting a tooth!*—is followed by a month of snowy blankness. Guiltily, Rae stares at all the empty days. Before her son's birth, she'd worked as a science journalist. This is a new kind of writer's block.

February 19. Dear Baby: Today, a little scratch disappeared above your left eyebrow.

All her life, Rae has been rehearsing for the worst imaginable scenarios. Her fears often get fact-checked, their validity confirmed. She's written about the acidifying oceans and sarin attacks. It's psychic whiplash to turn from these assignments to the baby's sleeping face koalaed against her chest, in a marsupial accessory recommended to her by the Old Moms. For $49.99, you, too, can convert your deflated abdomen into a pouch.

March 1. Dear Baby: I like the way you turn in half circles on the mattress, like a senile clock.

"The baby" sounds cold to Rae, but "my baby" sounds too cozily proprietary. "I am your mother," she tells him instead, reintroducing herself dozens of times each day. "We belong together."

March 22. Dear Baby:

She thumbs through the blank pages, shining and white. The happiness she feels is frightening to her. It's nothing she's ever rehearsed for. Only an idiot would try to write about it.

Her mother sends her a gift, a "smart" sock that will beep if the baby's heart stops in his sleep.

Two stars, the top-rated online review gives it. "I was expecting to get more use out of this."

"Look, I don't mean to sound harsh," one of the Old Moms says, in a Theraflu voice. "But you established a precedent. You set up this routine, and now it expects to be fed at the same time every night."

Rae nods miserably. She did!

"It's a vicious cycle."

Yvette has convened a special meeting, Friday at 8 p.m.,

which feels like midnight to Rae. The co-op is closed, its windows shuttered. Six women sit around the table, Old Moms with demonic experience. The seventh woman is another New Mom, Marie. She and her wife run the piano store on Franklin; Yvette put her in touch with Rae. Sometimes they meet at the park, trotting behind their strollers like bleary centaurs. Marie has also been feeding the devil, in a ditch behind the Windy Grove apartments.

Marie and Rae sit side by side. Under the table, Marie takes her hand. It feels a little traitorous to make a new friend, when she is out of touch with everyone she loves. But it's happening to them, a friendship. She pictures octopuses bobbing in the sea, their tentacles curling around each other. Diaphanous mothers with great swollen heads, bulbous with fear.

Shyly, Rae asks the Old Moms, "Did you bargain with it, too?"

A torrent of stories follows. What this devil once promised to do for them:

Stop the car from running the red light.

Shrink the tumor.

Jail the kidnapper.

Drain the water from her brain.

Return the bullets to the gun.

Swat away the infected mosquito.

Save the job that pays our rent.

Prevent the warhead from reaching western Oregon.

Keep our son safe from the police.

Reverse the spread of leukemia.

Bring them home to me safely, my babies, oh, please.

The interloper, it seems, arrives in a variety of costumes.

"Mine was a hawk. It descended on me every night and tore at my breast."

"Mine came as a horse. A miniature horse, or possibly a donkey. It had enormous buckteeth. I'm still missing pieces of my shins."

"Mine was a bear cub. It had a purple tongue. It sharpened its claws on the fire hydrant."

That nobody notices these deficits and bruises says something about the battered invisibility of the postpartum body. People tactfully agree to unsee the brown blood seeping onto their blue sofa cushions, the haunted bulges moving under a friend's sweater. When Rae was pregnant, these same Linda Blair undulations made strangers smile. "I saw a foot!" a bus driver once gasped, pointing at her abdomen, as if a blue whale had just fluked.

"I'm not sure what ours is," Rae admits. "Maybe a badger?"

Yvette holds up *The ABCs of Animals*. Together the mothers review the suspects:

"Was it an anteater? A bok?"

"It is a capybara," Marie says, with grave finality.

The capybara is the largest rodent in the world. It is endemic to South America, a barrel-sized hamster with gingery fur. Rae is not so sure, but she defers to her new friend.

"Mine was not a devil," Carol, an Old Mom with carroty curls, says. "It was an extraterrestrial."

Rae doesn't want to begrudge another woman her confidence, her certainly hard-won confidence in a society that prides itself on dismantling women's testimonies. At the same time, she thinks, *Bullshit, Carol. It was a devil.*

"Okay, ladies," Yvette says, addressing Rae and Marie. She

gives them an exhausted smile, and Rae recognizes the bludgeoned kindness of a mother of four children under the age of three. Wait, is that even possible? Three children under the age of five? Her mind is a fog machine. "Let's not mince shit. You have to stop feeding this thing."

Marie gives Rae a look of utter dismay.

"Does a problem go away on its own?" Yvette says. "It does not."

"Mine did!" Carol says.

"Carol. Please. This is not helpful."

"Look," Marie says. "This approach, I'm glad it worked for you. But I'm not ready to wean yet. I'm afraid of it! I don't want my family to suffer."

"Uh, hello? None of us want our families to suffer."

"It speaks with great authority about many calamitous possibilities. Then it promises me that if I feed it, these bad things will not come to pass."

"Rookie mistake," Yvette says. "It can't do that for you."

She sees Marie's face fall and adds, with surprising gentleness, "It's understandable, though. It's not like there's a manual."

Actually, there are hundreds of manuals. Rae has several on her nightstand, mostly unread.

"Do you know about Clever Hans?" Yvette asks. "No? This was a horse, believed by all to be a mathematical genius. 'What's two plus two, Hans?' his owner would ask. And Hans would stamp four times with his hoof."

"Wow. They really lowered the bar for genius for old Hans."

"Well, it turns out Hans was just a canny motherfucker.

He read cues from his owner, and he knew when to start and when to stop clomping. This thing is like that. A manipulator."

Marie looks unconvinced. Rae sees the echo of her own shining fear.

"What exactly is it promising you?" Yvette asks. "What does it tell you will happen, if you quit?"

"I . . . I can't say. I am afraid that speaking these fears will turn them into prophecies."

"Oh, boy. I have a whole shelf of bullshit for you. *The Treasure Is the Cave,* have you read that? Number one bestseller. Those authors are laughing all the way to the bank."

Then Marie explains that her little girl has a fever of a hundred and two. The temperature will keep climbing, she knows, unless it helps. And, to help, it needs her milk. What if she gently weans the devil?

Yvette shakes her head. Even her no is somehow balletic. Rae watches her swaying ponytail and hears wind in the treetops.

Couldn't she leave a bowl of milk out for it occasionally? Cold turkey.

Just this once? This extraordinarily terrible night? Cold turkey.

"We have to stop together," Marie tells Rae after the meeting. "Promise me. I can't do this alone."

Eight hours later, when she hears the scratching of the little claws on her porch, Rae bolts the door. For the first night since giving birth, Rae nurses only her son.

The next morning, when Rae opens the curtains, her devil is skulking along the road in broad daylight. "Get the fuck back in the gutter," she says. "Get the fuck away from my house." Instead it runs up a Douglas fir, whipping its long tail around the trunk. It bounces across the power lines, leering at her. Three black Priuses roll under the devil, unaware.

That night, it scratches at the door for hours. It crawls into her skull, whining over the giggling baby as he topples blocks. Angrily, then pitifully. Finally, when she can't take it any longer, Rae gets out of bed. She is midway down the stairs when the baby, her real baby, begins to cry. A cry of pure hunger. Beautiful in its fearless fullness, its expectation of an answer. She can't leave her son weeping in his crib. Nor, she realizes, can she fail to keep her compact with the creature in the gutter. A compromise, then.

Orange World. Suiting the poor baby up like a marshmallow at 5 a.m. Jerking on a hat, mittens. Letting him nurse hungrily on her right breast as she carries him down the steep stairs. Opening the door onto the gray, evolving film of dawn. Hurrying down the porch steps, her hand pushing through plushy snow to grasp the railing. (The snow keeps falling this year, breaking records.) Crossing a lake of street light to the gutter. It's easier than you'd think, to cross an icy road carrying a nursing infant. She commends herself on her good sense—she's chosen the right footwear, heavy-duty boots. Good soles. Okay. This can work. She can do this. Just this once—

The creature is waiting at the entrance to the storm drain, washing its paws in the falling water. She balks just as it starts loping toward them.

"No!" Her baby's eyes fly open; his mouth goes slack around her nipple. Her son absorbs her horror and pushes it outward in a long, blossoming cry. Together they retreat into the stillness of the house. Across the street, she can hear the devil hissing at her neighbor's cat, poor incontinent Rambo.

Two nights later, an emergency meeting is convened after hours at the Milk and Honey Co-op.

Marie looks haunted. "I broke," she confesses to the group. The veterans struggle to conceal their disappointment.

"So did I," Rae admits. "I went outside, and it ran right at me and my baby, like a rabid thing."

"You brought the *baby?*"

Orange World. Rae's face is hot. She nods.

"Okay," Yvette says, breathing loudly through her nose. "That's okay. Weaning is a process."

"Today, I saw it outside," Rae says. "Howling for me, in noon light. It's going to hurt my family!"

"Well," Yvette says. "This appears to be an extreme case. An extreme manifestation of will."

"I think it's just so hungry," Marie whispers.

"Ladies, any suggestions?"

"If anybody says the word 'binky' again, I will scream," Valerie, an Old Mom who has a sexy lisp and/or is maybe a little drunk, says. "They need help corralling a demon. We can use netting, or a Havahart trap."

Old Moms are nodding; sweet Zhaleh, a mother of twins and an oncology nurse, pounds a fist on the table: "We mothers of Southeast Portland cannot entertain this devil any longer!"

Marie stiffens beside Rae.

"Listen, you . . ." She leaves a beat for the unspoken noun, a very unfriendly noun. "It's easy for you Olds to tell us to drive it off. Nothing is at stake for you. Personally? It *has* protected my baby. My daughter's last MRI was totally normal. Not one of the nightmares has come to pass."

"Congratulations. Good for you." Yvette rolls her eyes. "You must think your milk is white gold or something."

"Excuse me?"

"Believe me, if I thought this thing could protect my kids? I would give it my viscera in a sippy cup," Yvette says. "But it can't do shit."

Rae and Marie exchange a long look, flaunting their complicity. So what if the Old Moms are judging them? The Old Moms have no idea what they are up against.

"Women like you love to play the martyr, don't you?" Yvette says. "You would rather this thing be the real devil than admit that you are powerless like the rest of us."

Anger tightens Rae's chest. She imagines lunging at haughty, gorgeous Yvette. *Women like you love to get Groupon plastic surgery and pretend to be twenty. Women like you—*

"You think I've never been tested? You think I've never begged for help?" Yvette stares at them. She was a cheerleader in high school, Rae can tell. She has that way of smiling even while screaming, a red-lipped control.

"My daughter died," she says. "Genevieve. When she was two months old. That is why I say I have four children. Because it would be a lie not to include her."

Rae pushes a fist into her mouth. Marie, beside her, starts to whimper.

"Do you want to know how she died?"

Yvette folds her manicured hands on the table. Her smile is terrifying. Nobody speaks.

"Right," she continues. "Tell me, honestly: If I had let that thing suck my tit at night, would she still be alive today? Should I have taken the deal when it was offered? Do you ladies think I killed my daughter?"

In the silence that follows, Rae hears the spinning of a thousand roulette wheels.

If you believe that, what else do you believe?

The stakeout begins at 3 a.m. Bonnie and her sisters run a wildlife-removal company, and she shows up in her van. There are enclosures ranging in size from squirrel to panther.

"Trap and release," Bonnie promises. "Nobody gets hurt."

Valerie donates a Wallababy sling.

Zhaleh brings a case of injectable sedative.

Ellen brandishes a cap gun. "It's just a toy. I hate guns, personally. Somebody went off registry."

Earlier in the evening, Rae had asked her husband if he could give their son his bottles; she was socializing with some new friends. "It's a sleepover, actually," she said. "A sort of initiation, for the New Moms Group. We take a night off and sleep like the dead. Yvette is hosting."

"A sleepover! That sounds awkward." But he'd sounded

truly happy for her; Rae could take a long time to warm up to people.

They park the van across the street from Rae's house. After so many nights alone, it feels strange to know that the others are watching her. She can't see their faces from the gutter. But she feels self-conscious, lying on her side in a cold sweat, waiting. Right at 4:44, the creature climbs out of the storm drain. Nothing in her lifetime has come to her as reliably as this monster. It keeps a faithful calendar. Yvette must be right—the real devil, Rae feels certain, would not be taken in so easily. Without suspicion, it bounds over to her and begins drinking ecstatically. She waits until its gelid eyelids flutter, then gives the signal. Valerie stands in front of the storm drain; Carol blocks off the exit to Powell.

As gently as she can, she inserts the needle. Drugging a devil is no easier and no harder than cutting her baby's fingernails. There is a plexus of vessels under the forked tongue where the detomidine is absorbed. *This isn't going to work,* she thinks. But, as it turns out, her fear of failure changes nothing. It does not slow the progress of the sedative, and soon the creature's chin dribbles against her shoulder. She brushes dirt from the leathery webbing of one paw. Sleeping in her arms, the creature feels no heavier than her own son.

In the back of the van, she draws her knees up to her face. Her devil is in a large cat carrier, its fur poking through the holes.

"You see?" Marie prods her. "Capybara, for sure."

Bonnie drives stick and knows the mountain roads. In the cage, the thing begins to howl in its sleep. Someone hands

Bonnie earplugs. The real danger, of course, is the ice on the road. "Fucking Portland," she says. "We need a cloud of salt to fall now!" On a sharp curve, the van fishtails. Every mother is thinking of her child, her children. Who will care for them if I die? The question floats above their heads in a collective thought bubble, like that wordless prayer that unites two hundred passengers during airplane turbulence: *Let me live, let me continue. Return me to the earth, alive.*

Who are you bargaining with? Rae wants to ask. *Who do you imagine is listening?*

"Bonnie! Watch the goddamn road!"

They drive for two hours and pull over at an arbitrary spot just shy of the sandy border where, if you look down at the glove box and up again, Oregon will have transformed from coniferous forest into high desert. Two women hoist the carrier, and together they push through the underbrush to a meadow of snow. It is Rae who kneels and opens the door.

"All right," Rae lies. "You're free."

They watch in silence as it scampers off. At first it has a pale, vulpine face. But, as it runs, it seems to shimmer in and out of view, its edges melting and revising themselves. Very quietly, almost undetectably, it begins to break apart. Huge-eyed and snuffling, it looks back at the women. A final trick: tugging at the heartstrings. It mewls pitifully, faking a limp. "Nobody move," Yvette cautions. But even her eyes are filling. It is hard to watch anything die. As the sun sparkles on the sides of Mount Hood, the creature continues to shape-shift: a wolf cub, a bunny, a kit fox, a spotted fawn. Every animal protagonist of their infants' board books.

"Oh dear. It's forgetting its shape."

"Poor motherless thing. Look at it looking."

"It's exhausted. It can't keep itself together. It doesn't know what it is anymore."

"It knows it's hungry."

It keens at Rae like something twisting on a spit, pinioned above leaping flames. Snow crosses Yvette's impassive face, and Rae understands why they had to travel hundreds of miles from their children's bedrooms. The sound is shattering and unforgettable. Its edges crisp and blacken. The creature bobbles off, unsteady on its legs and disintegrating where the sun pierces its furry body. It screams again, smoke rippling from its shoulders. It turns and fixes the pain-dulled saucers of its enormous eyes on Rae's face. "Mama?" it says. "Mama?"

It goes streaking into the woods, a burst sac of pure light. It calls to the women in the voices of their children, doing a nightmare karaoke. It shrinks into a whisper, a plea for more life. Hunger with nothing but itself to offer for barter. It seems to levitate, midway up a sunbeam, before disappearing from sight—not with anything as dramatic as a flash, but with a gentle scattering of motes, domestic and unremarkable. On a rock near the trailhead, Valerie discovers its skin, already bubbling with the forest's bright-bodied flies. There is no corpse to bury and nothing left to nurse back to life.

Yvette can't stop yawning, for some reason. She buries her face in her hands politely, but it continues for a very long time. The others touch her back and shoulders. Marie is crying openly. Bonnie shows them the hairline cracks in her glasses. "Its screams did that."

"I'll drive," Rae volunteers. "I'm a pretty good driver, actually."

———

And where has Rae's own mother been all this while?

Her mother is still on the other side of the globe, caring for Rae's grandmother in a shadow story, a solemn and uncertain leave-taking. Feeding her puréed fruits with a little spoon, combing her eight remaining hairs. They are so far apart on the parabola that Rae's morning is her mother's night. When the phone rings at an obscene hour, Rae knows it is her mother.

At the same moment, they ask each other, "Is everything okay?"

While Rae watches, her baby's eyelids crease and open. Sunlight splashes all around the kitchen. Joy threatens to take the roof off the house. The light is almost blinding today. She crouches over him to shelter them both.

A feeling leaps into her from the past: "Mother! You felt this way about me!"

"Yes," her mother says. "And I feel that way about you still."

Green World. Rae is learning to identify it very late in this life. Her feet push into the floorboards. Happiness travels through her, heels to skull. She cradles her son. She cradles the phone. Remotely, her mother is cradling her.

Acknowledgments

Thanks to the MacArthur Foundation, for their life-changing gift and their support of my work.

Thanks to Sam Chang, Connie Brothers, Kevin Brockmeier, and my Iowa Gill-Openers.

Thanks to the Tin House family and to that green dream incubator, the Tin House Summer Workshop.

Thanks to the MFA program in creative writing and the Department of English at Texas State University. It's been an honor and a true pleasure to serve as the endowed chair.

Big love and thanks to Tom and Jody Grimes—you make Texas feel like our home.

Thank you to my students for putting up with my jokes, and for opening my eyes to so many new worlds in progress.

Thank you to Willing Davidson, for your friendship and your invaluable help with these stories.

Thank you, Deborah Treisman, for your terrific insights and suggestions.

Thank you to my old pal and partner in weirdness, Michael Ray, for your brilliant edits.

Thank you to Cheston Knapp for your peerless echo-location.

Thank you to Denise Shannon, the world's most amazing agent.

Thank you to Jordan Pavlin, who sees right to the secret heart of things, and always lights the way for me.

Thanks to Nicholas Thomson, Kathleen Fridella, Susan Bradanini Betz, Emily Reardon, John Gall, Kate Runde, Sara Eagle, Madeleine Denman, Kate Berner, Kim Thornton Ingenito, and the wonderful folks at Knopf and the RHSB.

Thanks to Carey McHugh and Avery Gordon for permission to use lines from their excellent books, *American Gramophone* and *Ghostly Matters: Haunting and the Sociological Imagination,* as my epigraphs.

Andrew Moore, thank you for your photographs and particularly for *Basset Cattle Auction, Rock County, Neb 2006.*

Doug Johnson, thank you for teaching me about the nuanced beauty, resilience, and fragility of the High Plains.

A special thanks to the world's best grandmothers, Janice Russell and Claire Perez, for making it possible for me to spend time with the tornadoes and the ghosts and finish this book.

Thanks to Bruce Russell, Kent Russell, Lauren Russell, Alan and Fran Romanchuck, and my Perez family, for so much laughter and for the joy of this new chapter.

Hey, friends: thanks for turning the pages with me. I love you.

To Tony Perez and Oscar Perez, the great loves of my life: thank you for teaching me how to write such a happy story. T, thank you for spending so many hours dreaming and revising with me. This book is for you. I can't wait to see what comes next.

A NOTE ABOUT THE AUTHOR

KAREN RUSSELL won the 2012 and the 2018 National
Magazine Award for fiction, and her first novel, *Swamplandia!* (2011), was the winner of the New York Public
Library's Young Lions Award and a finalist for the Pulitzer
Prize. A recipient of a Guggenheim Fellowship, a Cull-
man Center Fellowship, a 2012 Fellowship at the American
Academy in Berlin, and a 2013 MacArthur Fellowship, she
lives with her husband and son in Portland, Oregon, and
currently holds the Endowed Chair at Texas State's MFA
program.

A NOTE ON THE TYPE

This book was set in Granjon, a type named in compliment
to Robert Granjon, a type cutter and printer active in Ant-
werp, Lyon, Rome, and Paris from 1523 to 1590.

Linotype Granjon was designed by George W. Jones,
who based his drawings on a face used by Claude Garamond (ca. 1480–1561). Granjon more closely resembles
Garamond's own type than do any of the various modern
faces that bear his name.

Composed by North Market Street Graphics,
Lancaster, Pennsylvania

Printed and bound by Berryville Graphics,
Berryville, Virginia

Designed by Cassandra J. Pappas